GOD OF VENGEANCE

A Medieval Romance

By Kathryn Le Veque

Part of the Executioner Knights series

It's another Executioner Knight's tale featuring the younger prince of Kitara—and he's about to blow Medieval England wide open!

Forced marriages, secrets, sins, and scoundrels run rampant in this blockbuster Medieval tale!

Essien al-Kort was not born in England. Having been exiled from his homeland far to the east, he has experienced more suffering in his lifetime than most. But the crusading knights were good to him and he grew up in a Christian world, eventually finding his way to England. As a fully fledged knight under Ajax de Velt and Christopher de Lohr, Essien is an elite warrior among warriors. He's also a highly skilled tournament competitor, like his older brother, and these days, he's making a fortune as the tournament knight known as the **God of Vengeance.**

But his fortune will only take him so far.

Enter Catalina de Barenton.

Catalina's father is an ally and neighbor of Christopher de Lohr (*Rise of the Defender*). Unfortunately, the man has expressed his desire to Christopher that his daughter should be well taken care of. Her first husband is dead, so he wants another husband who will assume her burden. Christopher sees Essien as a candidate, not only in marriage, but as an ally when he inherits the de Barenton properties through marriage.

The only problem is that Catalina has no desire to remarry… not even after she meets Essien. And her husband, who is presumed dead, may not be dead after all.

The mystery deepens.

Join Essien and Catalina in a unique and powerful love story as they navigate the complexities of a forced marriage that eventually becomes their lifeline. From the rocky start to the breathtaking conclusion, *God of Vengeance* is a story for the ages.

HOUSE OF KITARA (AL-KORT)

Motto: *a nullo victa*

Conquered by None

(In their native tongue of Urdu: Kasis se ftah nihen hoi)

LIST OF EXECUTIONER KNIGHTS

(Note: this list is around 1210 A.D.—1228 A.D..)

William Marshal—Earl of Pembroke, Pembroke Castle and Farrington House

Christopher de Lohr—Earl of Hereford and Worcester, Lioncross Abbey Castle

David de Lohr—Earl of Canterbury, Canterbury Castle, Bellham Place

Peter de Lohr—Lioncross Abbey Castle, Ludlow Castle

Gart Forbes—Dunster Castle, Devon

Caius d'Avignon—Richmond Castle, North Yorkshire

Maxton of Loxbeare—Chalford Hill Castle, Gloucester

Kress de Rhydian—Seton Castle, Scotland

Achilles de Dere—Caversham Manor, Berkshire

Susannah de Tiegh de Dere—a Blackchurch-trained knight, wife of Achilles

Alexander de Sherrington—Farringdon House for William Marshal (a year before he becomes Christopher de Lohr's son-in-law)

Bric MacRohan—Narborough Castle, Norwich Castle, Norfolk

Dashiell du Reims—Ramsbury Castle, Wiltshire. Also Thunderbey Castle, East Anglia.

Sean de Lara—King John's personal bodyguard

Kevin de Lara—Canterbury Castle (in the service of David de

Lohr). Also Hyssington, Caradoc, and Trelystan Castles—
Welsh Marches

Cullen de Nerra—Rockingham Castle, Northamptonshire

Cole de Velt—formerly William the Lion's personal guard, now
Pelinom Castle

Addax al-Kort—Earl of Deira

Essien al-Kort—Earl of Mercia, Lord Eckington

AUTHOR'S NOTE

Buckle up, kids. This is one heck of a ride!

I can't tell you how thrilled I am to finally present you with Essien's story. Our baby brother has grown up. It's funny how an author envisions characters, physically—I always envisioned Essien to be about a head taller than his older brother, Addax. Addax is big, broad, and powerful, while Essien was the tall, muscular brother who is a little… excitable. What younger brother isn't? (And I have a younger brother, so I can say that with confidence!)

If you've not yet read *The Black Dragon*, which is Addax's story, then let me fill you in a little on the situation of Addax and Essien. They are princes from the country of Kitara, which is situated in what is today the country of Pakistan. The location of the ancient city of Mohenjo Daro is the approximate area and, in fact, the city upon which I based my opening scene.

Speaking of the opening scene, it's basically the same scene from *The Black Dragon*, slightly different, because it is from Essien's perspective. He was very young, so his recollections are more vague than his older brother's, but the scene is an important setup to the story because it gives you, the reader, a peek into the night Essien was torn from the land of his birth. It gives you a glimpse into the trauma. As the younger brother, Essien didn't have the weight of the kingdom on his shoulders that his brother had because he is the "spare." But that means he needs to be prepared in the event his older brother can't take the throne, but of course, with no country, his position is kind of moot. I think that leaves Essien feeling lost in a sense—maybe even without a purpose. He's always lived in Addax's shadow.

But in this tale, he finds a purpose. And what a purpose!

I want to mention something because you're going to be reading it fairly quickly. In the first chapter, Christopher de Lohr and William de Wolfe meet yet again. In my novel *Lord of the Sky*, there was a brief moment when young William and seasoned Christopher were side by side in battle at the Tower of London, and in this book, they meet yet again, several times. What an honor it is to put these two in a scene together. They are a generation apart in age, with Christopher being the same age as William's father, and we discover in this book that William has a bit of hero worship when it comes to Christopher. But I don't want to spoil that part of it—you'll have to read it for yourself. Also, I'm not sure if you're aware of this, but Curtis de Lohr, Christopher's heir, was born a year after William, so they're essentially the same age. So many timelines to keep track of!

You are also going to notice a LOT of characters you are familiar with from other books. They just pop in and aren't really meant to have a big story arc, if any. A tournament is the kickoff of this novel and, of course, where there are tournaments, there are many visitors. I don't think you'll have trouble keeping up with them, but it is fun to catch a glimpse of them in other books. My universe is very connected, so de Lohr and de Wolfe and other worlds collide from time to time. The only world that really doesn't come into play during the thirteenth century is Gaston de Russe and the House of de Russe, mostly because his world happens about two hundred years after the glory of de Lohr and de Wolfe. That's essentially the same stretch of time between the Regency period and present day!

The usual pronunciation guide:

Essien—ess-EE-in

Kitara—kit-TAR-uh

Addax—ADD-x (it sort of sounds like "Attics" if you say it properly)

Amare—uh-MAR-ay

Kiya—KY-uh

Ines—I've heard it pronounced both ways—ee-NEZ or eye-NEZ. We're going with ee-NEZ.

And with that—enjoy Essien and Catalina. Get ready with that tissue box—you're going to need it!

Hugs,

Kathryn

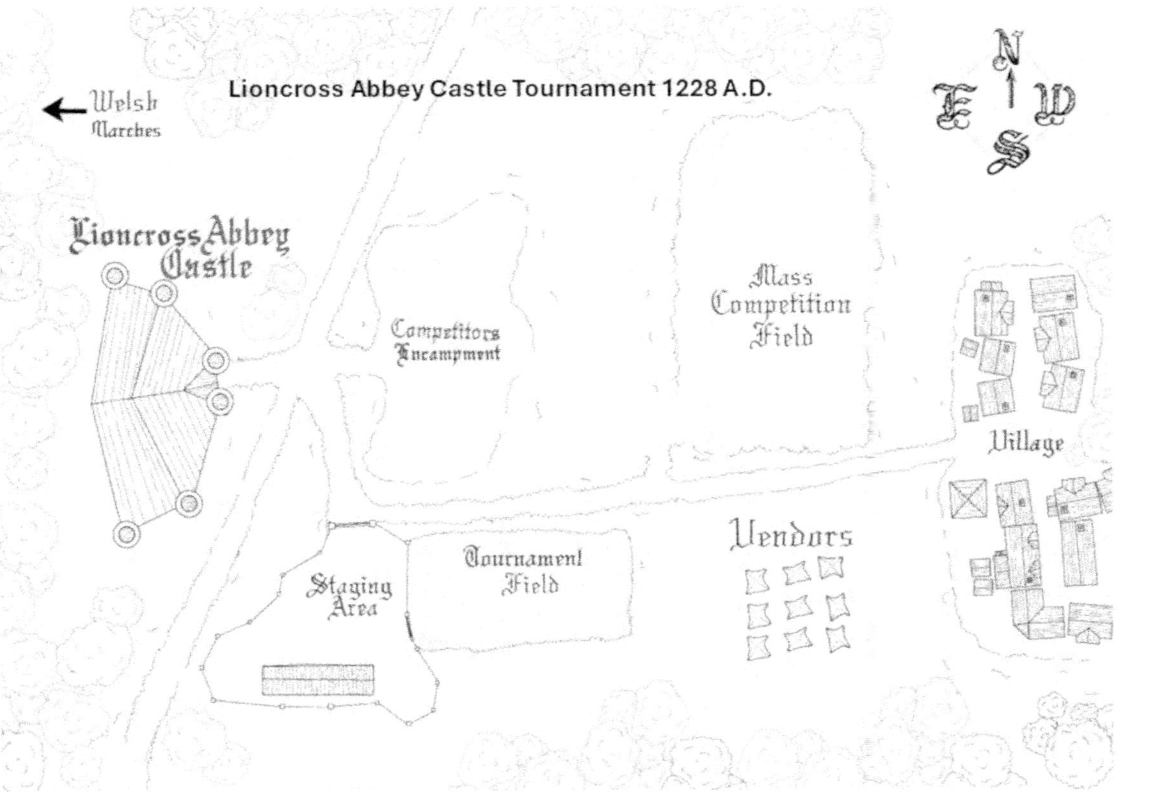

Lioncross Abbey Castle Tournament 1228 A.D.
Welsh Marches
Lioncross Abbey Castle
Competitors Encampment
Mass Competition Field
Village
Staging Area
Tournament Field
Vendors
N
E
S
W

PROLOGUE

Year of Our Lord 1190
The fall of the Kingdom of Kitara

THE SMELL OF smoke was heavy in the air.

That was all he really knew—that it was smoky and smelly and he was running. So much running. He was too young to know how critical this night was, how horrific in its measure. A kingdom that had existed for a thousand years was now in danger of going up in smoke and there was no way to stop it. A thousand years of life and love and beauty, of culture and joy, was about to become a pile of ash.

The hot desert winds were carrying the smoke and embers, flowing from one cottage to the next, igniting the thatched roof so that the dry grass went up like a torch. But the fire had been deliberate, set by the King of Kitara so that the Mongols from the north, and a leader named *Temüjin*, could not have his beloved city. He'd rather burn it than surrender.

But it was even worse than that.

They had been betrayed.

King Amare, tall and powerful, with eyes the color of jade and skin as smooth as polished stone, watched the fire from

1

Larkana Palace, the residence of more than two dozen generations of his family. But tonight would see that legacy come to an end, because the royal family of Kitara had been betrayed from within. Amare was so emotionally wounded by the betrayal that it was difficult for him to face the task ahead. One of desperation, one of reckoning.

But it had to be done.

He had to kill his brother.

Prince Ekon was four years younger than Amare and had coveted the throne since he was a young boy. There had been numerous attempts on Amare's life over the years, and the general belief was that most of them had been orchestrated by Ekon, who simply denied the accusations and threw himself on his brother's mercy. It wasn't mercy he wanted, but fragility. He played on his brother's one weakness—his love for his family.

Even for those who betrayed him.

Amare knew this. He was well aware of his brother's ploys. He was well aware of the man's movements, his subversion, and even his attempts to seduce Amare's own wife. Rumor had it that the youngest child, a beautiful daughter named Adanya, was Ekon's child. Since Amare and Ekon looked quite similar to one another and the daughter had the same green eyes, perhaps the truth would never be known, even though Amare's wife vehemently denied anything illicit. Given that Amare loved her, and she had always been quite loyal, he believed her. But the rumors continued, and Amare ignored them.

The price of his ignorance, however, would be high. Ekon had taken a journey some time ago into the north after he'd tried to assassinate one of Amare's generals. Amare had sent him north as a diplomat, trying to give him a useful position in the hope that it would satisfy him, but it didn't. The intent of

Ekon's journey was to seek trade with the tribes to the north and the vast empire that was established there, but Ekon had done something quite different. Rather than establish ties for his brother's kingdom, he'd managed to ally himself with the most feared warlord in the world.

A man he had promised his fealty, should he remove Amare from the throne.

And that was why Temüjin had come.

Amare and his loyalists had known of the approach of his army for a couple of weeks now, ever since the outposts began reporting the movement of the enormous army southward. Amare had listened to the reports in horror, and when he sent for Ekon, his brother was nowhere to be found. As the days passed and the army drew closer, Amare knew that his brother could be found somewhere in the approaching army, and he further knew that, given the size of the force, his own army, which was trained and sizable, would be facing a suicide mission.

And so would his people.

But Amare would have the last word.

It was with a heavy heart that Amare ordered his own city burned before the Mongols could get to it. His army was out there right now, helping the villagers flee and burning their homes behind them. When Amare had been told, by a double agent, that Ekon was indeed with the approaching army and was promised Kitara's throne, Amare knew he had to destroy everything. He'd rather do that than let his brother have it.

Ekon would be the king of ashes.

As Amare pondered the course his life would take, in the stone halls of the palace, something else was happening. Fear was happening as his wife, Queen Kiya, went on the hunt for her children. They were supposed to be with their nurse, but the old woman seemed to have vanished.

Kiya could only pray that she hadn't vanished with her children, but she had yet to find them. There was a caravan waiting to take them away and time was growing short, so Kiya and her women were running down the corridors, checking chambers, until they finally came to the chamber where the old nurse usually slept. It was a small chamber with a wide balcony and linen curtains hanging in front of the opening that led to the patios beyond. The glow of the city to the east was creating a silhouette of small figures through the linen, and she pushed through them to find all three children on the balcony, watching the fires beyond.

"Thanks to God," she gasped as she rushed to them, falling to her knees. "You are all safe!"

She was grasping Essien and Adanya, her baby. They were the youngest. Adanya had only recently learned to walk, but she was bright and quick and wanted to do everything her older brothers did. As usual, Essien had the baby by the hand. It was rare when he let her out of his sight, so Kiya put her arms around them, hugging them, as Addax stoically watched the fires.

"There is fire, Maman," the boy said, pointing.

Kiya looked up from her youngest children, noting that the fire, which had seemed distant only minutes before, seemed to be growing closer. Smoke was in the air, embers blowing about. She was trying so hard to be calm, but it was difficult.

"I know," she said. "We must go and find your father now. He will want us with him."

"Bam said that soldiers are coming," Essien said, referring to their nurse. "Are soldiers coming, Maman?"

Kiya swallowed hard, trying to hide her fear. "They are," she said. "That is why we must go to your father now."

Essien, two years younger than Addax, was nonetheless already as tall as his older brother. He had long arms and strong legs for his age, something Amare was quite proud of. He pointed in the distance, to the fire, and made slashing gestures.

"I will fight them," he declared. "When they come here, I will stab them and beat them!"

Kiya put her hand on his shaved head. "You are very brave," she told him. "Your father will be very proud of you. Shall we go and find him?"

She didn't give him a chance to answer. She swung Adanya into her arms and took Essien by the hand, leading them away from the edge of the balcony. She called softly to Addax, who was reluctant to tear himself away from the view. Even at his young age, he could sense his mother's fear.

Something evil was happening.

When they reached the large corridor that led to the throne room, Kiya handed Adanya over to one of her ladies and continued on to where her husband was. The boys were still with her, tagging along behind her, as she rushed into the room where Amare was watching the collapse of his kingdom.

"My love!" Kiya gasped. "What are you doing here? The caravan is ready to take us by river out to the sea. We must hurry!"

Amare turned to look at his wife. God, he was glad to see her. Kiya was such a lovely creature, so graceful and beautiful and kind. She had been an arranged marriage, a princess of her people in the land of the pharaohs known as Kemet, but the moment Amare set eyes on her was the moment he fell in love with her. Before he could answer, Addax and Essien ran up behind her, throwing themselves at their father. Amare laughed softly as he collected his sons. He was a warm and loving father, but tonight, he was perhaps a little more loving and warm.

He knew it would be the last time he ever held his children.

"Addax," he said, giving the boys a squeeze before he set them on their feet. "Essien, look at me. I have something very important to ask you."

Essien and Addax obeyed, at least at first. But a few seconds of obedience deteriorated into both boys trying to climb back into his arms, so his next request to them was more of an order.

"Es, stop climbing," he commanded softly. "Stand still. That's good. Something very important is happening tonight, and you must be part of it."

Addax, the less squirmy of the two, was watching his father seriously. "An army is coming, Abba," he said. "We have come to help you fight."

Abba. That meant father. It would be the last time he ever heard it from his sons, and Amare smiled at his brave boy. "And you are very courageous," he said. "I am honored to have you by my side. But I have an even more important task for you."

Addax cocked his head curiously. "What, Abba?"

Amare wasn't sure he could keep his composure knowing it would be the last time he was addressed as father. But time was not his friend on this night—it was passing more quickly than usual—so he pulled his boys against him one last time, hugging them fiercely.

But his heart was breaking.

"You must get your mother to safety," he said, indicating Kiya as she stood behind the boys and tried not to weep. "You must go with her and protect her. Will you do this for me?"

Addax and Essien looked at their mother before Addax returned his attention to his father. "But what about you?" he asked. "Who will help you fight?"

Amare forced a smile. "I have the entire army to help me fight," he said, making it sound as if it were nothing at all. "But your mother does not command an army. She has a few servants, but you two are her very best warriors. Will you please do this for me?"

Essien nodded solemnly, but Addax was still hesitant. "She has Bobo and Rani to help her," he said. "But you need me."

He was referring to the old women who served his mother, but Amare nodded sincerely. "Indeed, I do need you," he said. "I will always need you, Addax, and right now I need you to take care of your mother. Promise me."

Addax sighed heavily before finally nodding. Essien, who had the attention span of a mosquito at this age, stuck his finger up his nose and began to turn around, looking for his mother, looking at the people who were hovering on the fringe of the room. Men who had served his father for many years. He recognized them. As his father spoke to Addax about a dragon-headed dagger, Essien reached a small hand out to his mother, tugging on her gossamer skirt.

"Maman?" he said. "Maman, I am hungry. Can I have cheese?"

Kiya, who had been listening to Amare explain the significance of the dragon-headed dagger carried by every Kitara king back to the beginning, knelt down to speak quietly to her youngest son.

"Not now," she said, tightening up the little belt he wore to secure his trousers. "We must leave, and then I shall find you some cheese."

Essien watched her as she fussed with his clothing. "Maman?"

"What is it?"

"Why do you weep?"

Kiya came to a halt, lifting her eyes from the belt to his little face. Essien had always been her intuitive child, the one who could see beyond the façade, beyond the words that one spoke or the gestures one completed. He was interested in people. Though she'd not wept in front of him, he could see it in her eyes.

She couldn't lie to him.

"I weep because I am afraid," she said honestly. "I weep because I worry for you and your brother and your sister."

Essien cocked his head thoughtfully. "But you should not worry," he said. "We will be safe soon and I will eat cheese."

Kiya grinned. "You shall, indeed," she said. "But we must go on a journey first, before you will be safe. Do you remember the journey we took on the boat in the summertime? When we saw *Jido*?"

She was referring to the journey they'd taken across the sea. It had taken half of the summertime to reach a port where her father, Shadhi, the hereditary but deposed ruler of Cairo, had met her and her children. He'd never seen them before. Shadhi had taken great delight in his daughter's offspring, and in particular Essien, because he bore the characteristics of someone born in Kemet. *Egypt.* He had fine, sculpted features even at his young age and eyes the color of a tiger's eye stone. In fact, he looked strikingly similar to his *jido*, or maternal grandfather, and Shadhi had naturally taken to him.

Essien remembered it well.

"He called me Horus," he said. "He gave me sweets."

Kiya laughed softly. "He did, indeed," she said. "And your first name is Horus, in honor of the land of my birth. That is why he called you by the name."

"Adda calls me Essien."

Kiya nodded, still smiling. "Because that is the name from the land of his birth," she said. "You are Horus Essien Nazimuddin Mei al-Kort. You are named for the falcon-headed god of protection and healing. You *are* destined to protect, Essien. That is what you must do now—you must protect your sister and your brother, but you must never let them know."

"Why not?"

"Because Addax would not take kindly to being protected by his younger brother," she said. "But that is why you were put on this earth, my love. To protect and thrive. The gods of ancient Kemet watch over you, even now. They will see you safely through this."

Essien had to think about that. He didn't exactly understand all of it, but he felt proud knowing he bore the name of a god of protection. But behind him, his father and Addax had finished their conversation and Amare interrupted Essien's moment with his mother.

"Where is Adanya?" Amare asked.

Kiya looked up from her youngest son. "She is already at the river with her nurse," she said softly. "She is so young. She would not understand this parting. But the boys…"

Amare nodded quickly, for there was no reason for her to continue. It would be the last time their sons faced their father, so it was more important for them. And more important that Amare say what he needed to say.

"Thank you, my love, for allowing me to bid them farewell," he said. Then he cupped her face with one hand and gently kissed her mouth. "You must hurry. I sent word to your father when the army from the north approached. He will not receive the missive for some time, but you must be on your way so his ships can meet yours. The captain of your ship knows the way, and by the time your ship reaches the Red Sea, your father should be on his way to meet you. You and the children will be safe in Cairo."

Her tears started to come. "And you, my darling?" she whispered. "What about you?"

He forced a smile, kissing her again. "I must do what I was destined to do," he said bravely. "What I was meant to do. I will burn Lankara to the ground, and when there is only smoke and ashes left, I will kill my brother."

"What if he kills you first?"

Amare shrugged. "Then I will see you in paradise," he said. "But know… know that you have made my life paradise on earth, Kiya. No man has ever loved a woman more than I have loved you."

"And I love you with every breath I take," she murmured. "That will never stop, not in this world or any other."

"I know, *mere jaan.*"

"Promise me, Amare. If you can escape to Egypt, promise that you will come to us."

"I promise. But if I do not… this farewell was well made. It has given me courage."

She started to weep. Weeks of being strong had reached the breaking point. But Amare shushed her softly, turning her around and hustling her toward the servants who were waiting for her. Essien grabbed her hand, holding it tightly as they rushed along. Amare took them to the secret palace exit, where tunnels would take them to the river beyond, where ships awaited, and then the river would take them to the sea and westward. At the exit, Amare came to a halt and kissed his wife one last time, kissed Essien, and took a moment with Addax as the boy faced him.

"Be strong, my son," he whispered, struggling not to weep. "In the face of whatever this life will bring you, be strong, be honest, and be loyal to those you love. Promise me."

"I promise, Abba."

Amare smiled weakly. "Good," he said, turning him to his mother and the rest of the escort bound for the tunnels. The servants were already dressing Essien in a disguise as a servant's child. "Hurry, now. I will see you soon."

Even as Addax was facing the reality of the night with his father, Essien was watching it all carefully. His mother was worried, his father was being brave, Addax was focused on the blade in his hand, but Essien was simply drawing it all in. He still felt fear, but there was trust there, also. He trusted his father and his mother. Trust in the servants who were dressing him in smelly, unfamiliar clothing. The idea that this was a permanent situation had never occurred to him because he'd never known anything other than the Lankara Palace. To Essien, this was just some big adventure. He never thought he wouldn't return. As the servants began dressing Addax, Essien went to his father.

"Will you come?" he asked.

Amare smiled at his youngest boy who so favored his mother. "Soon," he said. "I will come soon."

"When?"

There was no time for a child's questions. Amare kissed his boy on the forehead. "*Jab tak ham dubarah nihen malin ge,*" he whispered. "Until we meet again."

And that was the last Essien saw of his father.

On that dark, terrible night, Essien, his mother, brother, and sister, along with several loyal servants, fled, out to sea.

But all did not go well.

A storm on the second night at sea pushed their convoy of three ships off course and into a gulf, where they were forced to dock at the city of Abu Samra. That was when the captain, who had been loyal to Amare for years and had established trade routes for him, decided to demand favors from Kiya. He'd never had a queen before, he'd said, something that confused Addax and Essien, but they knew instinctively that it wasn't good. When Kiya refused, he struck her. That was when Addax rammed the dragon-headed dagger into the man's kidney. *Protect your mother,* his father had said. So, he did.

After that, it was chaos.

Kiya and her children fled with her servants onto the streets of Abu Samra, but they became separated in the chaos. Dust and wind and terror swirled about them, and the group fractured further. The two old women, Bobo and Rami, fell afoul of a man they'd run into, and he threw them both into the sea. After hiding out for a day and a night, Addax and Essien searched for their mother and sister for days and days, until they found an old fisherman who said he'd seen a screaming woman and her infant daughter taken aboard another ship.

Distraught, the hungry and exhausted boys had no idea what to do when they came across one of the male servants who had accompanied them, only the man had been in a fight and left to die in an alley. He told Addax and Essien that, indeed, their mother and sister had been captured by the crew of the murdered captain and taken back aboard the ship. Now, the ship was gone.

So were their last links to their family.

Two very small boys found themselves alone in a strange land, their mother and sister vanished. There were no more servants out of the several who came with them, except for the dying old man. Therefore, Addax and Essien took up vigil next to the old servant, through heat and cold, night and day, learning to beg for food and receiving a pittance from the mosque in town. But it was enough to sustain them until the old servant finally passed away six days after they had found him.

After that, they were on their own.

But not for long.

Abu Samra was a crossroads for trade caravans throughout the region, and one day, when Addax and Essien went to the mosque to beg for more food, the holy man introduced them to a merchant who was bringing an enormous caravan from Abu Dhabi and heading for Damascus. The merchant needed small boys to run errands or complete little tasks, and the holy man made it seem as if it would be a great, fruitful adventure for Addax and Essien. It was better than begging in the streets, he said, and God would smile upon those who helped themselves.

So, they went.

Unfortunately, the merchant was not their savior. He enslaved them both, starving them and beating them, forcing them to tend camels and horses and load and unload merchandise. Addax was a little older and a little stronger than Essien, who was hardly more than a toddler. But he was a three-year-old who was forced to grow up very quickly as the hardships of life settled around them. It was either that or he would die, and neither of them wanted that. They had a strong will to survive, even in the worst of circumstances.

This went on for two very long years.

Two years of being beaten and abused, of hoping the next

day would bring relief or even someone with some kindness for them. At one point, the merchant, a man by the name of Abiram, was given a slave girl in Basrah in exchange for goods. She was young, but pretty and strong, and Abiram used her for labor. She worked alongside Addax and Essien, her nature kind and joyful in spite of her circumstances. Finally, the two young boys had someone to show them a measure of kindness and compassion, things they craved at their young age.

Amala was her name.

But Amala's presence wasn't to last forever.

Abiram had reached the Levant with his caravan of goods, and he found ready customers in the men protecting Acre, and other cities, from the onslaught of Christian armies. One night, Abiram sold Amala to a lord for his harem, and Addax would never forget her soft weeping as she was taken away. Somehow, Addax knew that he and Essien would not survive much longer. Abiram was growing crueler, and they were growing weaker. Once they hit the outskirts of Jerusalem, a vast and populous city, it was Addax who made the decision to run.

It was either run or die.

When Abiram brought the caravan to a halt and ordered the boys to go into town with a message for a friend of his, they willingly went into the citadel of Jerusalem and lost themselves on the dusty, ancient streets. Instead of searching for Abiram's friend on the Street of the Merchants, they escaped the city walls to the north, running through scrub and rocks, avoiding scorpions and snakes, rushing toward another village.

It took all night.

Once they arrived, there were very few people on the streets. Everyone seemed to be inside, even on what should have been a busy morning. Addax and Essien did what they'd learned to do best—hide in the shadows, trying to remain unseen, being as unobtrusive as possible. They'd learned that from Abiram, but more so now that they had fled the man. They didn't want to be brought back to him. But they were only small boys, after all, and by midmorning, they collapsed in a grove of olive trees from sheer exhaustion, and Essien fell asleep on his older brother.

But Addax couldn't sleep.

He had to remain vigilant.

Hollow-eyed, malnourished, and quite possibly as close to death as he'd ever been, Addax wondered if he would die in this place. He wondered what would become of his brother. Before Abiram's caravan, they'd begged for food because they didn't know what else to do. Now, it seemed they were to live on the street again, and Addax didn't relish the thought. He'd once had plans to find his mother and sister and return to Kitara to fight alongside his father, but all of those events had happened over two years ago. It seemed like a thousand years had passed. His father was dead, and so were his mother and sister, more than likely. Although he didn't want to believe that, deep down, he knew it was true.

He and Essien were the only ones left.

As Addax pondered what the future would bring, he heard horses in the distance. He was near the road, but still somewhat protected by the grove of olive trees. Turning his head, he could see enormous warhorses ridden by men covered with steel coats and great tunics and big, square buckets of metal on their heads. The tunics they wore were red, with yellow cats on them. There were so many that he couldn't see where the line of them ended, all of them heading down the road and into the village.

Somewhat fearful, Addax tried to move without waking up

Essien. His brother would likely cry at the sight of so many armed, unfamiliar warriors, and that would bring attention to them. If there was one thing Addax had learned as a young lad, it was how to be quiet. Noise was never a good thing. But he couldn't move enough, knowing he could be seen from the road.

And he was.

By dogs.

Two big gray dogs found him, licking his face furiously, wagging their tails, and evidently quite happy to see him. Even the dogs had steel on them, around their necks, and Addax was absolutely terrified. The dogs were very big, but thankfully friendly, and they licked Essien, too, who awoke to a giant dog head in his field of vision that was larger than his own head. He opened his mouth to scream, but Addax slapped a hand over his lips so the sound would go no further.

Then someone was yelling for the dogs. The dogs heard their names, but they were so happy that they'd found new people that they refused to leave the boys. In fact, one dog lay across Essien, and the other sat down next to Addax. It didn't seem to matter that someone was calling for them. They'd found something and they were proud of it. As Addax watched in terror, one of the heavily armed men on the road moved into the olive grove and dismounted.

He was heading straight for them.

"Argos!" the man boomed. "Artemis! Did you not hear me, you foolish animals?"

Addax had no idea what the man was saying. He didn't understand the language. But he was absolutely petrified as he clutched Essien, watching the big warrior approach. The man saw them fairly quickly, realizing his dogs had found the pair.

He slowed down, pausing a moment before removing his helm. He had hair the color of gold and a beard of nearly the same color around his jaw.

Addax had never seen hair that color in his life.

"*Aap kaun hain?*" the man asked, not unkindly.

Who are you? Addax recognized the language because he'd spent enough time in these lands to understand, and speak, a little of it. But he was so frightened, and so hungry and exhausted, that he started to weep.

"Addax," he said. "*Ana Addax.*"

I am Addax.

The warrior looked him over. He pointed to Essien questioningly, and Addax told the man his name. But that didn't seem to satisfy him. He didn't go away. He tried to get the dogs to come away, but they wouldn't. He finally gave up and crouched down a few feet away from them, even as other warriors saw what he was doing and reined their horses to a halt.

But the man's focus was on Addax.

"Do you understand me?" he asked in the language of the land.

Addax nodded. "Aye."

"Are you injured?"

Addax shook his head. "Nay."

"But you have bruises and blood on you."

Addax didn't know how to answer that. He was terrified to tell him the truth, so he made up something. Anything. "We… we are traveling."

"Where are you going?"

"I do not know."

The crouching warrior was joined by two more of the biggest men Addax had ever seen. One had the same gold hair, but the other man had black hair and blue eyes. They all had blue eyes. Addax had never seen that shade before, nor skin tone that color. It was quite pale.

"Where are your parents?" the crouching man asked. "Where do you belong?"

Addax shook his head. "We belong to no one," he said. "Please… will you let us go?"

The other blond warrior walked around the tree trunk, coming up on their other side. He, too, crouched down, closer to Essien. He spoke to the other man in a language Addax didn't understand.

"They've been beaten, Chris," he said quietly. "Starved, too, from the looks of it."

The man called Chris, the one with the blond beard, nodded. "I can see that," he said. "And they're clearly terrified. They are probably running from whoever did this. Why else would they be sleeping in an olive grove?"

The second blond man merely nodded and stood up. "We have some provisions we can give them," he said. "But we need to be on our way. Richard is expecting us."

The man called Chris stood up, too, but he was gazing down at the frightened boys. After a moment, he looked at the black-haired man standing next to him.

"Something tells me not to leave them here," he said.

The man with the dark hair frowned. "Why?"

"I do not know. It is a feeling I have." The man called Chris paused, looking indecisively at the boys huddling fearfully against the tree. "Those are very little boys who probably will not see another sunrise if they are not given food and help."

The man with the dark hair rolled his eyes. "So you come all this way to kill Muslims, yet you want to save these two?" he asked incredulously. "We do not have time for this. Give them some bread and let us be on our way."

With that, he turned and walked away, but the man called Chris didn't leave with him. In fact, he called after him.

"Mayhap God will be more willing to forgive me for the Muslims I've killed if I help two small children," he said loudly. But his focus returned to Addax and Essien. He'd made up his mind. He was going to help. "I cannot leave them here to die. David, pick up the one closest to you. I'll take the bigger one."

The other blond man looked confused. "And do what with them?" he said. "We bring them along like baggage?"

The man named Chris pointed to the dogs, still lying with the boys. "We bring them along like the dogs," he said. "Mayhap I will put them to work for us. In any case, I will not leave them. Pick up the smaller boy."

With a shrug, the other blond man dutifully reached down and picked up Essien, who screamed at being separated from his brother, but the man called Chris held up a hand to him.

"*Hadi, hadi,*" he said quickly. *Quiet, quiet.* "*Sawf 'usaeiduk.*"
I will help you.

That shut Essien up somewhat, but he was still crying. Addax found himself heaved up by the big blond man with the beard, being carried toward the warhorses that were tethered at the side of the road. No sooner were they put upon them than the warriors, men from a faraway land who spoke a strange language, were giving them water and stale bread.

But neither boy cared.

They wolfed it down.

Little did either one of them know that the food represented hope, and the Christian knights represented destiny. Hope and destiny came to Addax and Essien that day.

And they embraced it.

CHAPTER ONE

Year of Our Lord 1228
Tournament sponsored by the Earl of Hereford and Worcester
Lioncross Abbey Castle, the Welsh Marches

H E SAW THE lance lower a split second before it hit his shield. That gave him enough time to slightly move his own lance, hitting the knight in the left arm, which, in turn, jammed it into his chest, knocking him clean off his horse.

Crash!

The crowd went mad.

Essien heard the cheers of the crowd and would have liked to acknowledge them, but the problem was that he was covered with splinters from Paris de Norville's shattered lance and at least two of the splinters were big enough to pierce him. He could feel them rammed into the skin of his shoulder and had at least one that came through his visor. It hadn't hit his eye, thank God, but it was on his face.

He could feel the blood.

He was also going to beat de Norville silly because of it.

But first, he had a moment of victory to savor, and he did. He raised his arm, acknowledging the crowd, and they loved him for it. They particularly loved the God of Vengeance, as Essien was known on the tournament circuit, because he'd been known to throw coins into the crowd when he won. That always made him a favorite. But more than that, he was very handsome, with his bright smile and pale brown eyes, and women seemed to naturally be drawn to him. He was, as his friends so kindly put it, the flame that attracted the moths.

You attract bugs, his brother once teased him.

But there were no bugs on this day, only beautiful women, stiff competition, and food and gaiety all around. As he reined his blond stallion back to the staging area beyond the lists, he could see a host of knights and squires waiting for him.

"Well done, Es," his brother said, grasping the horse's bridle so Essien could dismount. "You showed de Norville how it's done."

Essien was helped from the horse by his dearest friend other than his brother, Cassian de Velt, a knight who also happened to be competing in the tournament. But, at the moment, Cassian was simply concerned with all the wood splinters in Essien, and he carefully turned the man around to examine him. But he wasn't the only one. Addax handed the horse to a pair of squires, and as they took the animal and equipment away, Addax joined Cassian in inspecting Essien's condition. The man looked like a pincushion with all of the wood sticking out of him. In fact, he held his arms out, away from his sides, and grunted unhappily.

"Pick out what you can," he said. "I have it everywhere."

As Cassian and another knight by the name of Ashton de Royans began carefully pulling wood out of his mail and tunic, Addax went to his brother's head and unlatched the helm.

"Careful," Essien said. "It came through my visor. I can feel it on my face."

Addax proceeded cautiously. He had the helm halfway off when another knight, older and seasoned, joined them. Christopher de Lohr, Earl of Hereford and Worcester, and the host of the tournament, peered closely at Essien's head.

"God's Bones," he muttered, helping Addax at that point. "Where do you feel it on your face, Es?"

"Near my left eye," Essien said, closing his eyes to protect them. "If you give the helm a shake, the shards might fall out."

Addax did just that. With a quick shake, three pieces of wood fell onto Essien's shoulders. Addax popped the helm all the way off at that point, giving him and Christopher a full view of Essien's face. There was a small stream of blood from a cut near his eye, trailing down his left cheek, but that seemed to be it. For the most part, he was intact and unscathed.

Luckily.

"Turn around," Addax said, pushing his brother gently to get the man to turn a circle for him so he could look him over. "I do not see any other damage. I think you were fortunate."

Essien ran a finger over his cheek, looking at the blood he'd scraped away. "I thought it was worse," he said honestly. "I knew he could not unseat me, but that lance exploded in a way I've not seen before."

"That is because it was made from Crack Willow."

The voice came from behind, and they all turned to see a young knight walking up. Sir William de Wolfe had spoken those words—a knight who had seen around twenty-seven years, but a man who had already earned himself an astonishing reputation in the north against the Scots. He was big, powerful, cunning, and the most brilliant man at any gathering. His intelligence was legendary. He also happened to be Paris' best friend, and when he saw that he had Essien's attention, he grinned.

"Crack Willow is supposed to be more flexible," he continued, clarifying his statement. "It can bend a great deal and then snap back, and that snap can push a man off his horse. Unfortunately, in your case, it simply shattered. I came to see if you were well, Es. Were you hurt?"

Instead of being touched by the inquiry, Essien went in the opposite direction. He flared, charging at de Wolfe. "So that idiot of a man you call your friend was testing something new on me?" he said angrily. "It could have killed me!"

William wasn't backing up. Essien was big and he was strong, but William was bigger and stronger. "I've been using the same wood myself," he said steadily, holding up his hands in surrender. "If it works as it should, it's lighter for a man to hold. It makes a joust easier when one has more control over the lance. But I am very sorry it broke on you."

Essien was on him by that point, his angry face a few inches from William's. He didn't swing at him or try to touch him—it seemed he mostly wanted to stare him down to get his point across.

"It shattered and a splinter flew in through my visor," he said, pointing to the smeared stream of blood. "What if it had hit me in the eye? I would be blind right now."

William looked at the blood, seeing the wound just along his hairline. "I'm sorry, Es, truly," he said sincerely. "I've never seen a willow lance explode like that one did. Paris wasn't deliberately trying to hurt you. You *know* that."

Essien did, but he was still frustrated. With a scowl, he turned away, back to Cassian and Addax, who began helping him remove his armor and protection. William's gaze was lingering on them when he felt a warm, strong hand on his shoulder.

"William," Christopher said. He'd been listening to the entire conversation. "Are the marshals aware that you are using a different wood?"

William looked at the man. His father, Edward, had been a close friend and ally of Christopher de Lohr during his lifetime, so William had been raised on the stories of the valor of Christopher, the right hand of King Richard, in his younger years. The man was like a god to him, a legend without equal. William drew every inspiration from Christopher, from the way he had trained to the manner in which he dealt with his men. He well remembered his father speaking about Christopher's "quiet authority." That was something that had left an imprint on a young boy who would grow up to be a great knight with skill and wisdom beyond his years.

And he owed everything to Christopher.

"Nay, my lord, they are not aware," William answered honestly. "We have used the lances in practice and wanted to test one out in competition. If it was a success, we would petition to use it regularly."

Christopher's blue eyes glimmered with some mirth. "You could be disqualified for using a lance with an unsanctioned material," he said. "Do you plan to use other lances like it?"

William nodded. "Aye, my lord."

"Then tell the marshals or I will."

The roar of the crowd suddenly caught their attention, and they turned to see that another bout was about to go off. It was one of the semifinal rounds, the same round that Essien had just competed in against de Norville. The start of a new game had them all momentarily distracted as they strained to catch a glimpse of who was about to compete.

"My lord, that is your son, Curtis," William pointed out. "He's riding against Kieran Hage."

Christopher frowned, taking a few steps toward the lists and spying his heir's standards on the body of a silver charger. "I thought he was going this afternoon," he said. "And when we last spoke, he did not tell me he was going against Hage."

There was some concern in that statement because Sir Kieran Hage was, perhaps, the strongest man in all of England. He wasn't the fastest, or even the most cunning, but he was as powerful as a bull and hell with a sword. He had no equal in battle. He also happened to be William's closest friend, along with Paris. The three of them were sometimes called the Terrible Trio, or the Troublesome Trio, depending on what they'd done and just how badly they had behaved. Stories of their gambling exploits were legendary, even at their young age.

But Christopher wasn't thinking about that. Three spirited knights didn't concern him. But his son going up against the knight known as Goliath on the tournament circuit did.

No wonder Curtis hadn't told him.

"Christ," he muttered. "De Wolfe, is Hage using that exploding wood for his lance, also?"

William hesitated for a moment. "Aye," he said. "We all have them."

Christopher whirled on him. "Then you had better stop this bout immediately and tell Hage to switch out his lance for one that is legal," he said. "If he makes a pass at Curtis and that thing breaks and drives wood into him, I will have you and your friends banished from every tournament from Kent to the Shetlands, and then I will take pleasure in beating each and every one of you until your backs are raw and my hands are broken. Do you hear me?"

William was on the run. He bolted onto the tournament field itself just as Curtis and Kieran were taking positions against one another. As Christopher watched the situation carefully, he felt a body standing to his right.

"What's that about?"

Christopher recognized the voice of his son-in-law, Alexander de Sherrington. The man had been helping Curtis prepare for his bout and now stood on the sidelines, watching like everyone else. Alexander had married Christopher's eldest daughter, Christin, several years ago and they had quite a brood of wild sons, in whom Christopher took great delight. He knew a little something about incorrigible lads because he'd fathered six of them.

Perhaps he understood them better than most.

"The Terrible Trio is at it again," Christopher muttered.

Alexander looked at him, puzzled. "Why do you say that?"

"Because de Norville was using a lance of softwood," Christopher replied. "William told me that they were testing them out because they hoped they would be more of an advantage in the joust, but they did not tell the marshals, so they are using illegal tools. Hage has one, too."

"And you are stopping the bout?"

"I am forcing William to inform the marshals."

Alexander frowned, looking out to the field once more to where de Wolfe was holding up the first run as he spoke with the marshals. "My God," he said in disgust. "Why can that trio not use their cunning and intelligence for good? Why must they always cause so much mayhem?"

Christopher snorted softly. "It is never evil," he said. "They aren't the type. But they're naughty children and have been ever since they learned to talk. Edward de Wolfe was constantly lamenting about his youngest son and how chaotically brilliant he was. William is, if nothing else, entertaining."

Alexander didn't happen to think so. "Why are they using softwood lances?"

Christopher shrugged. "Presumably to avoid the breakage like we saw on Essien," he said, turning around to see that Essien was stripped and Ashton was cleaning the blood from Essien's face as Addax supervised. "A softer wood would be more flexible in the joust. But you saw how that lance exploded, did you not?"

Alexander nodded. "I did," he said. "I was just at the base of the lists trying to explain that phenomenon to some worried women."

"Your wife and her mother?"

"Aye," Alexander said, pointing toward the middle of the lists. "Lady Hereford is in her usual seat, next to yours. When I was finished assisting Curtis, she wanted me to see to Essien. How is he?"

"Tell her that he is well," Christopher said. Then he looked pointedly at Alexander. "And tell Rebecca that he is well. That is why you really came, was it not?"

Alexander fought off a grin. "Rebecca saw the blow," he said. "She is… concerned."

Christopher sighed heavily. "She is too young to be concerned for him."

"She has seen eighteen summers, Chris."

"And he is twenty years older than she is," Christopher shot back. "Essien is too old for her."

"I am almost twenty years older than Christin," Alexander said softly. "Our marriage has been perfect."

Christopher grunted unhappily. "Why, Sherry?" he demanded weakly. "Why must you remind me of the age difference between you and Cissy?"

Alexander started laughing. "Because I like to be cruel," he said. "Honestly, Chris, I would not worry if Rebecca is infatuated with Essien right now. She was infatuated with someone else last month, wasn't she? A d'Vant son?"

Christopher just shook his head. "A de Nerra, not d'Vant," he grumbled. "I should be used to it by now, my daughters finding men fascinating, but the truth is that I am *not* used to it. Christin was never particularly interested in men until she met you, and Brielle only had one man in her life from the time she was a young lass. There was never anyone else for her than Cassius, so the truth is that Rebecca is my first experience with a daughter who seems to be infatuated with a new man every week. She is driving me mad."

Alexander continued laughing. "If it is any consolation, Essien is aware and he has no interest in her."

Christopher looked at him, frowning. "Why not?" he said, offended. "Is my daughter not beautiful enough for him?"

Alexander snorted, shaking his head. "To tell you the truth, Rebecca is probably the most beautiful of your daughters—aside from my own wife, of course," he said. "And that is saying something. Rebecca has that flaming red hair and Dustin's gray eyes, and it is an astonishing combination. You are going to have to protect her against the hunters looking for a lovely conquest."

Christopher sighed unhappily. "I already am," he said. "There are a few knights at this tournament who have tried to give her their favor. That is why Dustin is in the lists with her—to fight off the amorous horde."

Alexander continued to chuckle. Rebecca de Lohr, who had been a child with wildly curly, untamed red hair, buck teeth, and skinny legs like a chicken's had grown into a woman of magnificent beauty somewhere in the past few years. Her teeth were still a little bucked, but it only created a more charming smile. And she was utterly, completely fascinated with Essien, who came over to stand with Christopher and Alexander as William finished speaking with the marshals.

"What is de Wolfe doing?" Essien asked.

Christopher glanced at the source of his daughter's infatuation. "I told him to tell the marshals about the softwood lance that Hage is using," Christopher said, watching the marshals approach Hage. "I have a feeling this bout will be over before it starts."

"They will disqualify him?" Essien asked.

Christopher nodded faintly, his only answer, as he watched the marshals engage in conversation with Kieran. Essien, however, was more animated.

"They had better disqualify him," he fumed. "If he uses on Curtis what de Norville used on me, it will be a miracle if Curtis is not impaled. In fact, I will tell the marshals precisely that."

He started to move, but Christopher and Alexander held on to him. "Nay, lad," Christopher said. "The marshals will make their own decision."

By now, the marshals had taken the lance from Kieran and were inspecting it. As everyone on the grounds and in the lists watched, the marshals pored over the lance before finally shaking their heads at Kieran and indicating that he was disqualified. Without a word, Kieran turned his horse around and headed out of the arena as Curtis was awarded the victory by default.

By this time, several of the competitors were gathering around Christopher and Alexander, confused about what they'd just seen. There were more than twenty of them at that point, and two of them had already gone against William, Paris, or Kieran, since they were currently in the semifinals.

The questions were beginning to come.

Since Christopher didn't want a war party on his hands, men out for the blood of the three knights who had used the non-sanctioned wood, he had to think of something fast. Even Curtis, who had been poised to go against Kieran, came back into the staging area, completely confused. Christopher went to his son to see what the marshals had told him because he would base his reply to the other knights on what Curtis told him.

Curtis was disappointed. That was clear. He slid from his steed, an expensive and high-strung animal that his father had given him when he received his knighthood, and began unlatching his helm as his father approached.

"Well?" Christopher said. "What happened? What were you told?"

Curtis grunted as he pulled his helm off, revealing shiny blond hair, closely cut. "Hage has evidently fractured his lance and did not bring a spare," he said. Then he shrugged. "The man cannot compete and I win by default."

Christopher liked that answer. The marshals had used their discretion because they didn't want Kieran singled out as someone to mistrust because, in these games, men were dependent upon their reputations to be admitted and to compete.

A nasty reputation for underhandedness could follow a man for years.

"Ah," Christopher said, turning to the group of knights

behind him. He raised his voice so all could hear him. "Hage fractured his replacement lance and does not have another. He is out of the competition."

A short, sweet answer, one that satisfied everyone, and they began to return to their regular duties. Christopher looked at Alexander, who waggled his eyebrows in agreement over the little white lie. Kieran Hage was a man among men, most trustworthy, and given the fact that Christopher had known him, as well as William and Paris, for most of their lives, he knew the whole softwood experiment wasn't born from mischief, but from a sincere desire to use something in competition that might give them an advantage.

But not at the cost of the poles exploding on impact.

"Who is next, I wonder?" Alexander asked, looking out to the field as William followed Kieran out of the arena. "I haven't seen the list of competitors yet."

"Me," Curtis said, disgruntled. "I was supposed to triumph against Hage. I feel cheated."

Christopher eyed his eager son. "You will be able to compete in the next round, so I wouldn't feel so."

Curtis wasn't eased. He looked at Essien and the bloody scratch on his face. "At least you were able to humiliate de Norville," he said. "I was not even afforded that opportunity."

Essien shook his head. "De Norville is easier to humiliate than Hage," he said. "It is possible that Kieran could have bested you, but only by the remotest chance."

He was trying to be kind in saying that Kieran was a beast of a man who would not go down easily. There was always the chance of failure. Curtis was young and skilled and as strong as a bull, but Kieran was more than a match. Too bad, too.

It would have made for great competition.

As Essien mulled over the fact that Hage was out of the competition now, he turned away from Christopher and Alexander, heading back to his brother and their section of the staging area. They had a big tent set up and a small area beneath a tree where the horses were tethered. He could see Addax back by the tent now, preparing to inspect his reserve lance that the squires were polishing, when he heard someone calling his name. Curious, he looked over his right shoulder to see a woman with flaming hair waving at him.

Rebecca de Lohr had made an appearance.

Essien forced a smile, taking a deep breath and hoping her father would see her before she reached him. Essien had known Rebecca since she was born, but for some reason, she had decided over the past month or so that she was madly in love with him. He'd never seen her so attentive. In fact, she'd mostly ignored him for her entire life, so the latest surge of attention was both odd and unwelcome.

Here she came, waving her hand at him.

"Essien!" she called, smiling. "I had to come and see for myself if you were injured. Your bout was most exciting!"

Essien came to a halt, sighing with resignation. Given the fact that she was his liege's daughter, he couldn't very well be rude to her. Rebecca was a beautiful woman with extraordinary coloring—hair like molten metal and eyes the color of storm clouds. She had a pert little nose and a dusting of freckles across her cheeks, and her beauty was beyond compare. Even Essien was not hard pressed to admit that. But she was a child, and he saw her as a child, and he wanted nothing to do with her.

At least, not in *that* way.

"Thank you, my lady," he said. "Did you see the entire event or did you cover your eyes up like you did the last time?"

Rebecca laughed. "Did you see that?"

"I did."

She continued to laugh, and Essien had to admit that it was a charming gesture. Her two older sisters, Christin and Brielle, were rather serious, accomplished, and skilled women, more mature than most, so Rebecca's charismatic manner did not follow in line with her mother or her elder sisters. Not that Lady Hereford or Lady de Sherrington or Lady de Velt were any less charming, but Rebecca had a free manner about her, as if she didn't have a care in the world. She was sweet and captivating and a bit of a flirt, and she latched on to Essien's arm before he managed to move out of her range.

"Well, I did not do it the second time," she assured him. "Es, take me into the vendors' stalls, will you? I want to buy some sweets."

He shook his head, resisting the urge to pull his arm away from her warm fingers. "I cannot," he said. "The next round will probably be starting within the hour and I cannot be off gobbling puddings or pies. Go find someone else to buy you sweets."

Rebecca was undeterred. "Come with me or I will tell my father."

"Tell him. I do not care. He will tell you the same thing I just did."

Her eyes were twinkling mischievously. "Papa?" she called, knowing Christopher was within earshot. "Papa, come immediately. I have been insulted!"

Christopher did indeed hear her. She was hard to miss because of her high-pitched voice. He had been in conversation with Alexander, ignoring Rebecca's summons, until she turned to him and shouted.

"Do you not care that Essien has horribly offended me?" she demanded. "Come at once. I demand you punish him."

Christopher sighed heavily before turning to her. "I am glad he offended you," he said. "You probably deserved it. Now, leave the man alone and go back to the lists. This is no place for you."

"How cruel you are!"

"Do as I say. Go back to the lists."

"But I want sweets and Essien will not take me!"

Christopher cocked an eyebrow. "If I come over there, I will throw you over my shoulder and carry you back to your mother," he said. "If that is something you are unconcerned with, then by all means, continue to disobey me."

"I would be honored to escort your daughter to the sweets vendors, my lord."

An unexpected offer entered the mix and Christopher turned to see a knight he only vaguely knew. Lance le Kerque, blond and brawny and handsome, was standing a few feet away. A former bachelor knight who had spent a good deal of time on the tournament circuit as a competitor known as the King of Pain, Lance had only recently sworn an oath to one of Christopher's neighbors, an older lord by the name of Harald de Efford, Lord Eckington. De Efford was in bad health, however, so Christopher was surprised to see the man's new knight at the tournament and presumably away from his liege.

"Le Kerque?" he said, surprised. "I did not see your name on the rolls. Don't tell me that your lord accompanied you here?"

Lance nodded. "He did, my lord," he said. "He sends his greetings."

Christopher was surprised to hear it. "He must be feeling

better, then?"

"He seems to be, my lord," Land said. "He wanted very much to attend."

"Are you competing?"

"Tomorrow," Lance said. "I was supposed to enter the games for the joust, but we came too late for me to be added. I am, however, entered in the mass competition. I was here in the staging area, greeting some friends, when I saw Lady Rebecca. I am happy to escort her if your men are otherwise occupied."

Christopher looked at the men around him. He only saw men who served him, or his allies, and he had no idea what had happened to Curtis, but he didn't want to send Rebecca off with a knight he barely knew, even if the man did serve a trusted ally.

"Your offer is kind, but no need," he said. "Sherry will escort her."

"Papa!" Rebecca said unhappily. She'd been rather flattered at the handsome knight's offer, but now it was turning into an embarrassment. "*Nay*."

She drew the word out as if implying to him, in one small word, that she truly didn't want to be seen, yet again, with her sister's husband. Alexander seemed to be her escort all too frequently because he was a family member and a father with children of his own, so he tended to be judgmental and protective when it came to his ravishing sister-in-law. It was like having a personal guard dog, something Rebecca didn't want.

And Christopher was well aware of it.

"Then you may choose," he said. "It is either me or Sherry. Those are your choices."

Rebecca frowned in an expression that looked very much like her mother. In fact, she had a personality much like her mother's had been when Christopher first met the lovely Dustin, Lady Hereford. A spitfire was a fairly apt term. Therefore, when Rebecca turned on her heel and began marching away without either escort, Christopher wasn't surprised. With Rebecca, that kind of thing was expected. But he silently nodded to Alexander, who took the hint and began to follow Rebecca as she stormed off.

De Lohr women were feisty that way.

That left Lance standing there rather awkwardly, since his offer of an escort had been refused. Christopher realized that. Not wanting to offend the knight, he offered a brief explanation.

"She can be difficult to handle even in the best of times," he said quietly. "I meant no offense against you, because your offer was kind, but Rebecca is… headstrong. It would be unfair to put you in a situation where she might be unmanageable. At least she has a healthy fear of Sherry and that alone will keep her from running amok."

Lance understood. Sort of. "Of course, my lord," he said. "No offense taken."

"Good," Christopher said. Then he gestured toward the lists. "Take me to Eckington. I've not seen the man in some time and I should like to greet him. This is my tournament, after all. I should like to be a good host."

"My pleasure, my lord," Lance said. "At least I shall be able to escort one de Lohr today."

He grinned as Christopher conceded the point. As the pair of them headed off toward the lists, that left Essien still standing there, realizing that le Kerque had saved him from the predatory redhead. Better still, he'd come through it without raising her father's anger. It would have been easy to give in to her and become the son-in-law of the great Earl of Hereford and Worcester, but that wasn't what Essien wanted out of life. He loved the de Lohr family, so that wasn't the issue. But settling was. Marriage was.

He didn't want to do either at the moment.

Out on the tournament field, he noticed that the marshals were preparing another pair of knights, ready to run at one another. He recognized the colors, as one was a knight from Ludlow and the other was none other than William de Wolfe's elder brother, Jonathan de Wolfe. The bout promised to be exciting because Jonathan de Wolfe, or "Wolfie," as he was known, was as passionate a competitor as his younger brother. More so, even. The de Wolfe brothers hadn't gone up against one another in competition yet, but if things progressed the way everyone expected them to, William and Jonathan would go against each other at some point.

And that promised to be quite a match.

"Es!"

Essien was distracted from his observations of the tournament field by a shout, turning around to see Addax trying to catch his attention.

"What is it?" Essien called.

Addax waved him over. "Get over here," he said. "We've another bout later today, brother, and if you do not get over here to inspect your lances, I will damage them and you will fail."

Essien headed in his brother's direction, grinning. "It is the only way you will be able to beat me when we go against one another."

Addax snorted. "That is bold talk coming from a man who still sucks his thumb when he goes to sleep."

Essien rolled his eyes. "I do suck, but not thumbs," he said, a naughty smile on his lips. "At least, not my *own* thumbs."

Addax frowned at him. "Appalling," he said, turning back to the equipment. "You needn't remind me of the fact that you take tournament followers into your bed. I told you that is a very bad idea."

Essien was still grinning as he plopped down onto the nearest stool. "Mayhap to you, but not to me," he said. "I do not have a wife to go home to like you do. A man must take comfort when the opportunity strikes."

Addax pulled forth one of their spare lances. It was long and heavy, and he ended up inspecting the tip of it closely. "You need to find a wife," he said. "You are too old not to think about your legacy, Es."

Essien rolled his eyes. "That talk again," he said. "Just because you are married and have children, now that's all you talk about."

"Because I see how important it is," Addax said, perhaps a little forcefully. But he toned it down as he continued. "We owe our father that much. He sacrificed his life to ensure our survival, so the least you can do is breed sons to continue the family name. That is the greatest honor you can give our father."

The smile faded from Essien's face as he thought of those who had come before him, faceless men with names he still remembered, only the recollection of Kitara was like a dream. He hardly remembered it at all and, in fact, he completely identified as being English because he'd been part of the English culture far longer than he was ever part of Kitara. He'd been so young when everything fell apart.

Now, Kitara was just a memory.

"I am more English than I was ever Kitaran," he said quietly. "I do not remember the land of our birth other than whispers of memories. Feelings, mostly."

Addax knew that. It was something Essien sometimes wrestled with. Addax remembered a good deal more because he was older, but to Essien, Kitara was just something they spoke of. Like a distant relative he was familiar with but had never really met. People he knew in name only but had no emotional connection with.

"I know," Addax said. "But the fact remains that you *are* a prince. You are one of only two surviving princes of Kitara. It is time for you to find a wife and fulfill your destiny."

Essien closed his eyes for a moment, trying to remember things from the land of his birth. He remembered a big building with sand-colored stone and a pond with fish and flowers in it. Truthfully, he didn't mind his brother reminding him of where he came from. He needed reminding because it didn't come naturally for him like it did for Addax. He was the prince of one land, the resident of another.

"What do you suppose our lives would have been like had we remained at Lankara?" he said. "You would not have met Emmeline. Have you ever thought of that?"

Addax nodded. "Certainly," he said. "I would have married a princess from another land and we would have had a strong political union, much like our parents had. Hopefully I would have loved her."

"But that is not certain."

"Nay," Addax said with regret. "It is not certain. Emmy is my moon and my stars. She is all things to me. I cannot imagine my life without her, but on the other hand, had we remained in Kitara, I would not know what I was missing, if that makes sense. I could not mourn what I never knew."

"If you had to make a choice between Kitara and your wife?"

Addax waved him off. "That is unfair," he said. "Of course I would have wished for our parents to be alive, our country to still be ours. I regret that deeply. But I do not regret what I have now in life. It is not a substitute for what I lost. It is a life I have made for myself and I am proud of it. I am the Earl of Deira, Es. I am an important man in a country I was not even born in. De Lohr and his fellow warlords and even the king embraced me and gave me great opportunities. They have done the same for you, too. I will always be extremely grateful for that."

"As am I," Essien insisted softly. "I did not mean to make it sound otherwise. I was simply thinking aloud. I suppose I was thinking that we are all that is left of the House of al-Kort. We will marry Englishwomen and have sons, who will also marry Englishwomen and have sons. Soon, our bloodlines will be so diluted that any trace of Kitara will be in name only. Even the name may change in the years to come. Is that truly honoring our ancestors?"

Addax gave him an impatient expression. "And what is your solution?" he said. "Never to marry? Our father did not help us escape to a better life only to have you become a childless monk."

Essien knew that. And the truth was that he wasn't opposed to marrying an Englishwoman and having sons. But what he'd said about diluting their bloodlines was right.

Someday, the royal line of Kitara would cease to exist.

It wasn't something he liked to think about.

"Well," he said, rising from the stool, "I have no intention of becoming a monk, in any case. And tell your wife to stop trying to force her friends and ladies upon me."

Addax fought off a grin. "Emmeline thinks you need some encouragement," he said. "Her friends are quite lovely."

"I will pick my own woman, thank you very much."

Addax put the lance he'd been inspecting aside. "Then hurry and do it," he said. "Es, you are too old to be so directionless. Find a woman who puts you on the right path to happiness and I promise you will not regret it."

Essien curled his lip at his brother. "Spoken like a married man."

"Spoken like a *happy* man."

Essien didn't have a retort for that, but he was growing weary of the conversation. He didn't like it when his brother hammered him over the fact that he wasn't married. It had been happening with more frequency since Addax married a couple of years ago.

"Very well, happy man," he said, rather mockingly. "I am going to see to my horse and then mayhap take a lie-down. De Norville's exploding lance has given me an aching head."

"They will be drawing lots for the next rounds in about an hour."

"I will be there."

Addax let him go. He sat down to carefully file away a small crack in the tip of his lance, but his attention kept moving to his brother, who was heading off to the corral where the horses were kept. He knew Essien didn't want to hear about marriage or women, but the truth was that he needed to. He was a prince of Kitara, and those bloodlines were valuable and prestigious. Christopher had mentioned helping Essien find an advantageous marriage a couple of times, so Addax knew that de Lohr was thinking along those lines, too. In the absence of Amare,

Christopher was the closest thing they had to a father and, quite honestly, Addax was very grateful for it. He could only imagine how pleased and relieved his father would have been to know a man like de Lohr had taken care of his sons. As a father now himself, with a small son and another child on the way, Addax could appreciate that relationship more than ever. Someday, God willing, Essien would, too.

If the man's stubbornness didn't get the better of him first.

Thinking on his resistant, ridiculous brother, Addax went back to work on the lance. He suspected that an already eventful day was only going to become more eventful.

As he would discover later, he'd be right.

CHAPTER TWO

THEY COULDN'T GET enough of the trained dogs.

Lots of children were gathering near the food vendors' row, watching a man with five dogs that were very smart and well trained. One dog balanced an inflated pig bladder on his nose while still others leapt over little barriers, painted colorfully, and flying little banners. But her two daughters were mesmerized by the smart canines, so much so that wild horses couldn't have dragged them away.

Certainly not their mother.

Somewhere, her father was off conducting business at the Earl of Hereford's tournament. This was a major event on the Welsh marches and there were people from as far as Devon who had come to enjoy the sport and spectacle. Her father's knight had offered to escort her and her children to the sweets vendor, but her father had declined. That was a good thing, because she really didn't want to be alone with Lance le Kerque. Not after he'd mentioned that her daughters needed a father and that widowhood didn't suit her. He'd never come right out and made his intentions plain, but he didn't have to. He'd been making comments for weeks, nearly ever since he came into service for her father.

Catalina de Efford de Barenton didn't want another husband.

She just wanted to be left in peace.

"Mama! Look! Look at the dogs!"

Jolted from her reflections, Catalina smiled weakly at her youngest daughter, who was nearly out of her mind with joy at the little dogs who had just spun around in a circle at the owner's command. Ines was the excitable one, while Adabella, older by almost two years, was more serious and skeptical. She was a very intelligent girl and not given to flights of fancy like her younger sister was, although she seemed to be enjoying the dogs nearly as much. She wouldn't show it, however, as if embarrassed to be caught enjoying something.

Adabella was a complicated child.

"I believe the dogs are going to be here for the rest of the day," Catalina said. "If we leave them for a moment to purchase food, I am sure they will be here when we return."

Ines wasn't particularly happy to hear that. "Now?" she said, verging on tears.

Catalina was gentle with her. "I am hungry," she said. "Adabella is hungry and I know you did not break your fast this morning, so let us find something to eat and then we will return. I promise."

Ines was disappointed, but she nodded her head. Just once, so her mother wouldn't think she was being too agreeable. If Adabella was complicated, Ines was stubborn. Infinitely so. With a smile, Catalina had reached out to take her daughter by the hand when one of the little dogs suddenly bolted off.

"I'll get him!" Ines cried.

She was off and running before Catalina could stop her.

That had Catalina telling Adabella, very quickly, to remain with the dogs while Catalina took off after Ines. The youngest girl was very fast, as small children often are, and Catalina followed her daughter down the main avenue, shouting for her to stop.

Ines wasn't listening.

At some point, Catalina was certain her daughter was trying to outrun her mother more than she was actually trying to catch the dog. The more Catalina called to her, the more Ines ignored her, and Catalina was torn between terror and rage. She desperately wanted to catch her daughter to make sure the girl would be safe, but she also wanted to catch her daughter so that she could swat her on the buttocks for such foolishness. Ines wasn't a naughty girl, but she did have a tendency to be disobedient, even at her young age. Sometimes it was cute, but in times like this, it was horrifying.

The chase went on. Somehow, Ines had managed to end up running down an alleyway, and when Catalina fell in behind her, albeit quite far behind her, she couldn't even see the dog that Ines was supposed to be chasing. Now, apparently her daughter was running simply for the sake of running, and that absolutely infuriated Catalina. Ines had done that before, loving to take her mother on a merry chase simply for the laughs, but it was never in a situation like this. Never in a busy village where there were people and horses and conveyances that could quite easily run over a small child. Catalina was seriously thinking about putting a tether around her daughter the next time they went out in public. Hopefully that would eliminate moments like this.

Moments that took ten years off Catalina's life.

She was midway down the alley when Ines suddenly took a hard left and disappeared from sight. She'd evidently run in between two cottages, but by the time Catalina reached that point, a panicked glance down the alleyway showed no signs of her daughter.

That child had simply vanished.

God help me, Catalina thought, trying not to panic. *God help me to find her!*

Catalina's calls for her daughter resumed in earnest.

ℭℬ

HE HADN'T GONE to check on his horse, nor had he lain down to rest. Instead, Essien decided to go into the village.

The tournament was being held in a wide-open field to the southeast of Lioncross Abbey Castle. The precise location was in the space between the village of Lioncross and the castle itself, so the rather large vendor village that had popped up to the east also butted up against the village itself, integrating itself into the cottages that were on the fringe of the settlement.

That was how Essien found himself in the village.

He'd just wandered in. He could smell fresh bread baking somewhere and had followed his nose, but then the wind shifted and he found himself standing in a small avenue that was full of people but no bread. At one point, he thought he caught a flash of Rebecca's bright red hair, and that had him darting into an alleyway to get away from her. Pressed flat against the wall that he was next to, he dared to peek out from behind his protection when he heard sniffles.

Lots of them.

Curious, he looked around only to see a small girl sitting on the ground several feet away. She had been partially in the shadows, so he simply hadn't noticed her. She had bloodied knees, and her palms were scraped, and he turned to her purely out of natural concern.

"My lady?" he said gently. "Are you injured?"

The little girl looked up at him. She was a beautiful child, with dark blonde hair and enormous blue eyes. Those eyes were full of tears, running down her face, and her reply was to hold up her hands to show him the scrapes on her palms. She was quite young, and small, so he took a knee a few feet away to be more on her level.

"Did you fall?" he asked.

She nodded firmly, almost angrily, looking at her bloodied palms, but she didn't speak. She just kept sniffling.

"Ah," he said. "I see. Let me guess—you were chasing a very bad man whom you saw rob a vendor who was selling apples made from the shiniest gold. He took those golden apples, which were the only thing the vendor had to sell, because he has twenty beautiful daughters and he must buy silken dresses for all of them. Is that what happened?"

Her tears were fading. Sort of. "There were apples?" she said, wiping her nose and smearing mucus and dirt across her cheek.

Essien nodded. "Golden apples," he confirmed. "You were very heroic to chase the thief, but do not feel bad that you did not catch him. He had five hundred men helping him and not even you can fight off five hundred men, so you should not feel sad. Let me take you back to your mother and she can clean your wounds. I will tell her how brave you were."

The little girl wiped at her eyes but didn't move as he had requested. She simply looked at him, repeatedly wiping her eyes and smearing dirt all over her face. She didn't seem apt to speak again, even after his charming story, and he was running out of things to say.

He glanced at the child's clothing. It was rather fine, with expensive embroidery, and she had well-made leather slippers. This wasn't some lost peasant child. This was a child whose parents had means, perhaps even the child of a knight competing in the tournament.

Someone was surely looking for her.

"Since you are so brave, mayhap you will accompany me back to the lists?" he said, trying to convince the child to go with him. "Surely I will be quite safe with you as my escort. Will you not help me? Please?"

He held his hand out to her, but she continued to remain on the ground. She didn't seem too eager to comply with his request. He was certain that he was going to have to try again when she abruptly stood up. She didn't take his hand, however, and Essien stood up beside her, thinking that she really was a tiny thing, and with so many people and horses and wagons about, a child that size could easily be lost or crushed. Essien had always been thoughtful and chivalrous, something that had gotten him into trouble on occasion. Whereas many knights could simply discount a lone child in need, Essien wasn't one of them. His sense of compassion wouldn't allow it. If there was a need for assistance, he would always offer to provide it.

Even to a lost little girl.

"My name is Essien," he told her, reaching out to grasp her little hand. "What is your name?"

Surprisingly, she didn't pull away from him. "Ines," she said.

He smiled. "Lady Ines," he said. "I am honored to make your acquaintance. Do you know where your mother or father is?"

She shook her head and hiccupped again. "I was finding the

dog."

"Finding the dog?" Essien repeated. "What dog?"

She pointed down the alleyway, to the busy street. "He ran away."

He nodded in understanding. "I see," he said. "Was it your dog?"

She nodded, wiping at her eyes again. As they began to walk toward the end of the alleyway, Essien reached down to pick her up to keep her safe.

"Now you are high up," he said. "You can see more easily. We shall find your dog."

She didn't try to push away from him, thankfully. In fact, she'd been rather compliant. He'd taken about ten steps, heading toward the main road that would lead into the tournament village, when he heard someone shriek from behind. A faint sound, but unmistakable. Before he could turn around to see the source of the sound, however, he received a heavy blow to his shoulder and neck.

Down to his knees he went.

Someone was yanking the little girl out of his arms, who began screaming. Essien tried to grab her, because she was surely terrified, but there were two more heavy blows against his back. A third one hit him across the back of the head, but he was already falling forward, so it mostly glanced off. Still, stars burst in his vision. His survival instincts kicked in, and as he went down, he lashed out a big, booted foot and caught whoever was behind him in the legs.

Another shriek as his attacker hit the ground.

By this time, he was on his knees, launching himself at whoever had assaulted him. He could hear the little girl screaming, but he couldn't take the time to tend to her. He was in a fight, clearly someone who was trying to disable him, and he wasn't going to be an easy target. In the midst of the tussle, he came down on a soft, small body, his big hand on the area of the head and face. When his palm came down on a chin and mouth and maybe a nose, he heard another scream, muffled this time, but he really couldn't see who it was because of the stars in his eyes from the blow to the back of his head.

A hand came up and a bony finger poked him in the eye.

Grunting in pain, he faltered enough that the same finger went up his nose. It jabbed him right in his left nostril, so hard that his head jerked back in pain and surprise. As he staggered back, hand over his face to get away from the poking fingers, the hands that those fingers were attached to began slapping his head and face.

"Get off me!" the woman cried. "Get… off… get *off*!"

She punctuated the last four words with a slap. Realizing he was wrestling with a woman, Essien quickly leapt to his feet, backing away and trying to clear his vision.

"What was that for?" he demanded. "Why did you attack me?"

"How dare you abduct my daughter!" the woman said angrily. "You *stole* her!"

He blinked, several times, trying to focus on the woman, but he noticed a big piece of wood a few feet away, something he suspected she had used as a weapon.

"I did not steal her," he said. "I found her sitting on the ground with bloodied knees. She said she had been chasing her dog. What a poor mother you are to let that infant run around alone, chasing a dog."

The woman gasped in shock and outrage about the time his vision cleared and Essien found himself looking at a glorious vision. She was positively exquisite as she clutched the little girl against her.

"I did no such thing," she said indignantly. "She ran off and I have been looking for her ever since."

He blinked again, clearing his eyes as much as he could and raking his hair out of his face. He was fairly enraged himself, and he faced off against the woman who had swung the wood at his head with exceptional accuracy.

"She ran off because you are a poor excuse for a mother," he said sternly. "How could you not keep this child so close to you that she could not possibly run away? You should be ashamed of yourself."

The woman was growing increasingly angry. "You do not know what you are speaking of," she said. "You are an ignorant brute."

"And you are a worthless female."

The woman's face was turning red and she opened her mouth to clap back, but she refrained. Clutching her child against her chest, it was clear that she was stewing.

"Worthless or not, I shall report you to Lord Hereford," she said. "We'll see what he has to say about a man like you who steals children."

"Good," Essien said with enthusiastic irritation. "Tell him. Tell him that Essien al-Kort found your child alone and injured in an alleyway and was attempting to help her find her mother. Tell him that you let your child escape your custody and that *you* are at fault here. Not me, lady. I've got better things to do than argue with a fool, so leave me out of your dramatics. The next time your daughter runs away, I hope she doesn't run into someone who will truly do her more harm than your careless-ness has already caused."

With that, he turned and headed toward the main road. He was just drawing near when a little dog suddenly appeared in his pathway. He would have tripped over it had his reflexes been any slower. When he staggered, putting out a hand to brace himself against a wall and keep his balance, the dog stood on its hind legs and began to dance around in a circle.

"It's the dog!" the little girl shrieked. "Look, Mama! The dog!"

The child wormed her way out of her mother's arms in a flash, running for the dog as the little animal danced around. She descended on the pup, squealing with delight, before putting her arms around the little creature and hugging it.

Hand still braced against the wall, Essien watched the entire thing. It occurred to him that this was the animal in question, the whole purpose of the bloody knees and enraged mother. A dumb, adorable pup and his equally adorable owner.

Things were becoming a little clearer now.

"And that is your dog," he said quietly. "I suppose he was here all the time."

The little girl nodded eagerly, hugging the pup as it licked her face happily. She was so joyful that he found himself snorting at her, shaking his head at the ridiculousness of the entire situation. A little girl, a little dog, and it was clear how attached to each other the two of them were. He was starting to see just how she might have slipped away from her mother, loving the dog as she did. Now he was starting to feel the least bit remorseful for what he'd said.

Maybe it hadn't been the mother's carelessness, after all.

"It is not even her dog."

He looked over his shoulder to see the mother standing a few feet away. When their eyes met, she shrugged her shoulders.

"She saw the dog dancing with other dogs and became enamored with it," she said, sounding far calmer than she had just a few moments earlier. "When the dog ran off, she ran after it before I could catch her. I've been frantically searching for her ever since."

Essien gestured to the general area where he'd found the child. "She was over there," he said. "I was here because I smelled bread and thought I might find the street of the bakers through this alleyway. But she was sitting there, weeping, and I took pity on her. I was going to help her find you."

The woman sighed faintly, her gaze moving to her daughter, who was delighted that the dog was licking her chin. "When I saw her in your arms, I panicked," she said. "There are plenty of people who would walk away with a child and I would never see her again. If I was wrong about you, then I apologize."

Essien didn't feel so hostile toward her now. She was truly a beautiful woman, with long, wavy hair, gathered at the nape of her neck, and then braided down her back and secured with a silk ribbon. It was a shade of brown, light, with flecks of gold in it, and her eyes, from what he could see, were an intense shade of blue. The same color as the little girl's. Coupled with her delicate face, pert nose, and generous lips, she was truly a sight to behold.

"As I said, my name is Essien al-Kort," he said. "I am a man of honor and of good reputation. I am a knight sworn to Lord Hereford. If you wish to ask him about me, I am certain he would confirm what I have just told you. And I swear upon my oath that I was not stealing your daughter."

She nodded, seemingly embarrassed now that the fury and fighting had passed. Then she looked at him timidly.

"Did I hurt you?" she asked as if she didn't want to know the answer.

But Essien grinned. "Of course not," he said. "I face worse blows on the tournament field. Yours were nothing, I assure you."

She looked at him curiously. "Are you competing today?"

He looked down at himself, dressed in a dirty, padded tunic and breeches. "I know I do not look like it, but I am," he said. "I am in the coming final bouts."

"Oh?" she said, interested. "Then you must have great skill at what you do."

"I think so," he said, not modest about it at all. "Skill enough to survive a shattered lance and still keep my seat. The same cannot be said for my opponent."

The light of realization came to her eyes. "The shattered lance," she repeated. Then her entire face relaxed as she realized who he was. "You had a bout a little while ago."

"I did." He nodded. "You saw it?"

Her smile broke through, though it was hesitant. "I did," she said. "The lance that burst into a thousand pieces?"

"It burst on me."

"That was truly you?"

"It was," Essien said. "Ask Hereford if you do not believe me. He will tell you the truth."

She chuckled softly, perhaps with some embarrassment. "That will not be necessary," she said. "I believe you. The bout was very exciting."

He beamed. "Good," he said. "It is my pleasure to entertain you. And win money whilst I am doing so."

"And you were unharmed?"

"I am perfectly well."

For the first time since their acquaintance, the mood between them was lightening because the mother was realizing her child had never been in danger with Essien. He wasn't a random brute, but a knight of the highest caliber, one who had just come off the tournament field. The child was still hugging the dog, as happy as could be and clearly unharmed, and the tension was melting away between them.

It was a welcome moment.

"I truly am sorry I attacked you," she said quietly. "As I said, when I saw you carrying my daughter, I thought the worst."

He nodded. "Understandable," he said. "I cannot say that I would not have thought the same thing, given the circumstances."

"You are gracious."

"No harm done, though I'm not sure my left eye will ever be the same."

He meant when she'd tried to gouge the eye out. In fact, it was a little red and irritated, and as he grinned, she appeared exceedingly remorseful.

"I will wash it out for you if you wish," she said. "I shall be happy to make amends if you will let me."

He shook his head. "The offer is appreciated, but there is no need," he said. Then he eyed her, still smiling. "You are quite formidable, in fact. I would not wish to tangle with you again."

Her face flushed red and she quickly lowered her gaze. "It was only out of fear, I assure you."

He looked at her lowered head, thinking her to be quite enchanting. Ferocious, but enchanting.

He rather liked that.

"There is one thing you can do for me," he said.

Her head came up. "What is that?"

"Tell me your name," he said, a glimmer in his eye. "You know mine and I know your daughter's, but I do not know yours."

Her features relaxed, and she smiled, but with some chagrin. Usually, formal introductions were made by others, but with no one around, there was little choice when it came to propriety.

"I am Catalina de Barenton," she said. "My father is Harald de Efford."

"Lord Eckington?"

"You know him?"

Essien nodded. "I do," he said. "He and Hereford are friends and allies. He has come to visit us on occasion, but I did not know he had a daughter."

She nodded. "One child," she said. "He never mentioned me?"

"Not that I heard."

She sighed, as if that was to be expected. "I married young," she said. "I've been away from Eckington Castle for almost ten years, so I am certain my father felt childless at times. My husband served with Richard FitzRoy at Wallingford Castle. He remained there even after FitzRoy moved on to other properties, so that is where we lived until his death last year."

"I see," Essien said. "I am sorry for the loss of your husband, Lady de Barenton. What was his first name?"

"Alfred."

Essien pondered that for a moment. "Alas, I do not know him," he said. "Hereford has never had much to do with Richard FitzRoy, given that he is a bastard of King John, who was Hereford's mortal enemy."

"My father did not particularly like him, either."

Essien chuckled. "The man has good taste," he said. "Speaking of men, I saw your father's knight in the staging area this afternoon. Le Kerque?"

Her smile faded. "Aye," she said. "Lance le Kerque has served my father for a few months now. He used to be on the tournament circuit before that, but you probably already know."

"I do," he said. "Though he tended to ride the eastern circuit, our paths crossed sometimes. He called himself the King of Pain, you know."

She frowned. "What a terrible name," she said, chuckling at the distasteful moniker. "Do you know him well?"

Essien shook his head. "Nay," he said. "Only in passing."

The dog picked that moment to squirm out of Ines's arms, rushing back down the alley and disappearing. Stricken, the girl started to follow, but Catalina was faster this time. And closer. She grabbed her daughter and hauled the kicking, yelling child into her arms.

"I will *not* lose her again," she said firmly. "If you will excuse us, my lord, I must find my father. And mayhap tie this little one down so she cannot run off again."

Essien could see that the child was giving her mother a difficult time with flying feet and kicking legs. "I will escort you," he said. "And do not argue with me. There are many unsavory characters at these tournaments and I should not like you to have to fight off one of them. I think you've done enough fighting for today."

Catalina didn't argue with him. She simply nodded, smiling her thanks at his chivalry and trying to avoid being kicked.

"We must return to the man with the dogs," she told him. "I left my other daughter there to wait for me. She's the obedient one."

"It is good to have at least one obedient child."

"Do you have children?"

He snorted as they began to head back toward the tournament village. "Nay," he said. "But I know about them."

"How?"

He was still grinning. "Because between my brother and I, he was your older daughter and I was Ines. One obedient child, one… *lively* child."

Catalina cocked an eyebrow as she readjusted her grip on her daughter. "Is that what they call this?" she said. "Lively?"

Essien simply laughed softly. What had started out as a violent confrontation had turned into something quite the opposite, and he wasn't hard pressed to admit that he was relieved. He shouldn't like to have such a lovely lady as an enemy.

Definitely not an enemy.

… but nothing more.

Or so he thought.

CHAPTER THREE

THE GAMES THAT night were something to celebrate.

Lioncross Abbey Castle was an enormous bastion located on the Welsh marches, built solid and big, squatting amongst the rolling green hills like a predator ready to pounce. Before Christopher had assumed ownership of the castle, it had belonged to his wife's family for over one hundred years. The name came from the fact that the castle was built upon an ancient Roman fort, which had become a church, the foundations of which were still visible in the undercroft of the structure. It was surrounded by enormous curtain walls, twenty feet high in places, that neither the Welsh nor any other invading army had ever been able to breach. It was, in fact, an immovable object situated in a bucolic land that seemed to convey peace and serenity far more than it did war and conflict.

Lioncross was a legend as much as its owner.

It was the seat of the Earl of Hereford and Worcester, titles given to Christopher during the reign of Richard the Lionheart—which was a good thing, considering his brother, John, hated the very ground Christopher walked upon. Christopher had been close to Richard and, in fact, had earned the nickname the Lion's Claw for his unwavering support and duty to the monarch both in England and in the Holy Land when he had gone on crusade at Richard's side. He had returned from the Levant and Richard hadn't, but he was more or less Richard's will in England in the man's absence, something that had created a mortal enemy out of John. The relationship between Christopher and John was legendary, something that fortunately did not carry over into John's son, Henry, who loved Christopher and depended on him greatly.

Therefore, Christopher had kept his lands and his titles throughout the reign of three kings. Ironically, it was John who had given him the massive earldom, hoping to entice the man into supporting him. Christopher was mostly a knight, born and bred to battle, but he had been a hell of a tournament competitor in his day and racked up dozens of wins in both the joust and the mass competition. Over the years, however, it had been rare for him to put on his own tournament, as he simply didn't have the time to do it, but in this case, the tournament was supposed to be in celebration of his wife's birthday. At least, that was what he told her, and Dustin had promptly told him that she wanted no part of a bloody tournament and to stop making excuses simply because he wanted to put one on.

He'd put one on, anyway.

Therefore, he stopped telling people that this tournament was a celebration of Lady Hereford's birthday because every time he said it, she would contradict him, so he was tired of being called out as a liar. Even if it *was* true. Tonight, the feast promised to be the biggest one yet, because several more competitors had arrived due to the fact that the mass competition was in a couple of days. The joust had gone first and there had been seven days of it, the last day and the finals being tomorrow.

There was a lot to celebrate this evening.

The great hall of Lioncross was ablaze with the light of a thousand tapers on this evening, plus the enormous hearth was spitting out so much smoke and heat that no one could get within ten feet of it without risking being roasted alive. It was already half full of competitors and some women, but the truth was that most wives didn't attend things like this because they could be long, uncomfortable, dull at times, and dangerous at others. Therefore, there were a good deal of single men traveling around in gangs, and Rebecca and four of the wards entrusted to Lady Hereford to train and nurture had set themselves up at the very entry of the hall to cheer, or jeer, the men who came through the door.

They had created quite a spectacle.

If a man were handsome, they would yell and cheer and throw cherries at him, cherries they had stolen from the feasting table from numerous bowls because there had been a bumper cherry crop earlier in the season. Several men had been hit in the arm, shoulder, thigh, or cheek with flying cherries. When they turned angrily to the source, they would see clapping, laughing young women being led by a gleeful redhead. It was difficult to be truly angry at Christopher de Lohr's delightful daughter, so they simply brushed it off and moved into the hall, away from the flying cherries. But for men who were perhaps not so handsome—or worse, old—the reaction of the women was perhaps more stinging.

The first men who received that kind of treatment were a pair of older brothers from Devon. They didn't receive cherries thrown at them, but pebbles. Rebecca had a reed from the castle pond, hollow, and she blew hard to shoot the pebbles with great accuracy thanks to older brothers teaching her how to do it. She nearly blinded one of the Devon brothers before they got away from her. Because her mother and father were still in the castle, dressing for the evening, she could get away with such actions, including shooting a very soggy cherry at a knight named Rolf Deinhold and absolutely ruining his pale linen tunic. He was angry about it until Rebecca promised to dance with him later. Then he was willing to let it go.

But others weren't.

It soon became a spectacle for half the room to watch Rebecca and the young women as they jeered or cheered those entering the hall. Those around the young women began to cheer and jeer along with them. A handsome man would enter and a great chorus of cries would rise up in the hall, or a man considered unhandsome or dirty or slovenly would enter and there would be an entire chorale of catcalls and hisses. It was a competition once again, not on the tournament field this time, but inside the great hall. It went on for about an hour, men entering and dodging either flying fruit or accurate pebbles, until the elite knights began to arrive.

Then the stakes deepened.

William de Wolfe came through first, tall and exceedingly handsome, and Rebecca stood up and clapped loudly, cheering. A few cherries flew from her cohorts, dropping around his feet. William paused at the flying fruit, greatly confused, until he saw who was behind it. He'd had his own round with Rebecca a few days earlier when she tried to flirt with him and he'd politely brushed her off. Therefore, he was on his guard. But Paris entered on William's heels and instantly, the jeering started because Paris had been something of an arse to Rebecca around the same time she was flirting with William. Therefore, the pebbles started to fly. Paris had no patience for lively young women, and he began picking up handfuls of smashed cherries and pebbles on the hall floor and throwing them back at the women, who screamed and scattered.

The entire room erupted in laughter.

Only Rebecca didn't think it was so funny. She didn't like being challenged at her own game. She fired another pebble back at Paris and caught him in the arse. Stinging, he rubbed his bum and shook his fist at her, but she told him that she'd get him into trouble with her father if he didn't stop harassing her. William pulled him away before there could be more of a confrontation, and that was the end of that.

With Paris gone, Rebecca settled back into her role as judge and jury for the men trickling into the hall. Kieran Hage followed Paris and William, and he was cheered, with a cherry hitting him in the shoulder. He had no idea why, frowning at the lively women, before continuing on. After him came Jonathan de Wolfe.

That was when things began to change.

Jonathan had the dark de Wolfe looks, and hazel eyes that were gold in a certain light, but he was taller and wider than his sublimely beautiful younger brother. *Beastly* was how some people described him. Wolfie, as he was called, was a follower, not a leader, a man with more brawn than brains, but he was hell on a tournament field. He was one of the competitors to beat, much like his brother, and a de Wolfe-against-de Wolfe bout was highly prized by tournament fans. While William had a sensual male beauty, Jonathan's was more rugged. He was glorious to some and inglorious to others. Unfortunately, to Rebecca, it was the latter. The moment he walked in, the pebbles began to fly.

Jonathan came to a halt, turning with confusion to the jeering women, as a pebble hit him straight in the eye. He hissed, lowering his head and rubbing the eye that had been offended.

"What was that for?" he demanded, still rubbing.

Rebecca was quite imperious about it. "For being an eyesore," she said, pointing toward the main area of the hall. "Keep moving. Your presence here is not required."

He stopped rubbing and looked at her, frowning. "What are you talking about?"

Rebecca had a mischievous gleam to her eye. "Just what I said," she said. "We do not wish to look at you. Keep moving so someone more pleasing to the eye can take your place and entertain us."

As he stood there, trying to figure out what in the hell she meant, Cassian and Ashton came in behind him. When they saw Jonathan stopped in the middle of the entryway, they came to a pause next to the man.

"What ails you, Wolfie?" Ashton said, pointing toward the enormous feasting table against the far wall that was heavy with food and drink and where William, Paris, and Kieran were now standing. "Let us get to that table before your brother and his friends strip it of everything good to drink."

Jonathan waved him off. "In a moment," he said. "Lady Rebecca seems to think we are not worth looking at. She nearly blinded me with a pebble to prove her point."

That had Cassian and Ashton looking at Rebecca. Cassian, being her brother-in-law, knew she could be a handful. "Bebe," he said in a low voice, "behave yourself or I shall summon your sister. Keep on the path you have chosen and I'll even summon your father."

Given that he was family, Cassian could not only address her by the family nickname of "Bebe," but he could also threaten her. However, Rebecca was defiant.

"Summon Brie," she said, chin thrust into the air. "I do not care. My sister cannot stop me from having my fun, nor can my father, so your threats are empty."

"Mine aren't," Jonathan said, moving purposefully toward the table where Rebecca and her court were sitting. "The palm of my hand will fit quite nicely across your buttocks."

The women screamed and fled, and that included Rebecca. Jonathan went in pursuit as Rebecca tried to retain her decorum while fleeing an angry man. She ran around tables, leapt over chairs, and threw anything she could get her hands on at him. But Jonathan was undeterred. As the entire hall erupted in laughter at Rebecca's expense, Jonathan continued to pursue her.

"Leave me alone!" Rebecca commanded, throwing a hunk of cheese at him because it was the only thing she could grasp as she ran past a table. "Touch me and there will be consequences! My father will punish you!"

"Your father will thank me," Jonathan said, cutting her off as she tried to run around another table. "You have been rude and insolent since I arrived and now you must pay the price."

Rebecca shrieked and headed in the other direction with Jonathan on her tail. As this was going on and the room full of men were now trying to herd Rebecca in his direction, Essien and Addax entered the hall. They could see the commotion. Noticing that Ashton and Cassian were standing near the entry, watching everything, they went to stand with them.

"What's amiss?" Essien asked. "Why is Wolfie chasing Rebecca?"

Cassian shook his head at the antics. "Because Bebe and her friends were throwing things at the men who entered the hall, evidently, and Wolfie is going to teach her a lesson," he said. "This is one time her behavior will not be rewarded."

The four of them watched as Jonathan nearly got a hold of her, but she darted off once again. "Should you save her?" Essien asked. "Wolfie is frightening when he's not a happy man."

Cassian sighed heavily. "Truly, she deserves it," he said. "But Hereford probably would not take kindly to his daughter being spanked."

"By Wolfie?"

"By anyone."

Essien glanced at him. "Where *is* Hereford?"

Cassian shook his head. "In the keep, I suppose," he said. Then he sighed again. "Mayhap I should put an end to this before there are tears or more eyes gouged out."

Ashton bumped him in a gesture meant to get his attention. "Not right now," he said. "I want to see Wolfie put a good scare into her. Mayhap she will stop being such a tyrant."

Cassian cocked his head. "True," he said. Then he shouted out to Jonathan, "If you catch her, leave no marks, Wolfie. Do you hear me?"

Jonathan simply growled and tossed a chair that was in his way. Rebecca was running for a servants' alcove, but she was blocked by grinning knights. She tried to push her way between them but they wouldn't move. By the time she turned around, Jonathan was on her and she screamed in terror as he grabbed her, heaving her up over one enormous shoulder.

"Ha!" he said triumphantly. "I have the prize!"

The room roared with approval. Even Cassian grinned,

though he was trying desperately not to. Rebecca was about to face the consequences of her deplorable actions and she was both angry and terrified as she beat on Jonathan's back, demanding he put her down. Jonathan, of course, ignored her as he made his way back to Essien and Cassian, Addax, and Ashton.

"Now," Jonathan said, smiling broadly, "what shall it be? A good spank? A good pinch?"

Essien, fighting off a smirk, went around to Jonathan's back, where Rebecca was hanging upside down. Her face was red from all of the blood rushing to her head, but she caught sight of him and reached out in desperation.

"Essien, help me!" she demanded. "Help me and you shall be rewarded!"

Essien cocked an eyebrow. "With what?" he said. "There is nothing from you that I need or want. But let this be a lesson to you, my lady. Harass men at your own peril."

Rebecca didn't like that answer. She began fighting and kicking and twisting, making it difficult for Jonathan to keep his hold on her. He tried to keep his grip, but she twisted and lifted her knee at the same time, right by his face, and ended up kneeing him in the nose. His head snapped back and he grunted in pain as she slipped from his arms, falling to the ground.

"You wicked, terrible man!" she scolded as blood began to pour from Jonathan's nose. "You deserve everything coming to you! I hope you fail spectacularly tomorrow, do you hear? I hope you lose!"

She was on her feet by now, raging, but the four men who had been standing around, Essien included, were now crowded around Jonathan, helping him stifle the blood that was pouring from his face. Rebecca looked at Jonathan in anger, then confusion, then perhaps something that resembled concern. She hadn't realized she'd hit him in the face in the midst of her struggles. As she was focused on Jonathan's bloody face, perhaps trying to think of something less cruel to say to him that might even resemble an apology, a big hand came from behind her, full of cherries, and smashed them right into her face.

Rebecca began screaming again.

Paris had his revenge. While Rebecca had been distracted with Jonathan, Paris had managed to grab a handful of those cherries she'd been so fond of throwing and rubbed them into her face. Even as she tried to get away from him, swinging her arms and trying to turn her face away, he was smashing them into her. They went up her nose, into her mouth, into her eyes. One even got in her right ear. She was covered with cherries and juice all around her face and in her hair by the time he finished. As she gasped in outrage, he wiped his hands off on the tabletop.

"How do you like *that*, you little chit?" he said. "If you are going to play games with grown men, then you'd better be prepared for them to fight back. Now who's ugly and unappealing, Rebecca de Lohr? The answer to that question would be *you*."

Rebecca was covered with the stuff. It had dripped down onto the front of her lovely green frock, staining it. When she realized that, she quickly rushed away, but not before they heard her sobbing. As Paris lifted his chin triumphantly, Cassian came to stand next to him, watching Rebecca cross the bailey, heading toward the keep.

They could hear her crying from where they stood.

"She deserved it," Cassian said simply. "But do not be surprised if Lady Hereford gets involved. If I were you, I would stay out of the woman's way."

Paris cocked an eyebrow. "She raised the tyrant," he said. "It is her fault if her daughter's punishment has been left to others."

"She will not see it that way."

That was more than likely true. With a shrug, Paris headed back to his friends, who were over by the feasting table, while Ashton and Addax took Jonathan out of the hall to tend to his still-bleeding nose. That left Cassian standing by himself for a moment, hoping the evening didn't become much more violent than it already had. As he stood there pondering that very thing, he felt someone standing beside him and turned to see Essien.

He smiled weakly.

"An eventful evening already," he said. "Rebecca is the lively one of the family."

Essien grinned. "You mean the troublemaker," he said. "You forget that I've watched her grow up, too. She was always the dramatic one. Weeping if she didn't get her way, screaming if someone as much as frowned at her. I seem to remember her getting you into trouble on more than one occasion because you had eyes for Brielle and not for her."

Cassian snorted. "She was barely five years of age at the time," he said. "Every time I would speak to Brielle, she would pretend to hurt herself so my attention would shift to her. Do you remember that?"

Essien laughed softly. "I do, indeed."

"She was a nuisance."

"She still is," Essien agreed. "Only she's a woman now, and a beautiful one at that. If someone doesn't curb that wild streak in her, then there's going to be trouble. Hereford knows it."

Cassian eyed him. "Why not you?" he said. "Speaking on behalf of Sherry and myself, men who have married the daughters of de Lohr, we would welcome you into our pack."

Essien shook his head, throwing his hands up in surrender. "Not me," he said. "You'll have to find a lion tamer for Rebecca, because it will not be me."

Cassian continued to snort. "Truthfully, I do not blame you," he said. "You deserve a woman who is better suited as the wife of a prince."

Essien shook his head. "A prince with no lands, no country," he said. "That is what ambitious women want—men with titles and wealth, of which I only have the title, and a minor one at that. Nay, my friend, I am afraid the woman I marry will have to be a very unique blend of acceptance, beauty, and obedience. She will have to accept me as I am, be outrageously beautiful to behold, and obey every command I give her. And she will not care that I am a prince from a bereft house."

Cassian smiled at him. "There is a woman out there like that, I am certain."

"Are you? For I am not."

"When you least expect it, she shall appear."

Essien simply shook his head. He didn't care and he didn't want to continue the conversation. A wife was of no interest to him, much as he'd explained to his brother. In fact, he wasn't happy that he'd had to field that conversation twice in the same day. Noticing that the servants were bringing in a fresh barrel of wine, he headed in that direction, fully prepared to drink away his irritation.

Little did he know that he would be unable to run from that conversation from this night forward.

For Essien al-Kort, things were about to change.

CHAPTER FOUR

T HINGS WERE CERTAINLY lively in the great hall this night.
He'd watched the entire fiasco with the flame-haired
de Lohr daughter and the knights who were determined to
teach her a lesson. She was lively, that one, as he'd seen her
during the day around the tournament field and in the lists.
He'd even offered to escort her into the village for sweets but
was summarily denied by the woman's father. He'd been kind
about it, to be sure, but he'd denied him and then ignored him.
Or forgot about him. It was all the same to Lance le Kerque.

He was used to be ignored by the de Lohrs.

He didn't even know why he'd offered. He'd been pursuing
his liege's daughter since nearly the moment he swore his fealty,
but Lady Catalina, a widow, wasn't exactly receptive. She was
such a beautiful woman, elegant and graceful, and had an
ethereal quality about her that Lance found fascinating. Maybe
that was why he'd gone in pursuit of her, because he'd never
seen anyone like her, but it could also be because she was
Eckington's heir. She had also inherited a great deal from her
dead husband, some foolish knight who had gone off and
gotten himself killed. Or he'd just died. Lance really didn't

know. He only knew that the man was dead and had left behind his exquisite wife and two adorable daughters. Perhaps her latest rejection had damaged Lance's confidence enough that he had to find another lady to boost it, hence his interest in Rebecca de Lohr.

But he'd been denied her, too.

Such was his life.

His liege, Lord Eckington, was with the Earl of Hereford, somewhere on this property. Lance hadn't seen him in hours, ever since de Lohr had greeted him during the tournament and then the two of them had stolen away. That left Lance alone, in command of Eckington's escort and presumably in charge of keeping an eye on Lady Catalina and her children. He'd been so caught up in sending Eckington's escort back to their encampment to the east, where all of the competitors were camped, and then the list for the mass competition contestants when it was finally posted by the marshals, that he'd failed to notice Lady Catalina's disappearance until she returned with a knight who was introduced as Essien al-Kort.

God of Vengeance.

Lance thought he recognized him from tournaments in the past, and that suspicion was confirmed when he learned the man's name. Essien was polite and departed as soon as he delivered the women, but Lance was left feeling humiliated that another man had done his duty for him. He should have been paying closer attention to Catalina and her daughters. He was fairly certain her already mediocre opinion of him had grown exponentially worse because of his lack of attention.

He couldn't blame Essien. The man was in the right place at the right time. All he could do was blame himself and make the decision that, rather than pursue Catalina personally, trying to establish something between them, he would simply go to Lord Eckington and plead for her hand. She would have to do what her father told her to do, so perhaps that would be his best course of action.

If Eckington ever made it to the feasting hall.

In the meantime, Lance would enjoy the food and entertainment, which had been Lady Rebecca and her friends, but now that their spectacle was over, a group of men and women near the hearth had commenced playing musical instruments and singing. The hall was starting to settle down and more food was being brought forth to keep the guests satisfied until Hereford and his wife appeared and the meal commenced in earnest. But the truth was that Lance only had one goal whilst he was here at Lioncross Abbey, and it had nothing to do with the tournament.

He wanted to get Hereford alone.

This was the closest he'd ever come in his entire life. All of those years of serving various lords in his youth and ending up in Brabant and Vilinius, fighting other men's wars, before returning to England as a bachelor knight and riding the circuit until the opportunity with Eckington presented itself. He'd been wanting to serve a de Lohr ally for many years, but not any de Lohr ally—one that was close by sheer proximity to Lioncross Abbey and Christopher de Lohr. He had to be able to get close to the man with ease—physically close—and Eckington had been part of that plan. It had been sheer luck that he'd managed to obtain a position with him. But now, here he was. At Lioncross.

And he intended to get Hereford alone.

He'd come too far not to.

It was time.

CHAPTER FIVE

"**I** THINK WE'VE had too much to drink."

"What makes you say that?"

"Because the chamber is *sparkling*."

Christopher started laughing. He was sitting in his solar with Harald de Efford, Lord Eckington, and the older man had him in hysterics. Harald was congenial, wise, and humorous to the bone, something Christopher had always liked about him. He wasn't any good in battle or with a sword any longer, though he'd never been particularly talented with either, but he was very astute when it came to politics. Christopher had relied on his counsel in the past and the man had never failed him. But more than anything, he simply enjoyed the man's company from time to time. He'd long learned not to enjoy a man's company for fear he'd turn on him.

But not Harald.

He was loyal to the bone.

"Is it sparkling?" Christopher said, looking around at the old walls, the stacks of books, the big black cat that liked to nap on the shelves. "Harald, I do not think it is sparkling. I think there is something wrong with your eyes."

Harald was looking around, too. He rubbed his eyes and looked again. "Nay," he said. "It is definitely sparkling. Do you think God is trying to speak to me?"

"I think you would hear Him if He was."

Harald frowned. "Chris, he appeared to Moses as a burning bush," he pointed out. "Why can he not appear to me in a shower of sparkles?"

Christopher scratched his chin and continued to look around. "I think you are right," he said. "Wait… I am hearing something now."

Harald looked at him, wide-eyed. "What do you hear?"

Christopher cocked an ear. "He is saying that if we do not go into the great hall soon, my wife will come looking for us here and we shall both be in trouble," he said. "I have an entire hall full of guests, and as much as I would like to remain here with you, I cannot, but you will not let me go."

"That is *because*…" Harald said, using exaggerated hand gestures. "Because God wishes for me to speak to you about something most urgent. The sparkles in the room are encouraging me to do so."

"I see," Christopher said, grinning. "Now the sparkles are speaking to you?"

"Verily."

"What are they saying?"

"That I wish for you to help me find a husband for my daughter."

The light of realization came to Christopher's face. "Ah," he said. "The lovely Catalina."

"That would be her."

Christopher sat back in his chair. "Well?" he said. "What do you want from me? Suggestions on eligible husbands? I will tell you right now that my sons are too young to marry. Curtis and Roi are the only ones even remotely eligible by age, but they are still too young. Your lovely daughter cannot have one of my sons."

Harald waved him off impatiently. "I did not set my sights for Catalina so high that I was hoping for a de Lohr son," he said. "But you know people. Who do you know that has eligible sons?"

Christopher poured himself more wine whilst he was thinking. "Almost everyone I know has younger sons or sons that are already married," he said. "Does it have to be a son of an ally?"

Harald shook his head. "It only has to be a decent man with some means," he said. "Age-appropriate, of course. My daughter has seen twenty years and six. That is very old for a bride."

Christopher eyed him. "Very," he said, though he didn't really mean it. He happened to think that women in their twenties were perfectly acceptable as brides because it distressed him to see very young women being bartered as wives. "As I recall, she has two children, correct?"

Harald nodded. "She does," she said. "Girl children, unfortunately. But given my daughter is my heir, I would like her to marry and produce a few sons."

"Of course you would. That is reasonable."

"Do you have anyone in mind?"

Christopher took a drink of his wine, pondering the question and hearing strains of music, very faint, coming from the great hall in the bailey. The evening around them was cold and clear, and he could see the stars in the sky through the lancet windows that had not yet been covered for the night. This wasn't the first time Harald had brought up finding a husband for his widowed daughter, and it wouldn't be the last unless Christopher gave the man some help. Harald spent his time at his homes, with his solitary hobbies, and tended to socialize with the old guard and old friends rather than everyone else, newcomers included, so he was pleading for Christopher's knowledge and assistance outside of the scope of his tightly knit circle.

The truth was that Christopher did have some ideas.

"Your family descends from Cnut the Great, do they not?" he asked.

Harald nodded. "Through my mother," he said. "The kings of Mercia are in my blood."

"And, as I recall, your wife was from Catalonia."

"She was," Harald confirmed. "The House of Trastamara, though her family was from a cadet branch, the House of Antequera. My wife's uncle ruled Catalonia for years. She married me because I held the Earldom of Mercia, or her father would not have allowed it."

There it was. The ancient and prestigious title that the House of de Efford had held for centuries. Harald didn't go by that, however, as it came through his mother's family. He went by Lord Eckington because he didn't have the army to support the Earldom of Mercia title—such an old and grand collection of ancient lands that had a history of warfare, but Harald wasn't grand, nor was he truly a warlord. He was actually very simple, a modest man with ancient royal bloodlines and a grandiose title. Christopher held Hereford and Worcester, and he also held other titles, including Baron Magnis, an ancient title related to Mercia. But Mercia royalty wasn't his bloodline.

It *was* Harald's bloodline.

"When your daughter married de Barenton, did he know of

the Mercia title?" Christopher asked.

Harald nodded. "He did," he said. "Alfred was a good man. He may not have been the handsomest, or the wittiest, but he was wise and steady. That is why I selected him for Catalina. She needed wise and steady at the time. Oddly enough, now she is the wise and steady one. Alfred must have taught her that."

Christopher smiled faintly. "I remember him," he said. "A quiet man, but respected. He was close to Richard FitzRoy."

Harald nodded again. "He served the Crown in that capacity," he said. "FitzRoy, being the bastard son of King John, was afforded Crown support. He's hotheaded like his father."

"I know, all too well."

Harald looked at him, grinning. "I forget that you know the kings and princes better than anyone alive," he said. "I do believe Alfred was sent to watch FitzRoy more than actually serve him, but that was John's directive. I did not hold it against him. His family came to England with the Duke of Normandy, you know. He had an uncle or a cousin that was the Duc de Saint Hilaire. He had noble blood in him, but mostly, I simply liked him. This time… this time, Catalina deserves someone more prestigious, more powerful. The blood of Mercia flows through her veins and into the veins of any sons she has. They must have a prestigious father."

"Would a prince do?"

Harald's expression grew curious. "You know of an eligible prince?"

Christopher did, but he wasn't sure why he'd even said that. Perhaps it was because Catalina de Efford de Barenton brought a good deal with her, including an ancient and coveted title. In fact, the Mercia earldom had lands that surrounded Christopher's own, and he wanted an ally or relative as a neighbor. It was true that his sons were too young for Lady de Barenton, but he knew of another trusted ally that wasn't too young. Moreover, his royal bloodlines would be more than suitable for the Earl of Mercia title. Maybe that was why the idea came to him on a whim.

Essien al-Kort would be perfect.

"I do," he said after a moment. "But not an English prince. Not even a French or Saxon prince. Nay, this prince comes from bloodlines a thousand years old, and his brother is the hereditary king of his people. He has royal blood that an English prince could only hope for, and the bride he takes should also have such impressive lines. Catalina does. She deserves a prince, don't you think?"

Harald couldn't contain his excitement. "Who, man, *who*?"

"You do know him, but you must trust me that he is a good man."

"I believe you," he said. "Is he a cousin?"

Christopher shook his head. "Nay," he said. "A sworn knight who also happens to be an English lord. His brother, though king to his own people, is the Earl of Deira. The knight holds the title Lord Binchester."

Harald absorbed the information. "Lord Binchester," he repeated. "I do not know him."

Christopher snorted. "Aye, you do," he said. "You have seen him today, in fact, on the tournament field. You have heard me speak of the princes of Kitara before."

That seemed to bring a light of recognition. "Kitara," Harald said. Then realization dawned. "The knight with the dark hair in braids?"

Christopher nodded. "Sometimes," he said. "But that is Addax, the older brother."

"The king."

"The Earl of Deira."

"And you are speaking of the younger brother?"

"The God of Vengeance."

Now, Harald knew who he was speaking of. His eyes widened. "The tall lad with the dark hair and dark eyes?" he said. "The big lad with the loud voice?"

Christopher snorted. "Loud, indeed," he said. "He is at an age where he must take a wife or his brother will force him into a marriage that will more than likely not be nearly as impressive as one with Catalina will be. He is an excellent knight, a good friend, and intelligent. He is a man of good character. I would not tell you so if it were not true. He would make a good husband for Catalina."

Harald's features lit up. "Think of their children," he said. "Lads of royal blood inheriting the Earldom of Mercia. Chris, we must make this happen. We must!"

He was becoming quite eager, and Christopher held up a hand to ease him. "We shall," he assured him. "Let me speak with his older brother, who I am certain will be agreeable. But our God of Vengeance will more than likely not be at first, so tell me of your daughter's dowry aside from the earldom. What else shall she inherit?"

Harald was thinking quickly, so eager that he was nearly overwhelmed with it. "Her dowry is everything that comes from de Barenton," he said. "I gave the man five hundred pounds gold for her dowry, and when he died, I received it back and more besides. There is eight hundred and seventy-three pounds gold, plus another five hundred pounds sterling. Al-Kort can have it all if he marries her."

"Plus the earldom."

"Plus the earldom when I die."

Christopher nodded with satisfaction. "That will make Essien very, very rich," he said. "I will send for his brother and we will explain it to him."

That made Harald anxious. "Do you think he will agree?"

Christopher stood up, opening the solar door to send a servant to fetch Addax before he answered.

"I think he will," he said quietly as he came back over to the table where the wine was located. "I think he will be very eager for a marriage such as this for his brother."

He wiped out a nearby cup and poured a measure of wine into it as Harald stood up, staggering over to the table and collecting more wine for himself.

Christopher eyed him.

"If you have any more of that, the room will only continue to sparkle," he warned him. "It might even go up in flame. God presented himself as a burning bush once. He may do it again."

Harald took a long drink before answering. "I do not care," he said. "If God burns down this room in a divine moment that convinces Addax al-Kort that his brother should wed my daughter, I will make the sacrifice."

"It'll burn down with you in it."

"As I said, I'll make the sacrifice."

With that, he drained the cup and poured himself another. Christopher decided to put the wine out of his reach at that point, because they had to go through a rather serious conversation with Addax and the man was already drunk enough. In fact, by the time Addax arrived about a half-hour later, Harald was asleep in his chair, snoring loudly enough to rattle the walls. Christopher proceeded to tell Addax what had been proposed, pausing to awaken Harald, who was drunk and groggy but very agreeable. Not strangely, so was Addax.

Everyone was agreeable but the groom himself.

And that was a job for Christopher.

CHAPTER SIX

DUE TO THE fact that Lord and Lady Hereford had yet to appear at their feast, there had been no formal meal yet even if there was plentiful food, but there was also plentiful drink, so, not wanting to be rude to their hosts by eating before the formal feast commenced, the knights stayed mostly to the drink. The result was that within a couple of hours of their arrival to the hall, many of them were fairly drunk. A few were even smashed.

Essien was one of those who was rightfully plastered.

He was trying not to be. He truly was. But he'd had five cups of the strong Spanish wine that the de Lohrs favored, and before he knew it, the room was rolling as if he were on the high seas and he was holding on to the tables to keep from going overboard. He was sitting at a table near the dais with Ashton, Cassian, Addax, Jonathan, William, Kieran, and Paris, and they were all drunk to varying degrees. Alexander, who had arrived late to the feast with his wife, came across the group, noted their state of inebriation and ordered some of the egg dishes, bread, and boiled fruit juice over to the table to counteract the effects of the alcohol.

that answer. "Then you will marry the de Barenton widow?"

"I will," Essien said. "But if she attacks me during the wedding ceremony, I would expect you to protect me."

Christopher snorted, breaking into soft laughter, as Peter and Addax moved to congratulate Essien. The man didn't seem exactly pleased, but at least he wasn't fighting it or resisting it. As long as he knew he had a choice in the matter, he would buy what Christopher had so eloquently sold.

If only the marriage itself would be so easy.

They were about to find out.

CHAPTER EIGHT

"YOU HAVE A husband, my dear."

Catalina had no idea what Harald was talking about. In their small section of the competitor and visitor encampment on the outskirts of the tournament field, she had just settled her girls in for the night in the fortified carriage that she and her children had traveled to the tournament in when Harald summoned her. Leaving Adabella and Ines tucked into one of the small benches that doubled as a bed, she had just exited the carriage through the rear door when Harald had made his odd statement.

She looked at him curiously.

"A what?" she asked.

"Husband."

Catalina still wasn't clear on what he was saying. "Papa, forgive me, but you are talking nonsense," she said, pushing past him and heading for the small cooking fire next to the carriage. She picked up an earthenware pitcher. "Do you know where I can find fresh water? There must be a well around here."

Harald followed her. "Sit down," he told her, gently grasping her arm. "I must speak with you."

She let him direct her onto a stool near the fire. "What about?"

"Your husband."

She sighed with growing irritation. "I do not have one."

"You do now."

"What on earth are you speaking of?"

Harald sat on a collapsible chair, one made from leather on a sturdy frame, facing her across the fire.

"My dear, you must remarry," he said. "You know you must remarry. I have a great legacy and you are the guardian of that legacy. However, when I die, you cannot be unmarried. There must be a husband to pass that legacy on to, including the Earldom of Mercia. Including the wealth my forefathers have built over the years, a great deal of wealth. It must go to your husband."

Catalina had a horrible suspicion. "Papa, what have you done?"

"I found you a husband."

Catalina shot to her feet. "We have been over this," she said. "I will choose my own husband. You promised that I could."

Harald didn't rise to her anger. "And you have deliberately avoided choosing one," he said. "Do not deny it, for it would be a lie. You have had perfectly acceptable suitors, whom you have summarily dismissed."

She was angry, but he was right. There had been at least three suitors since Alfred had passed away and she'd brushed off all of them, not to mention the two friends of Harald's who had wanted her for their sons. She'd brushed them off, too.

"They were not of my choosing," she said, knowing it was a weak excuse. "I will choose my own husband."

"Who?" he said, almost sarcastically. "Le Kerque? For some reason, he seems to be fond of you, but I do not want him for you and I cannot wait for you to choose a husband because you might not do it until I am on my deathbed. At that point, there would be nothing I could do about it if he were unworthy."

"But—!"

"Nay," he said sharply, cutting her off. He pointed a bony finger at her. "You will listen to me and listen well, Catalina. This is not a matter up for debate. You did your duty and married, but all you could manage to produce were two daughters. We need a son from you if my legacy is to survive. If you remain a stubborn widow, with only two daughters to your name, then the king will swoop in, take everything from you, and force you to marry a man who could treat you like dirt beneath his feet, and there would be nothing you could do about it. I realize you want to choose your own husband, but you hardly leave Eckington as it is. How do you expect to choose a man when you refuse to socialize with anyone?"

Catalina was red in the face by the time he finished. "I am here, aren't I?" she snapped back. "I am out in the world, as you want me to be."

"So you are."

"Then let me start looking for a husband now," she said, trying to keep the panic from her voice. "Let me—"

He cut her off again. "Nay," he said. "It has been decided for you. I spoke to Lord Hereford and he has a prince in mind for you."

Catalina was gearing up for a major row, but his statement confused her. She faltered. "A prince?" she repeated. "What prince?"

Harald could see he had her attention. "The brother of a

king," he said. "Well, he would be king if his country had not been sacked. The man's brother is the Earl of Deira and your future husband is a prince from a family a thousand years old. He bears royal blood, as do you, so the sons you bear him will inherit the Earldom of Mercia. They will be men of royal blood, a fine legacy for my ancestors. You can do no better, Catalina. You are an old woman with two children. Decent, eligible men want virgins."

He was insulting her. But, then again, he always insulted her and never realized he was doing so. Harald could be oblivious sometimes, unaware how much he hurt his daughter, how much he battered her sense of self-worth. Sadly, Alfred used to do the same thing. She was beautiful, and bright, but Alfred's first unkind words came when she bore a daughter, and then more unkind words came when she bore a second daughter. The man had wanted sons and only got girl children.

Very difficult for him to swallow.

"If I am such an undesirable prospect, how did this prince agree to it?" she asked, her tone full of hurt. "Surely he would not want such an old hag as me."

Harald laughed softly, choosing to overlook the pain in her tone. "That is a good question," he said. "The truth is that he must take a wife, so he is being forced into this as much as you are. All you need to do is marry him and bear his sons, my dear. You do not have to like him. If he is intolerable enough, I will allow you to live under my roof. But you must marry. Am I making myself clear?"

He was. But he made it sound so transactional, as if there were nothing involved other than a contract. That was it. All the sentiment of buying a horse. Harald's disappointment in her being born a woman was never more evident than it was at that moment. Frankly, Catalina was disappointed, too.

Had she been born male, she'd at least have a choice over whom she married.

This was like a nightmare.

Disgusted and overwhelmed, Catalina turned away from her father, refusing to look at him. The truth was that she'd been away from the man for the duration of her marriage, several years at least, and had only returned after Alfred's death. They were only just coming to know one another again. They'd never been particularly close to begin with, as her father seemed to be aloof to women in general, so his heavy-handed control of her future didn't sit well with her.

"You have brokered this contract to simply perpetuate the de Efford name and titles," she said. "It has nothing to do with an alliance, or money, or even affection, but carrying on your bloodlines. I want to make sure I'm clear on this."

"What else is there?"

She did look at him, then. "The joining of two families is one," she said, annoyed. "Two allied families joining to strengthen a relationship or alliance. If it were that, I could understand it, but this… this man is not even a de Lohr. Or anyone of note. Is he? What is his name?"

Harald shook his head. "I do not know," he said. "But I know that he serves de Lohr."

Catalina looked at him with some horror. "You do not even know the man's *name*?"

Harald yawned, clearly bored with the conversation. "All I know is that he comes highly recommended by Hereford," he said. "You will marry him on the morrow and we will be done with this."

Catalina was dumbfounded. "And then what?" she said.

"My children and I go off with the man to his home, entering into a situation that could be dangerous or deadly or horrible? Do you even care what becomes of us?"

She was speaking through clenched teeth by the time she was finished, and Harald was no longer yawning. He was looking at her, brow furrowed, displeased by her words and her reaction to what he felt was as good a situation as she could hope for.

"Ungrateful," he finally said. "I have done my best for you and this is how you thank me?"

Catalina went swiftly from being dumbfounded to out-raged. "I have listened to you, so you will listen to me," she snarled. "If I die, if my girls die, then your legacy is finished once and for all. There will be no grandsons to carry on your grand legacy. Did you ever think of that?"

Harald sighed sharply. "De Lohr would not have recom-mended him were he the brutal sort, so you do not have to be hysterical about it," he said, standing up from the chair he'd been sitting on. "I am retiring for the night. Be prepared to marry on the morrow. That is all I have to say to you about it."

With that, he headed off for the canvas tent that had been raised for him by his men, the one bearing the dark blue, yellow, and white of de Barenton. Harald would sleep in his tent while Catalina and her girls had use of the carriage. It was cold in the carriage, without the brazier that would be in Harald's tent for warmth, but that didn't much matter to Harald. As long as he was comfortable, all was well in the world.

And his daughter was, thankfully, betrothed.

Catalina knew that was what he was thinking. He hadn't been thrilled when she returned home, even if it was because she'd had no choice, so certainly he wouldn't have any trouble finding her a husband with a hasty betrothal. He had promised her, once, that she could choose her husband, but he'd broken his word. That wasn't surprising, because he broke his word to her all the time. He didn't seem to think it meant much to keep it. Probably because he didn't think much of her.

Maybe he'd brought her to this tournament purely to marry her off.

Now, it was all becoming clear.

Frustrated, and upset, Catalina returned to the carriage to find her cloak, as the night was damp and temperatures were dropping. She checked on her sleeping children, both of them wrapped up in heavy blankets and sleeping well. She wasn't exactly tired, thinking that she needed to take a walk and reconcile herself to her future, which happened to be marrying a man she'd never met. Tiptoeing out of the carriage, she quietly closed the door and donned the cloak. There were a few soldiers on guard duty, so she knew the children would be protected. Her father's soldiers seemed to care something for the three women even if her father really didn't.

"My lady?"

Startled, she turned to see Lance coming out of the darkness. He wasn't wearing his armor, or the full regalia she'd seen him in since leaving Eckington, but rather clad in a simple tunic and breeches. His blond hair was combed back, hanging just above his shoulders. She'd seen him with his helm on so much that she'd forgotten the man had blond hair. She'd forgotten that he was rather handsome in an avenging-angel sort of way.

"You startled me," she said, hand on her chest to still her fluttering heart. "I thought you would be at the feast."

"I was," he said, coming to a halt a few feet away. "Is that where you are going? I would be happy to escort you to the great hall. There is enough food and drink there to feed most of London."

She smiled weakly. "I hadn't really thought about going there," she admitted. "I was simply going to walk around. The girls are asleep, but I am not tired."

"May I walk with you?"

Her smile faded. "Thank you, but I would prefer to go alone," she said. "It is not that I do not want your company—it is simply that everyone likes to be alone once in a while. Tonight is that time for me."

He nodded. "I understand," he said. "But with so many armed men here for the tournament, it is probably not safe for you to walk alone. I can follow well behind you so you will not see me, but I feel strongly that you should not walk without an escort."

So much for her walking alone to clear her head. Still, she wasn't going to give up without a fight. "I will not come to harm," she insisted. "I would rather go alone."

"I must insist, my lady."

That brought her temper. "Insist all you wish," she said. "Insist until the second coming of Christ. I do not care. I simply want to walk a little, alone, and I do not want an escort. I do not want you trailing behind me like a dog or walking alongside me as if we are companions. I am tired of men making decisions for me, so in this instance, I will make the decision myself. I am going *alone*."

He backed off a little. "I did not mean to upset you, my lady," he said calmly. "I am simply concerned for your welfare."

"I did not ask it of you," she said hotly. "Therefore, just leave me alone. If I need you, I will scream."

That didn't please Lance in the least. "My lady, I suspect

that not all of this anger is directed at me," he said. "If I have annoyed you, my apologies, but I am simply doing my duty. You cannot become angry at me for doing my duty."

She frowned. "I am *not* your duty," she said. "I am nothing to you. You serve my father and that is all. Go see to him if you are looking for something to do, because you will find no work here. I am simply going for a walk."

With the cloak pulled tightly around her, she headed off toward the warmth and light of Lioncross Abbey Castle. Lance watched her go, once again feeling disappointed by an interaction with her, but he wasn't going to give up. Lady Catalina was simply a challenge. A very beautiful challenge.

Nay, he wasn't going to give up in the least.

CHAPTER NINE

H E WASN'T EXACTLY sure why he was out in the bailey.
Essien wasn't feeling drunk anymore, but he knew he still was. The ground moved a little whenever he lowered his head, or looked up at the sky, and that told him there was still drink in his veins.

Frankly, he found that he needed more.

He'd left Christopher and Peter and Addax in Christopher's solar even though Addax wanted to come with him. Essien had waved his brother off. He needed some time alone after what he'd just been told.

A betrothal.

A wife.

A great title.

He wasn't sure how he felt about it all.

He found himself becoming increasingly annoyed at his brother, who seemed to want to invoke the name of their father every chance he had. If Addax wanted to make a point, he simply said that their father would want it so, or their father would be happy for it. That seemed to support whatever Addax was trying to drive home at the time, and Essien was getting tired of it.

It wasn't that he didn't care about their father's wants or wishes or desires for his sons, more that it simply didn't mean a great deal to him. As he knew, and as he'd said before, he didn't even really remember their father, and he barely remembered the land of his birth. The years between his departure from Kitara and their adult years were, quite frankly, a blur.

Of course, there were certain things he remembered. He remembered working shipboard for a cruel merchant who would starve them and beat them and force them to work. He remembered the kind woman that took care of him and his brother, a woman who was eventually sold or sent away. He didn't even remember her name, but he remembered her face. He remembered her kind eyes and the fact that she was young and beautiful. Other than their mother and their nurse, that enslaved woman had been the only one to show any measure of true affection to Essien and Addax.

And then she was gone.

The mind had a way of blocking out the unpleasant and the horrific, which was probably why he did not remember a good deal of his very young years. What he did remember, however, was being found by English knights who had saved him. That was when his life really began. He'd spent years with the knights on the sands of the Levant, mostly as a servant, but soon enough, the knights began to train him and his brother. The boys received experience by attending the battles against the Muslim invaders and in helping tend the wounded knights. It had been a baptism by fire, but both Essien and Addax had taken to it quickly. They'd lived and they'd learned.

They'd become men.

When it came time for the English to return home from the

hot sands of the Holy Land, Christopher was returning to face a new marriage, among other things, and his time for them would be limited. Not wanting to simply leave the boys behind, he'd arranged for them to continue their education with knights from Thuringia, education meant to expand their horizons beyond what the English knights had taught them, so they went off with a group of Thuringian knights and spent those years with more training and more battles. They learned of other cultures and languages before ending up in Flanders with a great warlord. The Duke of d'Acoz was an ally of Ajax de Velt, a great English warlord and Cassian's father, and after a visit to de Velt's fortress in Northern England, and becoming acquainted with Ajax's eldest son, Cole, Addax and Essien found themselves sucked into a secret spy ring administered by William Marshal himself.

England's greatest knight was also England's greatest spy.

They'd taken to that easily, too. The spy game came to them intrinsically, as if they were born to it, and that was how they ended up back in England permanently. Christopher was part of that spy game, too, and Essien was so glad to be back with the man who had essentially raised him as a child that he swore he would never leave. England had very quickly become his home, his favorite place, but it wasn't the same for his brother.

For him, it was a little different.

Addax remembered the land of his birth, remembered much of what had been left behind, so he was much more a man of two worlds than Essien was. That was where they had difficulty connecting sometimes, which was tragic, considering the land of their birth no longer existed and they were probably the only two people left in the world that could connect on that level, remembering the same things, remembering the same people and places.

Unfortunately, Essien couldn't even do that.

And that was why he became so irritated when Addax started bringing up their father, using the man as leverage to make his point or constantly reminding Essien of his ancestry. It was different when Christopher wielded Amare's name, because he was far more of a father figure than Addax was, and hearing Christopher speak of their father somehow wasn't annoying. It was more meaningful coming from him. Christopher spoke of Amare simply to convey his understanding of a father's wishes, while Addax spoke of their father as if Essien should know their father's mind and respect it. As if Essien remembered him.

And he simply didn't.

Addax may have been a man of two countries, but Essien wasn't.

He was England.

Now, Essien found himself out in the bailey, thinking that he should probably try to get some sleep. He didn't feel much like going back into the hall and filling his belly with more wine, so he began to head in the direction of the knights' quarters, which was really part of the undercroft of Lioncross. When the Roman temple had been converted by the Christians into an abbey, the monk cubicles remained, and they'd had many uses over the years. Serving as a prison was one of them, but with Christopher's expanding army, he'd moved the knights and senior soldiers into the area because it afforded them semiprivate room and some peace.

Essien was looking forward to a little peace.

But first, he headed to the gatehouse because he knew the de Lohr sons were manning the walls. Instead of feasting with their parents and guests, they were in charge of security, something that hadn't sat well with brothers Myles and Roi. They wanted to eat and drink, be merry. Curtis, much more solemn as the heir to the de Lohr empire, took the job seriously. Curtis and Roi had been known to fight from time to time because of this conflict, so Essien thought he'd make a sweep of the gatehouse to make sure the young men were being peaceful. The duty gave him a sense of normality, as it was a task he did most nights, and focusing on it took him away from the betrothal discussion. He was nearly to the gatehouse when a few people came in through the open gate—competitors, but walking behind them was a small female figure.

Alone.

That gave Essien pause because, sometimes, camp followers tried to sneak into the feasts, and he knew that Lady Hereford would have a fit if a prostitute made it into the great hall. That wasn't what she wanted around her family. Therefore, Essien came to a halt, watching the woman walk in. She was petite, with a dark cloak and a hood over her head. That was about all he saw until the hood came off when a breeze lifted it.

Then he found himself looking at Lady de Barenton.

His future wife.

For a moment, he was frozen where he stood. He didn't know if he should run away or go to her. Surely she knew they were to be married. If she felt toward the marriage what he did, which was mostly confusion, then surely the sight of him would be unwelcome. She'd already attacked him once. He wasn't going to make himself an easy target a second time. He very nearly turned away, hoping she wouldn't see him, but he wasn't fast enough. She caught sight of him, their eyes met, and his feet were rooted to the spot. He couldn't leave now. He'd braced himself for her fury when something odd happened.

She actually smiled at him.

"My lord," she said, heading in his direction. "You look as if you have not suffered any delayed effects from the shattered lance."

Pleasant. She's being pleasant! "Nay," he said, rubbing at his chest. "Mayhap a little sore, but nothing unmanageable."

"That is good."

"Are… are you alone?"

She nodded. "My father has retired for the evening," she said. "I was simply… walking. I am not tired enough to sleep."

Frankly, Essien was puzzled. Either she didn't know about the betrothal, she didn't care, or she didn't know it was him. One of those three possibilities. She seemed as if there were nothing amiss in her world, a woman who was simply walking because she wasn't ready for sleep. There was nothing unusual about that.

He wondered if he should say anything about the betrothal.

Probably not…

Truthfully, he didn't know *what* to say.

"Would some wine help you?" he finally said, indicating the great hall, glowing with light and warmth through the lancet windows. "Lord Hereford has some very fine wine."

She looked toward the hall, hearing the muffled voices, the laughter, and shook her head. "Nay," she said. "Thank you for the offer, but strong wine usually makes me very loud and very opinionated. I do not wish that side of me on anyone."

Essien grinned. "Why not?"

She eyed him. "Because it is embarrassing."

"It sounds intriguing."

She fought off a grin. "Most definitely not," she said. "And now that you know that about me, I will never trust you not to get me drunk should the opportunity arise. I should not have told you."

He laughed softly. "I promise, I would never do such a thing," he said. He sobered quickly. "If you are walking, would you allow me to walk with you? I am trying to tire myself out, also. The night before an important bout, sleep does not usually come easily for me."

She cocked her head curiously. "Are you nervous?"

"Excited."

She smiled faintly at that admission. "Then of course you may walk with me," she said. "I want to hear about your strategy on the morrow when you compete. There seems to be a good deal of strategy involved."

Pleased she had agreed to walk with him, he turned around and began to walk, very slowly, in the other direction.

She followed.

"That is astute of you to notice," he said. "Strategy depends on the opponent. Whether he will compete fairly or whether he is a trickster. There *are* some of those, you know."

"I can imagine," she said, walking beside him. "Have you ever been badly injured?"

He shook his head. "Never," he said. "Certainly, I've had wood driven into my flesh. I've been knocked off a horse backward before. By my own brother, I might add, and when a man is unhorsed, his opponent wins his horse. I had to fight my brother for a year to get my horse back. He did not want to return him."

"How unkind," she said as if in complete sympathy. "Is he always so cruel?"

"Always," Essien said dramatically. "Do you have any siblings?"

"Alas, I do not."

"Good," he said firmly. "You cannot know how utterly cruel and heartless they can be, although I will say that I would kill or die for my brother. He is a good man with a good heart. But he still vexes me, and he knows it."

Catalina broke into soft laughter. "Is that not what a sibling is for?" she said. "To annoy you to tears?"

"Exactly," he said. "You see? You may not have a sibling, but you know of the relationship between them. Of course, I am the younger brother, so I am the worse out of the two of us. I annoy my brother into madness at times."

"But that is your duty. He must accept that."

Essien guffawed, looking at her. "How clever you are," he said. "I can see that you are on my side. I am comforted."

"Good," she said, grinning at him because he was still snorting. "I am an excellent ally against annoying older brothers."

Essien suddenly dropped to one knee, grasping at her cloak. "My lady, this is the most marvelous news," he said. "Marry me and defend me against my brother. You are the only one who can save me from him. And myself. Mostly myself. Christ, I *am* completely annoying. Forget I said any of that."

He stood up, brushing off one knee, as Catalina giggled uncontrollably. "How many times have you proposed marriage out of desperation such as that?" she asked.

He shook his head. "Never," he said solemnly, hand over his heart. "You are the first. You are not betrothed, are you?"

Her smile faded, quickly. It was as if someone had doused a flame. One moment she was smiling and in the next, her face was as dead as stone. Where there had been laughter moments earlier, now there was silence. His smile faded, too.

"My apologies," he said. "That was forward of me. Forgive me."

She shook her head. "There is no need," she said. "As it happens, I was informed tonight that I am, in fact, betrothed."

He almost decided not to admit it, carrying on the charade until the moment was right, but he had a feeling if he didn't confess what he knew, she wouldn't take it very well. If he wanted to build a life with this lovely creature, forced as they were being, then he was going to have to take that first step.

Tell her.

He had to.

"I know," he said softly.

She looked at him, brow furrowed. "You know what?"

"That you are betrothed."

Her confusion grew. "How?"

"Because I was informed of the same thing."

That didn't make sense to her, still. "You... you were informed that I was betrothed?"

He sighed faintly. "I was informed that *I* was betrothed," he said. "I was told that I was betrothed to the daughter of Harald de Efford, Lord Eckington. She is a widow with two children. Does she sound familiar to you? Mayhap you know her."

Catalina stared at him. Then her eyes widened and a hand flew to her mouth in shock. "It's you!" she said through her fingers. "*You* are the prince?"

He nodded. "I am," he said. "I am Horus Essien Nazimuddin Mei al-Kort, named for the falcon-headed god of protection and healing from my mother's native country. In the country of my birth, Kitara, my father was the king. I am a *shehzadah*, a prince, known as the *dosara beta*, or the second son. My brother is the heir, now presumably king of a bereft country. It was destroyed, and that is why I find myself in England. My lady, I do not know how you feel about this betrothal, but if you are disappointed, know that I had no choice in the matter. I am very sorry if you are unhappy about it."

Catalina still had her hands over her mouth. She was looking at Essien with bulging eyes, ready to pop out of her head. Her breathing seemed to come in odd gasps until she finally pulled her hands away and emitted something of a cough.

"I think I need to sit down," she said, sounding weak. "Forgive me… I do not mean to be rude… but I must sit down."

Essien immediately went to take her arm to steady her. He didn't even think about it. The lady was in distress and he meant to help, so he quickly took her arm and escorted her over to the wall where there were several thick logs, tree stumps, that the soldiers used to sit upon. Catalina lowered herself onto one.

He could see her hands shaking.

"May I fetch you something to drink?" he said, unsure what to do at this point. "Or would you simply prefer to be left alone?"

She didn't say anything for a moment. She just kept breathing and blinking, with a sort of dazed expression on her face. Then she took a deep and rather ragged breath before looking up at him.

"You should stay," she said. "You should stay and sit down. We seem to be in a predicament together, and rather than avoid each other, we should probably discuss it."

Essien sat right down, his back straight, facing her as she struggled to regain her composure. "We are certainly in a shocking situation together," he said. "Well, shocking for us, anyway. A marriage contract is not shocking. But it can be when it is forced upon unsuspecting victims."

She nodded. Then she took another deep breath and blew it out. "My God," she said. "You have my deepest apologies, my lord. I know how my father is, and if he browbeat you into accepting this, I cannot adequately express my embarrassment. Please know that I did not know about any of this until he told me a short time ago."

"You did not know this afternoon when we met?"

"Nay," she said. "Did you?"

"I did not," he said. "However, when I was told of the betrothal, and whom it was with, I will admit that I had visions of you attacking me from behind and trying to gouge my eyes out as we stood before the priest."

There was a glimmer of mirth in his eyes. Catalina saw it. She tried not to smile but couldn't help it. She tried not to laugh, but she couldn't help that, either. Suddenly, she was ringing with laughter, her hands over her face in shame.

"God's Bones, what you must think of me," she said. "I swear to you that I am not a violent person by nature. Quite the contrary."

He held up a hand to ease her, a grin on his face. "I know," he said. "You thought I was absconding with your child and you protected her, as a mother should."

"Exactly," she said sincerely, sobering. "Only a madwoman would take on a man twice her size if it were not something truly important."

He nodded. "I realize that," he said. "But you were most impressive. And fearsome. Those are excellent traits for a woman."

Those were kind words, but it didn't distract her from the subject at hand. The smile faded from her face as she looked into his eyes, the color of a pale cat's-eye stone.

"I probably should not ask you how you feel about the betrothal, but I will," she said. "Since neither one of us can break it, it does not matter how we feel. But mayhap we should speak of what you expect from me."

His brow furrowed curiously. "Expect?"

"Aye," she said. "For example, if you wish for me to marry you but remain living with my father, I will do so. Having a wife must be shocking enough, but having the burden of a wife and her two children must be a truly horrific thought for a man such as yourself."

His furrowed brow had turned into a frown. "What kind of man do you think I am?"

She gestured in the direction of the tournament field. "I meant that you must travel with the tournament circuit, so a wife tagging along must be quite a burden," she said. "You have had your freedom. I do not wish to impose on the life you have lived."

He scratched his chin as he thought on her statement. "Then you wish to stay with your father?"

She snorted softly, with bitterness. "Nay, but I will if that is what you wish."

His gaze lingered on her for a moment. "You and your father are not close?"

"Not even a little."

"You dislike him?"

"I have no real love for him if that is what you are asking," she said. "He has never been particularly kind to me. I was not born a male and, in his opinion, that was a terrible sin."

Essien was coming to understand the situation a little. "Are we betrothed because he wants to be rid of you?"

She nodded. "Aye," she said. "But more than that, I suspect an ulterior motive."

"What is that?"

"He wants a grandson to carry on his legacy," she said simply. "When I bore two daughters, he did not speak to me for years until my husband died. Then he had no choice because I had nowhere to go. My lord… I am afraid you are caught up in my father's ambitions."

Essien could hear the genuine sorrow in her voice. She was quite apologetic for her father and his actions, a man that Essien only knew through the eyes of Christopher. *A wise man, a fair man,* Christopher had always said. But that wasn't what Essien was hearing from the man's daughter.

Every man lets us see of himself what he wants us to see.

Harald was evidently a man who was more concerned with perception than truth.

"Every man has ambitions," he said after a moment. "That is nothing new. That is how the world of men functions, each to his own ambitions and gains. You needn't apologize for that."

She shrugged. "I feel the need," she said. "You do not wish to marry, do you?"

"Do you?"

"I asked first."

The corners of his mouth turned up, a hint of a smile as he shook his head and averted his gaze. "Nay," he said honestly. "To be truthful, it is not that I never wish to marry. I simply hadn't thought of marrying now, at this time in my life. It is an old argument between my brother and me. Given the fact that we are the only two survivors of the royal family of Kitara, he feels strongly that it is my duty to marry and have sons who bear the blood of Kitara."

"Is your brother married?"

Essien nodded. "Aye," he said. "He already has one child, with another on the way, so he feels that he is an expert in all things having to do with marriage and children."

There was some annoyance as he said it. Catalina could hear it. With a sigh, she pulled the cloak around her more tightly, against the damp night, and gazed up at the stars.

"Having children and a marriage does give you a different perspective in life," she said softly. "It teaches you things."

"Like what?"

She looked at him, then. "Like thinking of your children before yourself," she said. "Like attacking a man you thought was trying to harm them. It makes you think more of your family than yourself."

He smiled faintly. "I can understand that," he said. "But you have not answered my question."

"What question?"

"Do you wish to marry?"

She averted her gaze again. "Since you were honest, I suppose I can be also," she said. "Nay, I do not wish to marry again. Once was enough. More than enough."

"Because you loved your husband?"

She shook her head even before he'd finished the question. "There was nothing as fragile as love in our marriage," she said. "It was a business arrangement. A contract. Alfred came from a good family, a family with property and money, and his father and my father were great friends. When I was old enough to marry, I did. We spent ten years together. Ten years and two daughters and memories I'm happy to leave in the past."

Essien watched her face as she spoke. There was no self-pity there, simply fact. "It was an unhappy marriage?"

She shrugged. "Alfred had his own life," she said. "I was not part of it. Truthfully, he never should have married. He simply wasn't the type of man who cherished home and hearth."

"What did he cherish?"

"His friend."

"What friend?"

From her expression, it was clear that she hadn't meant for the conversation to go in that direction. "It does not matter," she said. "Forgive me. I did not mean to ramble about a man who is dead and buried. Alfred de Barenton wasn't a bad man. He was simply in a bad situation, in a marriage he did not want. You asked me if I want to marry, and the truth is that I want what every woman wants from a marriage—a kind husband. Mayhap affection. Safety and security. But that is not what I got the first time, and I am wary to do it again. No offense intended, my lord, but we do not know one another. We are being forced into this union, so mayhap we should discuss our expectations from the onset so there will be no mistake."

Essien thought about that for a moment. "I believe that is fair," he said. "But I could not tell you what my expectations are at this moment. I've never had to think about it at all, so I will need some time to consider the question. This is quite new to me."

She nodded, understanding the magnitude of her request. But in her case, she didn't need time.

She already knew.

"My expectations are quite simple, I hope," she said. "All I will ever ask of you is honesty and kindness. For my part, I can promise you loyalty and honesty. I know what it means to be a wife. I will not shame you, no matter… well, no matter how you decide to conduct your life. Your life and choices are your own. I will accept them. I will tend our children, if any, with dignity and support your household. You will never have to worry about me."

He thought that was a strange thing to say. "Something tells me that you have been in that situation before."

"What situation?"

"Where your husband's choices were not to your liking?"

Catalina shook her head. "It does not matter," she said. "I do not mean to be mysterious, but my marriage to Alfred has nothing to do with our betrothal. Any choices he made are irrelevant. I am simply saying that I will do as you wish when it comes to our marriage. You'll have no argument from me, whatever decisions you make. Whatever they are, I will remain loyal to you, as my husband."

Essien's gaze lingered on her. There was so much more that she wasn't saying when she made a statement like that. He wanted to ask her, to dig deeper, but it didn't seem like the right time. Maybe someday, when they came to know one another better, but not now. Not today.

Today, the realization of a betrothal was enough to deal with.

"Thank you for telling me," he said. "I appreciate your candor."

"I will always be honest with you, my lord."

He held up a finger. "We'll start with that," he said. "You need not address me formally. My name is Essien. Please use it."

She shook her head. "Though I appreciate the honor, I cannot," she said. "Not until I know you better. It would seem rude and informal to me not to address you properly."

He gave her a half-grin. "As you wish," he said. "Would you prefer I address you formally, also?"

"Would you be offended?"

"Of course not," he said. "I will do what you are comfortable with."

"Thank you," she said sincerely. Then she spoke hesitantly. "I do not mean to cause trouble. It is simply that we do not know one another, and it would seem incredibly ill-mannered to address you by your name at this time."

"My lady, you need not explain yourself," he said. "You are correct—we are strangers. But we are strangers who are going to come to know one another very well. Very well, indeed. I am looking forward to it."

That statement seemed to surprise her. "You are?" she said. "Why?"

He laughed softly. "Because I should like to know my wife very well," he said. Then his smile faded. "You should know that my parents loved one another. They were devoted to one another. One of the last memories I have of them is of the pain and horror of their separation. My brother also loves his wife. They have a strong, enduring relationship. You asked me what I expect from this marriage? Mayhap I expect that we will be fond of one another. Mayhap more, with time. You see, I am surrounded by men who love their wives. I see what it has done for them. Mayhap I want the same."

His answer gave her a great deal of pause. After a moment, she simply shook her head. "And I have been surrounded by the opposite," she said quietly. "My own marriage was an existence, nothing more. I would not even know how to go about expecting more, because if you do not expect such things, you cannot be disappointed."

Essien thought that was a rather sad answer. He'd opened his mouth to reply when he suddenly caught movement out of the corner of his eye. It was somewhat dim where they were sitting, so all he could see was a figure coming toward them in the dark. The first thing he did was put himself between the lady and the approaching figure.

Lance le Kerque came into view.

"What is the meaning of this?" he demanded, then quickly looked to Catalina. "My lady, are you well? Is he harassing you?"

Catalina stood up. "Of course not," she said. "And what are you doing here? I told you that I did not wish to be followed."

Lance's gaze moved to Essien, his eyes narrowed menacingly. "It is a good thing I did," he said. "I told you that there were men about and it was not safe. Now I find you sitting with al-Kort in a darkened corner? What would your father say?"

"Nothing," Catalina snapped before Essien could reply. "He would say nothing because he has betrothed me to Sir Essien. The man is to be my husband, so it is his right to speak to me alone in the dark if he wishes."

That statement brought Lance's rage to an abrupt halt. The anger drained from his face, replaced by surprise. Perhaps even shock. Whatever it was, Essien could see the transformation right before his eyes.

The man was stunned.

"Betrothed?" Lance finally repeated. "You have been betrothed?"

"Aye," Catalina said, perhaps a little more gently. "My father and Lord Hereford have come to an agreement regarding me and Sir Essien, so there is no need for your intervention. I do not require, nor do I want, your assistance. When I ask you to leave me alone, I meant it."

The man stared at her, stiffening in indignation. The shock was quickly wearing off, replaced by something darker. Without another word, he spun on his heel and headed off into the darkness. Essien watched him go, fading off into the bailey and the open gates beyond.

"I must say that your words to him were rather sharp," he said, turning to look at her. "Is that how you treat all of your father's men?"

There was something disapproving in his tone, and Catalina caught on to it. "Nay," she assured him. "I believe servants and soldiers must be treated with respect. But you must understand that Lance le Kerque has been trying to woo me since nearly the day he came to Eckington. He is persistent and annoying and tries my patience because he will not accept my refusal. That is what you saw, my lord—my insistence that he stop his pursuit of me, once and for all. He seems to think that, somehow, I will change my mind, but now that he has heard of the betrothal, he will have to accept it."

Essien's focus lingered on her for a moment before returning to the bailey, where le Kerque had been. As if somehow he could see the man who was now evidently some kind of competition. Perhaps he was even a threat, though Essien couldn't know that for sure. Not now. But time would tell if le Kerque accepted his loss like an honorable man or if he was going to make something out of it.

Something told Essien that he would have to be on his guard.

"I will accept your explanation," he said. "Mayhap I should be plain with you—I do not treat my servants or men poorly, nor does my brother. To do so shows a lack of moral character."

He was telling her what he expected of her, and Catalina wasn't stupid. She understood. A glimmer came to her eye. "You behave like a prince," she said, a smile tugging on her lips. "You are benevolent to all, and that is admirable. I will say that I have never treated a servant or soldier poorly in my life, and if you do not believe me, you may ask any of my father's men. But do not ask le Kerque. Due to his relentless pursuit, my only choice was to be brutally frank with him, and even then, he probably would think I was flirting with him. The man does not know when he is not wanted."

Somehow, Essien believed her. He didn't know her, but he believed her. Time would tell, of course, and he thought he very well might ask one of her servants what kind of mistress she was, but for the moment, he was satisfied. He'd known enough scheming, dishonorable people in his lifetime and she simply didn't seem the type.

"It is difficult to chase a woman when she does not want to be chased," he said after a moment. "I do not know le Kerque well, of course, so I cannot speak to the man's relentless pursuit except to say that I do not blame him. He saw something of great beauty and set out to claim it. You cannot blame a man for trying."

She gave him a quirky smile. "Are *you* flirting with me?"

He shrugged coyly. "If you do not know, then I must be terrible at it," he said. "Either that, or you are impervious to men's charms."

"Do they have any?"

He burst out laughing. "I would hope that I do, but if you must ask, then I must be a failure at that, too."

She chuckled as he continued to laugh. "You are not a failure," she said. Then she glanced up at the sky again, noting the rise of the moon. "And I fear I must return to my children. Ines usually awakens an hour or two after going to bed because she becomes thirsty, so I must be there when she awakens."

"May I escort you?"

"I believe that is your right."

"Right or not, I am asking permission."

It was her turn to give him a coy expression. "Granted."

Essien extended his elbow to her, as a mannerly man would, and she accepted. As they began to walk across the bailey, heading toward the gatehouse, he was feeling exceptionally pleased to have this glorious woman on his arm. She was witty and beautiful, not to mention uncommonly brave, and that was something that impressed him. His first encounter with her had been interesting, to say the least, but his second encounter was enlightening.

He was definitely looking forward to the third.

"Where is your encampment?" he asked.

They were approaching the open gatehouse and she pointed off to the right. "Almost right on the edge of the competitors' encampment," she said. "The blue, yellow, and white tent is my father's, and there is a fortified carriage where my children are sleeping."

He couldn't really see it, but he took her word for it. In fact, he was rather enjoying the walk with her to the point where he slowed his pace a little. He didn't want it to come to an end. They were nearly to the gatehouse when someone ran into him from behind and big, hairy arms went around his shoulders. He was being jostled about, so he tried to protect Catalina from the buffeting going on even as he turned to see who had crashed into him.

"Es!" It was Jonathan. "We have been looking for you. We have games going on in the hall and you are needed!"

Essien came to an irritated stop, turning to Catalina. "My apologies for what I am about to do, my lady," he said politely. "I will get rid of him."

He gently took her hand off his elbow before turning to

Jonathan and shoving the man back by the chest. "Do you not see that I am walking with a lady, Wolfie?" he said angrily. "You nearly bowled her over with your rude behavior."

Jonathan wasn't alone. Ashton was there, also, the enormous blond knight with the dashing looks. Someone had once said he looked like an archangel, and he did, if one believed the paintings of those divine beings. He was also the less drunk of the pair, grabbing hold of Jonathan to steady the man.

"We were heading to the garderobe, but Wolfie saw you and went running across the bailey," he said. Then he focused on Catalina. "My apologies, my lady, if he has upset you."

Catalina shook her head. "Not at all, my lord."

Ashton merely smiled and tried to pull Jonathan away, but the big knight wouldn't move. "I am not leaving until Es promises to come inside and be on my team," he said, reaching out to grab Essien. "De Norville has a serving wench on his shoulders and we are battling in the hall. The women are trying to push each other off our shoulders."

Essien frowned. "God's Bones, Wolfie," he said. "Someone is going to get hurt."

Jonathan frowned. "No one is going to get hurt," he said. Suddenly, he pushed past Essien and grasped Catalina by the wrist. "Come inside, my lady. You can ride on Essien's shoulders. We are betting money on who will win, so you could win a purse!"

Catalina was faced with a very big, very sweaty man who had hold of her arm. Under normal circumstances, she probably would have shoved a finger in his eye, but she knew he was a friend of Essien's. He wasn't trying to hurt her. God knows, the man was drunk. Quite drunk. She saw Essien move to grab him out of the corner of her eye and she held up a hand to him, holding him off.

Her focus was on Jonathan.

"Come closer," she said to him, crooking a finger. "I must tell you something."

Jonathan leaned into her, weaving drunkenly. "Will you come?" he asked.

Catalina shook her head. "I cannot," she muttered. "Sir Essien was taking me to see my dying mother and you are preventing him from doing so. Will you please let me go so that I may see my mother before she dies?"

Jonathan appeared stricken. He released her immediately. "Forgive me," he said, too drunk to realize that she probably hadn't brought her dying mother to a tournament. "You must go immediately. Forgive me."

She smiled sweetly and reached out to take Essien's arm again. "Thank you," she said to Jonathan. "Good eve to you, my lord."

She was pulling Essien along, who had heard what she said and was quite impressed by the way she handled that big, bumbling idiot. A loveable idiot, but an idiot nonetheless.

"Well done, my lady," he muttered, his voice full of approval. "You handled Wolfie perfectly."

She smiled modestly. "I can tell he has great regard for you," she said. "He was not trying to hurt you or me. He simply needed to be gently handled."

He looked at her, at her lowered head as she watched the ground beneath her feet, and thought that, perhaps, she was potentially a woman of substance. It was difficult to tell after having known her less than a day, but he was usually a fairly good judge of character when his emotions didn't get in the way. He wasn't feeling emotional about her other than polite interest for now, so he could see her more clearly at the moment than he might in the days and weeks and years to come.

So far, he liked what he saw.

"Well done," he said again, patting her hand as he clutched his elbow. "You are a woman of tact."

Catalina didn't say anything. She was smiling, her head down, watching the ground pass beneath her feet. They came through the gatehouse and she once again pointed toward her father's section of the encampment, and it was, indeed, right on the edge of the encampment as a whole. For safety's sake, competitor encampments were always next to the castle in case they had to quickly move inside in the event of an attack, so that was simply the tradition at most locations. They were just heading into the fringe of the encampment, with her father's area about thirty feet ahead, when they began to hear shouting.

Bellowing, in truth.

Catalina came to a brief halt. "That sounds like my father," she said, puzzled. "But why would he be yelling so?"

Essien wasn't sure, but the closer they came to the tent and the general de Barenton encampment, the more yelling there was. Two voices. Then Lance shot out of the big blue tent with Harald behind him, swinging something at him. Essien couldn't tell if it was a club or a mace, but it was something. Harald was brandishing it like a weapon, striking Lance on the shoulder before the man swiftly moved out of his range.

"Get out!" Harald was screaming. "Take your things and leave my encampment. You will leave my sight, le Kerque, and never return. Do you hear me?"

Essien came to a halt, but Catalina ran toward Harald. "Father?" she said, concerned. "What is the trouble?"

Harald saw her coming and the rage on his face was evident. "*You,*" he said angrily. "You are the trouble. Women are nothing but trouble. Now le Kerque is enraged that I betrothed you to Hereford's man and he is calling me a charlatan and a liar. He wanted to marry you, but I gave you over to another. He is questioning my honor because of you! He is threatening me!"

Essien stepped into the fray, putting himself between Lance, who was busy grabbing his things out of a smaller tent, and a nearly hysterical Harald.

"Did you promise le Kerque your daughter's hand?" he asked the man. "Did you give him any indication that you would grant his petition?"

That only seemed to make Harald angrier. "That is none of your affair," he said. "Who are you?"

"Essien al-Kort."

Very quickly, Harald calmed. Too quickly. He struggled with his anger, looking Essien over in the dim light of the nearby torches.

"The prince," he said, almost to himself. "You are the one Hereford chose."

"I am, my lord," Essien said. "But if this man had a claim before me, that must be discussed."

"There was no claim," Harald said. "Only a wish. He wished it."

"I *requested* it." Lance had heard him. He had his broadsword, in its scabbard, in his hand because he'd been in the midst of securing it when he heard Harald's claim. "Over and over again, I requested it. I begged him to consider it. He never gave me a direct answer, only smiled and walked away. He has toyed with me for the past month about it and now I find he has betrothed his daughter to you."

Essien was calm as he faced him. "I did not know any of this," he said. "I doubt Hereford did, either."

Lance was livid, red in the face with emotion. "Then you understand why I feel cheated," he said. "I may not be a prince of Kitara, but my birth is not entirely unremarkable."

Essien shook his head. "I never said it wasn't," he said. "I've never said anything at all because I hardly know you. But I must tell Hereford of this situation. He may wish to speak to you."

"Why?" Catalina wanted to know. She'd been listening silently, confident that Lance's suit was ended for good, but Essien's words had her concerned. "Why would you tell Hereford about this?"

Essien looked at her with regret. "Because le Kerque may have a claim if your father never clearly denied his request," he said. "A magistrate might see it that way."

Her eyes widened. "Nay," she gasped. "I told you… I do not wish to marry him. I do not even like him. It would be another miserable marriage, and I will throw myself in the river before I marry him."

Essien could see how distressed she was. Truthfully, he was also, but he had a point. If le Kerque took his grievance to the local magistrate, which happened to be Christopher, there might be a problem because Christopher would recuse himself and pass it to another magistrate who might rule against Harald. If the man had been ambiguous enough in his response to le Kerque's suit, enough to imply he would consider it, there might be something in the law that gave Lance the right to compete for Catalina's hand. At this point, there was no written contract, only verbal, and a verbal one was easily dissolved if both parties agreed to it.

But Catalina wasn't having any of it.

"Be at ease," Essien said softly, reaching out to grasp her gently by the hand. "I am not saying that he will win, but he could cause… trouble."

"There will be no trouble," Harald shouted, shaking his club at Lance. "You are a knight with no name, no money, no title, and no prospects. My daughter is a valuable heiress. You are not good enough, le Kerque. Not in the least."

Lance's jaw was twitching with emotion. "I was good enough for you to take me on as your knight," he growled. "I may bear the name le Kerque, but I am not a le Kerque. I am my father's bastard and a man of great and noble birth. I am more than a match for your daughter."

"You are the dirt beneath my feet!"

Essien put his hand up in front of Lance before the man could respond, a silent request to keep his composure.

"You must do as he tells you to do," he said quietly. "If you maintain this argument, it will only get worse and Hereford will get involved, so do yourself a kindness and walk away. Get your things and walk away. Go into the great hall and stay there. Let the situation calm, and if you feel you have enough of a grievance, see Hereford on the morrow."

Lance eyed him in the darkness. "Why should you encourage me to do that?" he said. "You do realize that I am protesting your betrothal, don't you?"

"I do," Essien said. "Mayhap you have been treated unfairly. I don't really know. I was only told today of this contract, so I do not know what de Barenton may, or may not, have implied to you. But if you feel strongly about this, I suggest you see Hereford."

Oddly, those words seem to calm Lance. Essien was being

understanding, if not neutral, and considering he had a stake in this situation, it was surprising. He seemed to want to be fair about it.

That was most shocking.

Without another word, Lance collected his saddlebags, traveling bags, and a lad who had been squiring for him. Everything was packed up and the warhorse gathered. As Harald went back into his tent, for he didn't care what became of Lance at this point, Essien watched the man head toward the bailey of Lioncross Abbey. When he disappeared through the gatehouse, Essien turned to Catalina.

"I know this is distressing," he said quietly, "but I can only imagine how I would feel if I wanted to marry you and my suit had been toyed with. To be truthful, I do not think he has a claim of any kind, but I do not want the man feeling that he's been cheated and disrespected, most of all by me. If he tells others, that kind of thing will get around and put me in a bad light. So, I have to make him feel that he has recourse. Even if he does not pursue it. Do you understand?"

Catalina nodded. "I do," she said. "You show wisdom and kindness."

He shrugged. "Mayhap," he said, his gaze drifting over her in the dim light of the distant torches. "All I know is that if I had asked for your hand and was denied, I might have been quite upset myself."

She fought off a smile. "You flatter me."

"I speak the truth."

Catalina wasn't quite sure what to say to that, so she simply let her smile blossom as a silent gesture of thanks.

"It has been quite an evening, my lord," she said. "I am certain you have other things to attend to, so I will bid you a good night."

"Indeed," he said, dipping his head as he prepared to walk away. But he stopped as if a thought had just occurred to him. "My lady, would it be too bold to ask for a favor to carry for tomorrow's bouts? Something that will bring me luck?"

She appeared surprised by the request. "A favor?" she said. "From me?"

"You are my betrothed, are you not?"

Catalina almost had to think about that. It was such a strange thing to consider, but he was right. She *was* his betrothed. Without hesitation, she pulled her hair, thick and wavy, over her shoulder and untied the blue silk ribbon that was securing the braid at the bottom.

"Will this be acceptable?" she said, extending it to him. "I do not know what else I can give you."

He took the ribbon gratefully. "This is perfect," he said. "I can tuck it into my tunic easily. Thank you, my lady. This is very kind of you."

"I hope it helps."

He chuckled. Then he reached out and took her hand, bringing it to his lips for a gentle kiss.

"It already has," he said softly.

With that, he turned and headed for the gatehouse, but he turned back around to look at her a couple of times as he walked. Catalina grinned, waving at him both times, watching him as he finally picked up the pace and jogged through the open gates, disappearing inside.

Sweet Jesú… Is this really happening? Is Essien too good to be true?

She couldn't help but wonder. Certainly, he was beautiful to look at. He was quite tall, with long, muscular arms, broad chest, and narrow torso. His eyes had an ethereal quality to them, a sublime color that was a shade of golden brown. It was pale and lovely. But his smile was his most brilliant feature, for his big white teeth positively lit up the sky when he smiled. That smile made her feel the least bit quivery, too. She'd never felt that way before, so it was both intriguing and exciting.

He was intriguing and exciting.

Her prince.

With a smile playing on her lips, she headed off to bed.

CHAPTER TEN

E VEN IN THE dark, he could see the tournament in the distance.

The Welsh marches were historically a brutal and mysterious place, lands that were both Welsh and English, lands that had seen more battles than most. There was a certain aura that settled over the area, an aura that conveyed ancient tribes and great passion. There were two kinds of people who loved these lands and loved them enough to fight to the death for them. Those battles had been going on for centuries for reasons that probably would not be decided in his lifetime. Truthfully, he'd never been to the Welsh marches before, but here he was.

He was seeking something.

But finding it was difficult. It had all started on a ship sailing for Calais, one that had caught fire when they were in sight of the shore. It had started when the stove on the ship's middeck used for cooking and heat ignited some nearby bed fodder. After that, everything went up like a torch. He didn't even remember why he'd been on the ship, only that he had, and the one thing he had managed to take with him was a small gold cross pendant. The front of the cross had semiprecious carnelian stones on it, and on the back there was an inscription. It read *Allez avec Dieu*. Go with God. He remembered stealing the cross off someone as the ship went up in flames, a man who was already dead. A friend of his, he'd remembered later. *Al*. Al with the expensive gold cross he liked to flash around. He'd been flashing it around that night.

That was how he'd remembered to take it.

But that fire, for him, had been the first step in a journey where God was not present. That little cross with its inscription mocked him, because he'd stolen it and God did not reward thieves. When he'd grabbed it off Al's neck, it had been searing hot, so the imprint of it was on his right palm. The fire had been so hot and so terrible that it had damaged most of the skin on his body, including his nose and most of his hair. Men still cringed when they looked at him, and women still fainted, so he'd quickly learned to cover himself up so no one would see the horror he had become.

A caricature of his former self.

A man with no name, no past, and no future.

Along with the external damage had come the internal. The fire had also scorched his lungs and prevented him from breathing properly, so he'd been deprived of enough oxygen that his memory was gone and his way of thinking was rudimentary at best. He could speak still, but the words were slow and simple. He could walk, but it was stilted. He could dress himself and feed himself, but barely.

That damnable fire had taken everything from him.

It had taken him a full year to recover, enough so that he could function without assistance. He, and the few others who had survived the blaze, were tended by the priests at St. Joseph's church in Calais. His memory was so damaged that he didn't even remember why he'd been on that ship until someone at the church mentioned that it was a ship belonging to a Flemish warlord. It had been going to Calais and carried one hundred soldiers, but that information didn't really help him. He still didn't know who, or what, he was.

All he had was that little cross.

And then, one day, it came to him.

Eckington.

Al had mentioned the name Eckington, though he didn't know what it meant until he spoke to a man from England who happened to be at the church one day when he was strong enough to sweep off the steps. They got to speaking, mostly about the fire that had burned him so badly, and the man told him that he was from the West Country and Eckington was a town in Herefordshire. That led him to believe that Eckington was where Al was from or, at the very least, where he could seek answers. Perhaps Al had a wife who would welcome her husband home.

The man who carried the cross.

With his features burned so badly, she would never know the truth.

Armed with the name, and that gold cross, he'd decided to go to Eckington and see what he could discover about Al's past.

And his future.

But traveling to the Welsh marches wasn't without peril. From doing odd jobs around the church, he'd had enough money for passage to England, but he needed a horse once he got there. Because he was so horrific to look at, the first two livery stables had turned him down. They basically told him to go away and not come back. At the third livery stable, the man did the same thing, so the man now calling himself Al had killed him and stolen one of the horses. He didn't much have a sense of morality, so killing and stealing seemed to come naturally. He headed west, following the main road and keeping an eye out for anyone who might be looking for a murderer. Perhaps the family of the man he'd killed would come after him, but he couldn't be sure.

He couldn't be sure and he didn't much care.

All he knew was that he had to go west.

That apathy kept him on the main road, making his way east and really having no idea where he was going. He just kept going west. He would stop at taverns at nighttime, letting a bed or finding a warm corner to sleep in. He'd long learned to keep his face covered up, so he wore a scarf that covered his head and his face so that only his eyes were showing. By doing that, people would just focus on his eyes and not on the horrific scars all over his face and head.

By traveling that way, he could keep himself relatively un-seen. No one bothered him as he traveled from town to town on his stolen horse. The night before he reached Eckington, the tavern keep in a tiny village just south of his destination told him of Harald de Efford, Lord Eckington, and how the man had traveled to Lioncross Abbey Castle on the Welsh marches for a great tournament. Everybody in the shire was talking about the tournament and many had traveled to see it, including de Efford. The same tavern keep mentioned Lord Eckington's widowed daughter and her two children in the course of gossiping about Harald de Efford, as well as a local farmer's wife that de Efford evidently bedded on occasion. The rumormonger was quite gleeful about it. Al didn't care about the farmer's wife, but he was quite interested in Eckington's daughter. Somehow, he didn't even have to ask her name.

He already knew.

Catalina.

The real Al had told him that.

That realization had him heading for the Welsh marches and the tournament at Lioncross Abbey. It hadn't been difficult to find, and now he was finally here. Riding on a damp night, with the moon high overhead and listening to the sounds of the darkness around him, he was focused on the glowing settlement ahead. He would find Lord Eckington, and Catalina, and show them the cross he still kept in his pocket. Perhaps then they would accept him as Al returned.

Perhaps they would even welcome him with open arms.

That was the hope, anyway.

In the darkness, he pushed on.

CHAPTER ELEVEN

T HE BLUE SILK ribbon was pinned safely to the neck of his
tunic.

It was dawn as Lioncross Abbey and the tournament field
began to come alive. A glistening of dew covered the ground,
making everything smell fresh and new, as the sun's golden
fingers began to caress the land. The world was lighting up,
glowing, and a new day was upon them.

The competitors for the tournament finals were ready.

That included Essien.

He'd been up before dawn, seeing to his horse, a muscular
steed named Peggy. It was a stallion, in truth, and his name had
been Pegasus, but over the years, it had been reduced to Peggy
and that was all anyone ever called him. Peggy was a glorious
roan, gray-brown in color, with a dappled rump and four black-
and-white socks. He was quite a handsome horse and much the
envy of other competitors.

Essien treated the horse like a pampered dog.

The grooms were fussing over the horse this morning, making sure his tack was precisely placed, precisely fastened, as
Essien stood by and watched, chomping on an apple that he

eventually gave over to the horse because Peggy ate like a pig. If there was food around, he wanted it. And much like the horse, Essien had his own preparations to go through, so he began to don his clothing for the coming joust with the help of Christopher's sons, Douglas and Roi.

Douglas had seen fifteen summers and Roi was about nine years older. They were good lads, and Essien liked them a great deal. He'd watched them grow up, so they were more like brothers to him than his liege's sons. He stood still, arms raised, as Douglas and Roi dressed him for the day. Essien didn't normally utilize squires, although he had a couple of lads back at Raisbeck Castle, his garrison, who tended to him. They simply hadn't made this trip.

Therefore, Douglas and Roi were more than happy to prepare the man they expected to win the tournament today. The God of Vengeance was a hell of a competitor and they were honored that he'd asked for their assistance. The pairs for the finals hadn't been drawn yet, but one of the stable boys had been running back and forth from the marshal's station to see if anything had been posted yet. They knew the pairs would soon be drawn.

Finally, they were.

The stable boy came running back to the staging area at high speed, his flushed face full of excitement.

"*Oy!*" he exclaimed. "Sir Essien against Sir William!"

Essien started laughing. "So I've drawn the Wolfe, have I?" he said. "That's fine with me. I will beat that dog to a pulp. And my brother?"

"He drew Sir Jonathan!"

Essien laughed harder. "Wolfie?" he said. "Now, that's the bout I want to see. God's Blood, that is going to be a battle."

As he stood there, snorting, he was joined by Ashton. The big blond knight wandered over, an amused expression on his face as he came to stand next to Essien.

"Did you see the matches?" he asked.

Essien nodded. "I was just told," he said. "Me against the littlest de Wolfe. He's going to be spanked today, I can feel it."

Ashton chuckled. "Not strangely, he has said the same thing about you."

Essien's smile vanished unnaturally fast. "Did he?" he said. "That little whelp. Once I unseat him, I'm going to put him over my knee and lash the arrogance right out of him."

That only made Ashton laugh harder. "Again," he said, "not strangely, he said the same thing about *you*."

Essien looked at him, scowling. "Ash," he said frankly, "in a bout between the two of us, who would you put your money on to emerge the victor?"

Ashton scratched his head. "Let me think a moment," he said, watching Essien fume. "The littlest Wolfe has size and strength going for him. William is taller than you are."

Essien frowned. "Taller and dumber," he said. "Do you honestly think that whelp can beat me in a tournament?"

Ashton shook his head. "Nay," he said. "Riding tournaments was your business for quite some time, and no one does it better than you and your brother. But do not underestimate William, because he is more devious than you are. If he can figure out a way to take you down, he will."

That both flattered and worried Essien. He knew William and knew the lad was crafty. Not evil, but crafty. With de Norville and Hage out of the competition, at least all he had to worry about was the youngest de Wolfe brother.

And his own brother.

Or Wolfie.

Hell, he had to worry about all of them.

"Who else made the finals?" he asked. "I did not see the rest of the matchups."

"Not me," Ashton said indignantly, referring to being knocked out in the semifinals. "Your brother saw to that. But to answer your question, Cassian and Rolf Deinhold make the third pair."

"Ah," Essien said. "The Dark Conqueror and the Sword of Tyr. That should be exciting. Deinhold may look like someone who was scraped out of the sewer, but he is nothing to be trifled with on a tournament field. The man will send you to the ground if you are not careful."

Ashton knew that. "Indeed," he said. "You are up first. According to the marshal's list, the winners between Wolfie and your brother, and Cassian and Deinhold, will ride against each other. Then you will ride against the winner. What will you do if you must face your brother?"

The only reason Essian had the privileged position of facing the final winner between four competitors was because he'd won the overall joust at the last exhibition on the tournament circuit in Bath. Because he'd made it this far in this particular tournament, the marshals were giving him the honor of only having to face one more competitor should he win his bout. He could do away with de Wolfe and then…

"Addax and I have faced each other before," he said. "Nineteen times over the years, to be exact."

"And?"

"And Addax has me beat, ten victories to nine."

Ashton shook his head, putting a hand on Essien's shoulder. "Not this time," he said in a low voice. "This time, you will send him to the ground and take your horse back. He'll be riding it, you know. He is preparing that animal right now for today's bouts."

Essien grinned. "He's doing that on purpose," he said. "He will not give my horse back to me, or sell him back to me, but he'll let me win him. It's an incentive."

Ashton chuckled. "Will it work?"

"Let's hope so."

"My lord?"

A call came from behind, and they both turned to see one of the marshals standing there. He was looking at Essien.

"Your bout is coming up shortly," the man said. "You are requested to attend to the field immediately."

Essien nodded and the man walked away. Ashton began helping him with the rest of his protection, instructing the two de Lohr brothers to gather his things and get the horse ready. As the activity picked up in preparation for the coming bout, Ashton finished securing what amounted to a stiff leather breastplate that would remain underneath the tunic Essien would wear. It was meant to protect the chest area from the blow of a lance, a little extra reassurance.

"De Wolfe sits low in his saddle," Ashton muttered as he secured the straps on the breastplate. "That makes him difficult to unseat, so you are going to have to force him out of that crouch."

Essien was listening. "Aim for his head."

"Exactly," Ashton said. "Aim for his head, and when he realizes that, he'll try to move to the side. That will shift his balance. Hit him on the shoulder he drops, which will probably be his right, and he will fall. That is, if you can get past the lance. The man uses a sword with his left, but a lance with his right. You may not be able to go around the lance unless you, too, shift your position in the saddle. That leaves you vulnerable."

Essien took it all in. He'd gone against William before, twice, and each of them had a victory. This time, however, Essien was going to come out on top. He wasn't going to let the knight who'd tried to hide exploding lances get a win out of this.

William de Wolfe was going down.

Ↄ

"WE DID NOT arrive in time yesterday to see the bouts," Harald said. "At least, we did not make it over in time once our encampment was established. Today should be excellent entertainment, and given that your betrothed is competing, I'd say we're in for a fine day."

Catalina, Harald, Adabella, and Ines were sitting in the lists this morning, facing the vacant tournament field. It was a chilly morning, and damp, but the sun was up and the sky was bright. A light breeze wafted through the tournament grounds, lifting the standards that were flying over the field.

As Harald had said, they were in for a fine day.

Catalina sat next to her father with Ines on her lap, wrapped in one of her mother's cloaks because she was cold. Adabella sat next to her mother, the cloak partially on her legs. She was cold, too, but she would never admit it, so Catalina simply put the cloak over Adabella's legs and said no more about it.

This morning, her father had insisted they all go to the tournament field at dawn, being unusually nice to Catalina, and she knew why. She was now betrothed to Essien al-Kort, a good man of means, a prince to his people, so there was every reason to be nice to the daughter he would soon be rid of. She would have every chance in the world now to provide him with grandsons, so he could afford a little benevolence. He'd behaved in much the same way when she married Alfred, so this wasn't unexpected.

But it was disappointing.

"I've never seen a championship bout," she said, pulling the cloak more tightly around Ines. "I'm looking forward to it."

Harald seemed particularly interested in the marshals that were starting to come onto the field. That meant the bout wasn't far behind.

"The marshals are carrying the standards of today's competitors," he said, trying to get a good look at them. "I did not look at the list of competitors today, but your betrothed is one of them. We know that for certain."

"Do you know the color of his standard?"

"Nay," Harald said, finally standing up to gain a better view of the standards on the field. "I see a green standard with a wolf's head. That belongs to William de Wolfe because I've seen it before. And next to it… Wait… I see a yellow-and-black standard with a falcon head and a shield. I wonder if that is al-Kort?"

"Greetings, Lord Eckington."

Harald was distracted by a polite greeting and turned to see Lady Hereford on the approach with a few of her children. Dustin Barringdon de Lohr, Lady Hereford, was a petite woman with a thick, long mane of blonde hair, bound up in a bun at the nape of her neck, and a face that could only be described as angelic. She had been married to Christopher for many years and they had nine children between them. In fact, right behind her were her daughters, all four of them, and the eldest two had their younger children in tow.

Harald found himself looking at a parade of de Lohrs as they took the row immediately below him and Catalina, spreading out on the benches while Dustin stood next to the only chair facing the field. Next to it was another big chair, meant for Christopher.

The great Lady Hereford had arrived.

"Ah," he said. "Lady Hereford, how good to see you again."

Dustin smiled. "And you," she said, her gaze moving to Catalina and her girls. "And these lovely young women are with you?"

Harald nodded. "My daughter, Catalina, and her children," he said. "We've come to see her betrothed compete in the finals this morn."

Dustin's smile faded a little. She knew all about the betrothal of Essien to Lord Eckington's daughter because her husband had told her last night. She'd simply never met Harald's daughter before. But Rebecca didn't know about the betrothal and Dustin didn't particularly want her to hear about it. At least, not at the start of a new day because it would surely ruin it for her and, consequently, probably everyone around her when Rebecca reacted to the news. The girl had never been subtle. Therefore, she tried to veer away from the subject a little.

"And it is a glorious day for such competition," Dustin said, mostly to Catalina. "We've not met, my lady, but your father is a good friend of my husband's. We are delighted to have you here today. And your young ladies, of course."

Catalina smiled at the woman, who seemed genuinely kind. "Thank you, my lady," she said. "We are very happy to be here. I was just saying to my father that I do not ever think I've seen a tournament final. Sadly, my experience with tournaments is rather limited."

Dustin winked at her. "Then you are in for some excitement today," she said. Then she indicated the young women sitting nearest her. "These are my daughters—Olivia, Rebecca, Brielle, and Christin."

The four women looked over and politely acknowledged Catalina, who smiled and briefly waved. The daughters of Christopher and Dustin all looked quite different from each other, but the shape of their eyes was very nearly the same. Olivia, the youngest at eight or nine years of age, had blonde hair and blue eyes, while Rebecca, about seven years older, had flaming red hair and big gray eyes. Brielle, sitting next to Rebecca, was quite a bit older than the two younger women and had a dark-haired toddler lying on her shoulder, while Christin, around the same age as Brielle, was elegant with her nearly black hair and gray eyes. She, too, had children around her, demanding her attention, but she gave them a few coins and sent them off to have some peace. Only then did she turn to Catalina and properly greet her.

"I see that your children are far better behaved than the animals my sister and I have raised," she said, giggling. "Have they been enjoying the tournament?"

Catalina smiled as Ines, seeing that a woman was speaking to her mother, sat up in her lap. "So far," she said, pushing Ines's hair out of her eyes. "We saw some dogs who were trained to do tricks. That was delightful."

"Of course," Christin said. "The dancing dogs. My younger children love to see them, too. The man lives not far from here and he goes around to villages, performing for coin. Last year, on my younger son's day of birth, he requested those very dogs. We had them for the entire day."

"I want to see the dogs!" Ines suddenly piped up. "Mama, may I see the dogs?"

"Not now," Catalina told her. "We are going to see horses in a moment. We will see the dogs after, I promise."

Ines would have to be satisfied. She lay back down in her mother's arms and Catalina rolled her eyes at Christin, a silent gesture indicating that a crisis had been averted. Christin grinned, understanding that it was time to change the subject away from dancing dogs and back to the tournament field.

"It will be very exciting today," she said. "Brie's husband is riding in this round against Rolf Deinhold."

Catalina had no idea who that was, but she smiled anyway. "I am sorry that I do not recognize the names."

Brielle turned her head slightly, over the top of her dozing toddler. "My husband is Cassian de Velt," she said. "He goes by the name of the Dark Conqueror on the tournament field. He used to ride the circuit before we were married. His opponent is a Teutonic knight who calls himself the Sword of Tyr. He is quite good and, unfortunately, he will be out for blood against my family because my dear sister insulted him last night. Didn't you, Bebe?"

Hearing her nickname, Rebecca flipped that glorious hair back over her shoulder. "He should not have been so sensitive," she said indignantly. "Only women are so sensitive. It was just fruit. It is not like I launched bolts at the man."

Brielle snorted at her silly younger sister. She wasn't like Brielle or Christin, accomplished women in their own right. In the de Lohr family, the two older girls were, in fact, the eldest children, followed by a gaggle of boys. Rebecca was born in the middle of the boys and Olivia Charlotte, the fourth sister, was the youngest of the group. There were fourteen years between

Rebecca and Brielle, fifteen years between Rebecca and Christin, and then eight years between Rebecca and Olivia Charlotte. Having no sisters close in age, Rebecca had been somewhat on her own growing up. Left to her own devices, she was strong, bold, sassy, and most definitely man-crazy. Brielle and Christin loved her, but they didn't understand her half the time. Throwing cherries at a respected knight was one of those things they just didn't grasp.

And Rebecca knew it.

"He may have been sensitive, but you were rude," Christin said. "You had better hope he does not take it out on Cassian, because if he does, Papa will have something to say to you about it."

Rebecca's chin was up defiantly. "You cannot blame me if Cass falls from his horse," she said, but she knew she was without a leg to stand on. "Look! The competitors are coming to the field. And there's Essien!"

She abruptly jumped to her feet and began waving at him, trying to catch his attention, while Catalina looked at the young woman with surprise and some puzzlement. Because Rebecca was now blocking her view of the field, she had to look around her to see what the fuss was about.

"Bebe, sit down," Dustin scolded quietly. "Stop making a spectacle out of yourself."

Rebecca sat down, but she wasn't happy about it. "I bought him a favor," she said, pulling a small silk kerchief from her sleeve. "I want to give it to him."

"Sit," Dustin commanded. "Just… *sit.*"

Rebecca listened, but only for a moment. Essien came onto the field to the roar of the crowd, making a pass in front of the lists, and Rebecca bolted to her feet again, waving the silk kerchief and calling his name. Much to her delight, he came to the front of the lists, right where she was sitting, and pointed a finger at her.

Or so she thought.

"My lady," he said, muffled through his lowered visor. "I shall win this tournament for you!"

Rebecca was stumbling all over herself trying to climb over the people in front of her in order to reach Essien. But Dustin held her back, commanding her to sit yet again, which Rebecca didn't take kindly to. She began to fight with her mother. As they argued, Essien called out again.

"Lady de Barenton!" he said loudly. "Your favor shall bring me great luck on this day. I thank you for it, my fair beauty."

With that, he pulled forth the blue ribbon that Catalina had given him. He rubbed it against his metal visor, right where his cheek was located, before pushing it back under his tunic. Spinning his horse around, he thundered back toward his starting point at the western end of the guides.

The silence in the de Lohr party, at his departure, was deafening.

Rebecca had stopped arguing with her mother. She was baffled by what Essien had just said, while Dustin, Christin, and Brielle held their breath to see how she would react. Rebecca was not known for tact or restraint, so the results could be explosive.

And so they waited.

"Lady de Barenton?" Rebecca finally repeated. "Who is that?"

"My daughter," Harald said. He'd watched the entire scene with glee and was oblivious to Rebecca's feelings. "She and Sir Essien are to be married."

He pointed to Catalina, seated directly behind Rebecca, who turned to what he was pointing at. When she set her gaze upon Catalina's lovely face, with her dusky blue eyes, plump lips, and glorious hair, her mouth popped open in disbelief. It began to occur to her just who Essien had been pointing at.

And it hadn't been her.

"*You* gave him your favor?" she said in a tone somewhere between anger and disappointment. "Do you know him?"

Catalina nodded. "I do, my lady," she said evenly. "As my father said, we are betrothed."

Rebecca's eyes widened. "That's not true!" she declared. "You are lying!"

"*Rebecca,*" Dustin snapped quietly. "Behave yourself. This is your only warning."

Rebecca opened her mouth to lambast Catalina, but her mother's warning held weight. Dustin was not beyond spanking a daughter who was too old to be spanked. She'd done it before. Stunned, and crushed, Rebecca plopped back down on the bench, looking at Catalina as if the woman had just stolen her kitten.

"Is it true?" she begged, her tone full of agony. "Is it really true?"

Catalina could see the pain in the woman's face. "It is," she said, sensing that, clearly, the young lady had feelings for Essien. "I believe your mother can confirm it."

Rebecca looked to her mother, who nodded. "It is true," she said softly. "Essien and Lady de Barenton are, indeed, betrothed."

Rebecca was now beyond crushed. All of the life and love was draining out of her as they watched and she was quite sure her existence, as she knew it, was over. All of it, over. *She* was over.

Such were the dramatics of Rebecca de Lohr.

"But... when?" she said. "He was not betrothed yesterday. He would have told me if he was, but he did not tell me."

"It is none of your affair," Dustin said, but not without some sympathy. "Essien's life is his own. Lady de Barenton's life is her own, and you do not question them. It is not your place. Come now; turn around and let us watch the tournament. You will enjoy it, my love."

Rebecca turned around as instructed, but the moment she laid eyes on Essien, she began weeping. Big, fat tears rolled onto her cheeks, something Catalina couldn't see, but Dustin could. She leaned forward, catching Christin's eye and silently begging the woman to remove Rebecca before the young woman caused a scene. Even as Christin reached out to take Rebecca by the wrist and pull her out of the lists, the young woman's tears were gaining steam. By the time they hit the stairs, she was openly sobbing. As Christin took her sister away, Catalina couldn't help but feel bad about it.

"I did not know your daughter... and Essien," she said, stammering over her words. "I am very sorry if she is upset."

Dustin shook her head. "Please do not be concerned," she said "Rebecca's feelings for Essien were not mutual in the least. She has a new infatuation every month and he just happened to be her infatuation this month, so do not feel bad about her reaction. She will overcome and find someone new to obsess over."

Catalina forced a smile of gratitude at Lady Hereford's words, but she was still feeling bewildered about the entire thing. She didn't have time to dwell on it, however, because William de Wolfe made an appearance opposite Essien and the crowd in the lists went mad. The buzz of excitement was in the air as people began to stomp their feet, calling for the champions. Horses snorted, knights gripped their reins, and children screamed with glee because the time had finally come.

Let the games begin.

CHAPTER TWELVE

THEY WERE ALL on the rail.

David, Peter, Rhys, Maddoc, Ashton, Kieran, Paris, Christopher, Curtis, Roi, and Douglas were all standing on the rail, just below the lists, watching the tournament field from a bird's-eye vantage. When the competitors lined up on their assigned ends and the marshal dropped the flag, Essien and William thundered toward one another, lances brought to bear, pointing at one another. As an entire arena watched in anticipation, de Wolfe's lance glanced off Essien's hip and Essien managed to catch William in the shoulder. There was a lot of noise, and Essien's lance splintered, but both knights remained upright.

The crowd roared.

"That was a good pass," Rhys said to Christopher.

Christopher grunted. "Aye," he said. "Essien is immovable in the saddle. If de Wolfe is able to unseat him, I will be surprised."

Rhys smiled faintly as they watched the knights swing around and return to their starting positions. "It is still remarkable to me that the dying child we found in the Levant has grown into such a powerful man," he said. "The last time I saw Essien and Addax was, in fact, before we left the Levant. They had gone over to serve the Thuringian knights right before we departed."

Christopher thought back to that time for a moment. "It was difficult to let them go, but I had little choice at that point," he said. "I was returning home to face an unwanted marriage, and I would be preventing John from stealing the country from Richard, so I simply could not watch over Essien and Addax any longer. I knew the Thuringians would be good to them. And they were."

Rhys grunted in agreement. "It would seem so," he said. "I heard they trained in Flanders and ended up on the tournament circuit before coming to England."

Christopher nodded. "That was a few years ago," he said. "When they came to these shores, Cole de Velt recruited them for the Executioner Knights. They became part of the Unholy Trinity."

Rhys bobbed his head faintly in acknowledgment. "The Devil, the Fallen Angel, and the Unholy Spirit," he said, referring to the Unholy Trinity that was a running joke in the Executioner Knights organization because the work they did was often quite morally gray. "Thankfully, my days as an Executioner Knight are over, but it was great fun while it lasted."

"Does Maddoc ever express interest?"

Rhys shrugged. "He has," he said. "But David keeps him busy, so the distraction is welcome. Being an Executioner Knight is a difficult life. I do not know if I want that for my son."

Christopher couldn't disagree. "It is not for the faint of

heart," he said. "But it can also make a boy become a man. The spy business has a way of doing that."

"True," Rhys agreed. "It was certainly instrumental in my life, although I wasn't involved to the extent that some men were. After the mission involving my wife, and all that entailed, I landed in France and remained there. I left the intrigue and danger of England behind me for a bucolic life in Navarre."

Christopher was watching William as the man seemed to be having difficulty with a strap on his lance. "I think de Wolfe would serve the Executioner Knights well, but he is too headstrong," he said. "He is a free thinker, a man who follows his own heart, so I am not entirely sure that he would remain satisfied with the constraints of the Executioner Knights. He's destined for great things, that one."

"You and his father were great friends," Rhys said. "It is a tragedy that Edward did not live to see his sons reach their potential."

"I think he did," Christopher said, referring to Edward de Wolfe, one of his closest friends, who had passed away some years back. "He saw William fight in great battles when he was not even knighted yet. He saw Jonathan serve the Crown with distinction. Edward was very proud of his boys, you know. The man was a bore because he could speak of nothing else."

Rhys chuckled. "Speaking of distinction, there is something I wish to discuss with you."

"What is it?"

The marshal shouted at that moment, driving everyone's attention to the arena floor as William and Essien lined up for the second time. All conversation halted as a marshal dropped the flag and the two competitors charged at one another.

That was when a potential tragedy unfolded.

The guide that separated the competitors, a big wooden pole with several pillars that held it aloft and steady, suddenly lurched a little in William's direction. One of the pillars had come loose and leaned slightly, probably brought on by the shaking of the ground as the horses charged one another. But that movement into William's path of travel startled his horse so much that the animal stumbled, pitching William off and sending him crashing into the guide.

Essien had only a split second to avoid trampling William as the man fell in front of him. He reined his horse sharply to the right, away from the guide, narrowly missing de Wolfe's head. He had his lance in his right hand, however, and the sharp motion of turning his horse away from the guide knocked the weight of the lance back into Essien. He was forced to let it go so he could keep his balance, and his lance crashed to the dirt as he finally reined his horse to a halt.

Then he was off the animal, running in William's direction.

"William!" he bellowed, reaching the downed knight just after two of the marshals had reached him. "William? Are you injured?"

William was moving. He rolled onto his back as Essien fell to his knees and pulled the man's helm off. William's hazel eyes stared up to the sky, dazed.

"William?" Essien said again. "Can you hear me?"

"I can," William said, blinking his eyes as if to shake off the bells ringing in his ears. "I'm not dead, am I?"

Before Essien could answer, Christopher was crouched next to him, as were David and Alexander, who had been standing on the west side of the arena. He'd seen the entire crash from his vantage point. Paris, too, came running up, standing at William's feet with his fair features full of concern.

"Nay, lad, you're not dead," Christopher replied to William's question. "Come on, now. Let's get you to your feet."

William let a host of older, seasoned knights pull him to his feet. He was still a little dazed, and his ears were ringing because his head had hit the dirt, but he was alive. The moment he stood up, the crowd cheered wildly for him, and he lifted a hand to acknowledge them. Servants were rushing about, collecting what had fallen on the arena floor when he'd been pitched through the guide, but the horse was being tended to by Kieran. As Paris went to bolster his friend up, they made their way over to the horse.

"Is he injured?" William asked. "Did the broken guide pierce him?"

Kieran was kneeling down by the horse's left front leg, his hands on the fetlock. "Nay, it did not pierce him," he said. "But he is lame. He took a bad step, William. He cannot compete any longer."

That meant William was done for the day. Even if he'd had another horse, he wasn't entirely sure he could ride it. Or if they would let him ride. When he'd fallen, he'd gone head over heels, essentially landing on his head and shoulders. Everything was still ringing and he was woozy. It was difficult for him to admit defeat, but he had no choice.

"I suppose I cannot compete either," he said, looking over at the two marshals who were standing around him. "I will not continue. I will withdraw."

One marshal walked away to signal the end of the bout while the other one nodded in agreement. "Understood, my lord," he said. "You will not be given a loss, but a non-finish."

That was almost as good as a victory. In any case, it did not go against his tournament record, so William would have to be satisfied. Standing next to the disappointed knight, Essien put his hand on the side of William's head.

"Are you sure you are well?" he said. "That was a hard fall."

William smiled weakly. "I am lucky to be alive," he said. "I thought for certain I was going to be trampled by your horse, but you saved my life with your superior control of the beast. I am in your debt, Essien. Thank you."

Essien smiled in return. "The next time I see you on the ground, I will charge right for you and make sure you are ground into a pulp," he said, watching William chuckle. But then he noticed Paris standing next to him and, realizing they'd not really spoken since the exploding lance incident, narrowed his eyes at the fair-haired man. "And you—the next time you use an unsanctioned lance on me, I will beat you with it and throw your body in the river."

Paris was unmoved by the threat. "What are you complaining about?" he said. "You are in the finals, are you not? Do not be ungrateful, al-Kort. My failure was your gain."

He meant it, too. Greatly annoyed, Essien was about to throttle the man, but Peter pulled him away. He pushed him toward Ashton, who escorted Essien back to his horse, who was nervous and sweating from the unexpected incident. Peggy was a sensitive creature, and Essien patted the animal affectionately on the head, trying to comfort him. As the arena floor cleared, Essien and Peter led the horse back to the staging area to regroup for his final round. That left Rhys and Christopher standing in the middle of the arena, watching the marshals and a couple of carpenters struggle to repair the guide.

"It must have jarred loose when Essien's lance struck it on the first pass," Rhys said. "Did you notice that?"

Christopher nodded, watching the men hammer the post

back into place. "I did, but I did not think much of it," he said. "I certainly did not think it dislodged the pillar. Thank God a disaster was averted."

Rhys agreed with him. "Indeed," he said. "Thank God two excellent competitors were not compromised. Essien was gracious in his victory."

"He was," Christopher said. "He's a well-respected competitor."

"The little lad has certainly grown up," Rhys said, looking off toward the staging area. "I must greet him and his brother at some point. I did not get the chance to do it last night, and they are competing this morning, so I do not wish to distract them. I wonder if they'll even remember me."

"They will," Christopher said. "You were one of the first people who found them starving on the side of the road those years ago. You changed their lives."

Rhys waggled his eyebrows in a modest gesture. "They'd certainly had difficulty up until that point," he said. "But I remember their story, how they fled their homeland of Kitara. In fact, that's partially why I came to Lioncross. I had no idea that Essien and Addax would be here, of course, but I have a need to speak with you about something I discovered."

"About them?"

"Possibly."

David, who had been over looking at William's horse, chose that moment to join them, interrupting the conversation.

"That was a hard fall," he said to his brother. "William is fortunate that he can walk away from that. He's fortunate that Essien didn't stomp his head."

Christopher nodded. "For certain," he said. "Is the horse well?"

"Well enough," David said. "He'll be lame for a while, but he'll heal."

"Good," Christopher said. Then he looked back at Rhys. "You were starting to say something about Addax and Essien? You discovered something about them?"

Rhys nodded. "I very well may have," he said. "As I said, that is part of the reason for my visit here. I had business in London first and then went to visit Maddoc. I was planning on coming to Lioncross when Maddoc and David told me they were coming here also. I simply traveled with them."

"I see," Christopher said. "What is so important that you had to come all the way from Navarre to tell me?"

"A mystery, to be sure," Rhys said. "It is not something I could put in a missive for fear it might fall into the wrong hands, so I had to come personally."

"Now I *am* intrigued," Christopher said. "What is it?"

Rhys cast him an expression that suggested he'd better prepare himself. "This is going to sound like madness, I fear, so bear with me, because I do have a point," he said. "The Dukedom of Navarre is strategic and there are several allied neighbors. One of them, who is particularly close to my brother, is a man named Etienne Lavaur. He has a rather large castle just south of my brother's properties, and he breeds sheep and produces wine. The man has several ships moored south of Montpellier that take his wool and wine all over the great sea. He has traveled extensively. In fact, he has done so much business in Tripoli and Alexandria that he is friends with the sultan who rules Cairo."

"Interesting," Christopher said. "But what has that to do with the al-Kort brothers?"

Rhys started to reply, but he caught movement out of the

corner of his eye and turned to see Addax, astride his horse, rolling up to the west end of the arena. His helm was off, his long black hair glistening in the early morning light. He was next up, riding against Jonathan, so Christopher and Rhys and David began to move off the field.

"I think it may have everything to do with the al-Kort brothers," Rhys said as they walked. "About a year ago, Lavaur returned from a very long journey overseas. He was gone for almost a year. When he travels, my brother sends men to help guard his lands, so that is how I know he was gone. When he returned, it was with a new wife and her parents. In order to thank my brother for protecting his lands, he had a great feast and introduced his wife and her parents to my brother. I was there, of course, because it was mostly my men who guarded his property, but the point is this—the woman he married and her parents are refugees from a country far to the east. When I asked the name of their country, I was told that it was called Kitara."

They'd come to a halt by this point, back behind the rail where the other knights were lined up, awaiting Addax and Jonathan's bout. But Rhys had Christopher and David pulled off to the side, in a huddle, as he delivered what was potentially important information. In fact, Christopher's eyebrows rose as Rhys mentioned the name of the country.

"Kitara?" he repeated in shock. "You mean they escaped the destruction?"

Rhys nodded. "They did," he said. "I suppose it is perfectly logical that people from a country under siege escaped the carnage, but I've never heard of anyone else having come from Kitara, and especially not coming so far north into France."

"Addax and Essien came all the way to England," Christopher pointed out. "It is not entirely far-fetched, but the news is astonishing. What an incredible stroke of luck."

Rhys nodded. "That's what I was thinking," he said. "But there's more, Chris."

"What more?"

Rhys scratched his head. "Now, I've not seen Essien or Addax since they were children," he said. "I came here to tell you about the people from Kitara personally because when a country is invaded, you never know where their enemies might be. If Addax and Essien migrated all the way to England, it is very possible that their enemies have migrated, too. I did not want a missive from me, about the remaining royal princes of Kitara, to fall into the wrong hands."

"Understood," Christopher said. "That was smart. But why did you say there was more to it?"

Rhys sighed sharply, watching Addax take his position at the end of the repaired guide. "As I said, I've not seen Addax or Essien in years," he said. "But this new wife of Lavaur, and her parents… I swear to you that they look like Addax and Essien. Mayhap everyone in the country has a similar look, or mayhap it is my imagination, but I swear that they all look similar."

Christopher stared at him a moment, digesting what he was being told. "Do you think they are related?" he asked.

"It is possible."

"Did you get their names?"

Rhys nodded. "I did," he said. "I do not remember the names of Addax and Essien's family. Do you?"

Christopher had an ominous feeling hovering over him like a cloud waiting to clap thunder. He couldn't help it, but he did. Something was about to break open all around them.

He could feel it.

"Their sister's name was Adanya," he finally said, his voice hoarse.

Rhys' eyes widened. "Christ," he hissed. "That is the name of Lavaur's bride. But it could be a common name, couldn't it? Like John or Mary or Eleanor?"

"Aye, it could be," David said, entering into the conversation because it was bordering on the fantastic. "It could be a wild coincidence. But what are her parents' names?"

Rhys looked between the brothers, completely focused on the conversation even though the marshals were preparing to drop the flag and start the bout.

"The mother was referred to as Sitt Kiya," he said. "They referred to the father as the Pasha, but beyond that, I do not know his name. From what Lavaur told me, his wife's grandfather, the mother's father, was a sultan in Egypt who was recently deposed, so the entire family fled to France when Adanya married. It was not safe for them to remain in Egypt."

Christopher simply closed his eyes. Rhys and David were watching him closely until Rhys finally spoke.

"Chris?" he murmured. "What is it?"

Christopher took a long, deep breath and opened his eyes. "Addax told me that his mother's name was Kiya," he said. "God's Bones, is it actually possible that Addax and Essien's parents made it out of Kitara alive? And somehow made it to France?"

Rhys could only shrug. "That is why I had to come and tell you this," he said. "I knew that Essien and Addax had come back to England because David told me, and if it is their mother and father and sister in France, then…"

He was suggesting that Addax and Essien should be told, but Christopher shook his head. "Nay," he said. "Do not tell them anything. It is too fantastic, and you do not want to encourage their hope and then have it all dashed. Not after what they went through as children. That would be particularly cruel."

Rhys understood, even if he didn't really agree with him. "Then you do not wish for them to know?" he said. "At all?"

Christopher shook his head. "I simply do not think we should," he said. "Rhys, can you send for them? Have them come to England, but we will not tell Addax or Essien. If they recognize them as their family, then the reunion will be joyful. But if they are not their family, then it will simply be a pleasant introduction between them and others who escaped Kitara."

"You want to surprise them."

"For lack of a better term, aye," Christopher said. "I think that would be the safest thing to do."

Rhys could see his point. "Very well," he said. "I'll send word to Lavaur and explain the situation. I'll ask him to have them escorted to England, but not tell them why. He'll have to think up an excuse."

"Good," Christopher said. "We'll decide when, and how, the meeting shall take place."

"For their sakes, I hope it is their family," David said softly. "I cannot imagine going through life without mine, as they have. Mayhap God will be merciful."

It was a sentiment well supported by Christopher and Rhys.

The marshals picked that moment to drop the flag, and the roar of the crowd exploded.

CHAPTER THIRTEEN

Somehow, watching the tournament was far different than competing in it.

It was an incredibly depressing day.

Lance had spent the night in the great hall, as Essien had suggested, and he'd been up before dawn at the tournament field watching the preparations at hand. He still couldn't believe he had lost his position with Lord Eckington, but in hindsight, he didn't much like the man anyway, so he supposed it wasn't any great loss.

He'd simply join the tournament circuit again.

He'd been good at it, good enough to win prizes and pay his debts. He didn't live like a king, but he was able to eat and feed his horse and pay for the young man who took care of his possessions. It had been a farmer's son, and when he had taken the position with Lord Eckington, he'd sent the lad home.

It looked like he was going to have to bring him back.

The only thing that gave him pause about not serving Lord Eckington now was the fact that he would not be seeing Catalina any longer, but that created a whole new issue. Somehow, under his nose, she had been betrothed to Essien al-

Kort and he hadn't heard anything about it until everything was said and done. Did he truly feel cheated? The truth was that he didn't because he really didn't have a claim on her. He'd only expressed his interest to Lord Eckington. The old man had never really led him to believe that there was a possibility he would accept his suit, so the reality was that Lance was simply disappointed that he hadn't been chosen.

So, he spent the night brooding and drinking, and, after a couple of hours of sleep, he found himself back at the tournament field, watching none other than Essien prepare for the first bout of the day. Try as he might, he couldn't seem to hate the man, because Essien had been decent to him in the heat of the situation. He hadn't threatened him or postured angrily. He'd actually been kind. That was something Lance appreciated, since he'd spent his entire life with people who had not shown him anything beyond polite regard.

Therefore, kindness made an impact on him, no matter how small.

On this morning, Lance positioned himself in the staging area just outside the arena where he could see all of the action. He could see the lists and he saw, clearly, when Catalina and her father arrived. He could keep an eye on her from where he stood, but he made sure to stay out of Essien's way. He didn't want the man to see him and regret being polite to him if he thought Lance was making a nuisance of himself.

He didn't want to be on Essien's bad side.

The reality was that Lance didn't have many friends still in the tournament circuit that he could turn to in his time of need. He'd had a couple of friends, but both of those men had returned to their families and now served fathers or uncles or grandfathers. Lance had been a good competitor, but he hadn't been at the top of the food chain like the al-Kort brothers, or Cassian de Velt, or the de Wolfe brothers. They were elite knights with a massive network of family and friends, people they could depend on. Lance didn't have that.

But he wanted it.

And that was really why he was here.

He had heard last night in the great hall that David de Lohr, the Earl of Canterbury, had arrived, so he tucked himself into a quiet corner of the hall and waited for David to appear. There were dozens of senior soldiers and visiting knights and, at some point, he spied Christopher entering the hall in the company of a couple of men, one of whom was a shorter man who looked a good deal like him. Lance had never actually seen David de Lohr, so he wasn't sure if he was at Christopher's side. There were other young knights around, young men with blond hair who bore the de Lohr name, but Lance really didn't know who they were, either. Riding the tournament circuit had kept him away from fine homes and feasts like the one at Lioncross that evening, and that meant he wasn't too familiar with who the people were.

But he knew who Christopher was, and he was going to introduce himself to the de Lohr brothers if it was the last thing he ever did.

Even now, as the sun rose and Lance planted himself in an inconspicuous place in the staging area, he was watching a group of knights at the rail beneath the lists. Christopher was there along with a couple of older knights, the shorter blond man included, and once William de Wolfe went down and Essien won the bout, Christopher remained at the edge of the field in conversation with those men.

Whatever it was, the subject was intense.

But Lance's interest in them soon waned as his focus shifted to Catalina. She had her daughters with her, with the little one bundled up on her lap, and Lance watched her from afar. The more he watched her, the more regretful he was that he would not be marrying her. True, it was for the inheritance. It was for the companionship. It was because he wanted someone who belonged to him, but what he wished simply wasn't going to materialize.

He was going to have to get over his disappointment, but that was never going to happen if he stared at Catalina and mourned what would never be, so he tore his gaze away from her, returning his focus to the staging area where Addax al-Kort was fully dressed and ready to compete. Two other competitors were preparing for their bouts, too, and Lance recognized Cassian de Velt and Jonathan de Wolfe.

But he wasn't the only one watching them from the shadows.

There was another.

Across the staging area, near the gate that led out into the lists and the street of vendors, stood a figure swathed from head to toe in dirty cloaks and tattered scarves. His entire head was wrapped up so that only his eyes were evident, eyes that were watching the competitors intently. Lance could see the man from where he stood, and as he watched, the figure turned toward the lists, evidently studying the crowd as well. It occurred to Lance that the man might be looking for someone to rob. He was certainly dressed in a way that would prevent identification from witnesses.

That thought had Lance's focus shifting. If he couldn't be of service to Lady de Barenton any longer, then perhaps he could be of service to the men in the staging area and protect them from a thief.

It gave him something to do, anyway.

As the morning proceeded, Lance settled down to watch the stranger in the tattered cloaks.

CHAPTER FOURTEEN

I T WAS TIME to eat.

That was what Ines thought, anyway. She'd been groggy throughout Essien and William's bout, but by the time it came to the next, she decided to wake up and declare her hunger—tremendous, great hunger, and she was literally starving to death. Seated in front of her, Brielle's toddler, Luciana, suddenly came alive also, and the two little ones started smiling and pointing at one another. Ines was a little older than Luciana, but Brielle's older daughter, Celestine, was about Ines's age.

Suddenly, the lists were filled with chattering little girls.

Brielle had brought some food for them, which she generously shared with Ines. There were apples and pieces of soft white bread along with little cakes made from oats, honey, and currants. Ines sat down on the footboards of the lists alongside Celestine and Luciana, and the three of them had a picnic under Brielle's supervision.

Catalina thought it was quite sweet to see Ines interact with other little girls. She even tried to convince Adabella to join, but the older girl was too shy to make new friends. She sat with her mother, timidly taking an oatcake from Brielle and thanking her for it at her mother's prompting. But that didn't last long—even as Ines was having a grand time with her new friends, Adabella was tugging on her mother, asking for porridge.

"I did not bring any," Catalina told her daughter. "I can find you something to eat if you are hungry, however. Do you want to see what the vendors have?"

Adabella nodded firmly. As Catalina dug in her purse to see how much money she had, the competitors for the next bout were lining up and everyone seemed to be quite excited by it, including Harald. Catalina realized she just had a few coins with her and tried to gain her father's attention, but he was too busy watching the field. He wouldn't even look at her. As the marshal dropped the flag and the competitors charged toward one another, Catalina helped herself to her father's coin purse, which was tied to his waist. He didn't even notice. She took several coins, tying off his purse about the time the two competitors clashed. Wood went flying into the lists, the result of both lances hitting the heavily armored left shoulder of each knight.

The match was a draw.

As the competitors circled back around to start again, Catalina went to collect Ines, but she cried at being taken away from her new friends. Brielle convinced Catalina to let the child stay, since the three little girls were playing so nicely, and Catalina was grateful. Tasks, and life in general, were so much easier when she didn't have Ines to deal with, so she took Adabella by the hand and left the lists. With the smell of fresh bread heavy in the air, they followed their noses.

There was much to choose from on this morning. Adabella finally settled on a round bowl of stale bread filled with beef, beans, and gravy. It was warm and filling and delicious, and she gobbled hers down as they headed back to the lists. Catalina only had a few bites of her bowl, saving the rest of it for Ines, who had probably eaten all of Brielle's food and was now looking for more. She knew her daughter. As they reached the stairs that led up into the lists, they were next to the gate that led to the staging area. Catalina could see Essien standing inside, speaking to another man.

Just seeing him again did something to her. Her heart thumped against her ribs and she couldn't seem to keep the smile off her face. Simply seeing the man brought her joy in ways she could hardly comprehend because it had never happened to her before. It was something new and thrilling, but it was difficult for her to embrace it with abandon. She'd been disappointed before. Her entire life had added up to disappointment.

But with Essien… she hoped she was wrong.

"Go into the lists and sit with your grandfather," she instructed Adabella, keeping her eyes on Essien. "I will join you in a moment."

Adabella was too timid to go into the lists by herself. "Where are you going?"

Catalina gestured at Essien. "Over there," she said. "I will join you shortly."

"I want to come!"

Catalina didn't argue with her. She took Adabella by the hand and entered the gate, heading in Essien's direction. There were horses and men between them, but soon enough, he looked up and saw her coming.

The smile on his face was clear.

"My lady," he said, breaking away from the man he'd been

speaking with and quickly moving toward her. "How good of you to come. And you have brought me food!"

He took the bread bowl out of her hand before she could say a word. As Catalina and Adabella watched, he devoured the stew, and the stale bread, in about five bites. At least, it seemed like five bites, though it was surely more. He was positively delighted that she'd brought him something to eat, so she simply let him think that she had.

"I hope you enjoy it," Catalina said, chuckling as she watched him shove the gravy-soaked bread into his mouth. "I think you have earned it."

Mouth full, he was trying not to be rude by speaking. "I won the bout in your honor like I told you I would," he said, swallowing what was in his mouth. "You bring me good fortune. And so does your lovely lady-in-waiting."

He was looking at Adabella, winking at her, and she flushed a bright red and tried to hide behind her mother.

"This is my daughter, Adabella," Catalina said, grinning. "You've not properly met yet. Adabella, this is Sir Essien. You saw him yesterday as he helped Ines. Please greet him properly."

Adabella let go of her mother long enough to bob a swift curtsy before she was back to hiding behind her mother again. Catalina laughed apologetically.

"I am sorry," she said to Essien. "She can be a little… shy."

"Not to worry," Essien said, shoving the last of the bread in his mouth. "I think shy young ladies are very nice. Usually, they are very bright and can read and mayhap even paint. I suppose that Lady Adabella can do both of those things, can't she?"

"I can," Adabella said, summoning her bravery.

"Oh?" Essien pretended to be very interested. "What do you

like to paint?"

Adabella was so red in the face that she was in danger of bursting into flame at any moment. "Flowers," she said.

"Flowers sound lovely," Essien said. "What else?"

Adabella thought on the question. "Cats," she said. "I like cats."

"Do you have a cat?"

Adabella shook her head. "Nay," she said. "They make Mama sneeze."

Essien looked at Catalina. "And you think your nose is more important than your daughter's happiness?" he teased. "For shame."

He said it so dramatically that it was clear he was teasing her, and Catalina went along with it. She laughed softly.

"I like cats, I truly do," she said. "But my nose does not."

"What about puppies?"

"Puppies are not so bad, fortunately."

Essien held up a finger, begging for patience. There was a stable behind him, a long, permanent structure used when there were tournaments or when storage for grain or other things was needed, so he disappeared inside. Catalina looked at Adabella questioningly and the girl shrugged her shoulders. Neither of them seemed to know where Essien had vanished to. But he emerged a short time later carrying something. Catalina didn't really see what it was until he was just a few feet away, and by then he was extending it to Adabella.

It was a puppy.

Adabella squealed in delight as Essien carefully put a puppy in her hands. It was a long-legged puppy, perhaps a couple of months old, and it licked Adabella's face furiously, much to her delight.

"One of the stable dogs had a litter of puppies," Essien said, smiling as he watched the happy girl and equally happy pup. "I saw them yesterday."

Catalina wasn't quite as happy as Essien and her daughter seemed to be. She watched with uncertainty as Adabella hugged the puppy, clearly thrilled with the pet. There must have been something in her expression that suggested disapproval, because she heard Essien's low voice.

"Did I do wrong?" he asked quietly. When she turned to look at him, he smiled apologetically. "I can take him back to his mother. I just thought she might like to play with him."

Catalina softened a little. "She would like very much to play with him," she said. "But I am not certain we can keep a puppy. My father has dogs, but they are big and mean. I am afraid they might hurt it."

Essien was watching her carefully. "But you have no objection to your daughter having a pet?"

"Not really."

"I know I should have asked first," he said, his tone soft. "I did not even think to. I will not do it again."

Catalina shook her head. "You are forgiven," she said. "But we should probably leave the dog with its mother."

Essien understood. He'd been impulsive in giving the child a dog. He realized that now. But at the time, he'd simply wanted to make her happy. She seemed like such a solemn little thing. He was precluded from replying, however, when the shouts started up again on the tournament field. Addax was ready to go against Jonathan again and the marshals were preparing to drop the flag.

"Come," he said quickly. "My brother is about to compete. We can see it from the edge of the field."

He grasped Catalina by the hand and pulled her along. That had Catalina grasping Adabella by the sleeve, towing her daughter and the dog behind her. They made it to the edge of the arena just as the flag dropped and the horses began to charge. The crowd was on their feet, cheering and yelling, as the riders approached one another.

And then the contact happened quickly.

Addax had been sitting high in the saddle, with his lance higher than usual, which had Jonathan aiming for his left shoulder. But as they came close, Addax suddenly lowered his profile in the saddle by hunching down, dropping his lance, and planting it right into Jonathan's abdomen. Addax threw his weight behind the lance as well, which meant Jonathan was hit with everything Addax had right in his center of gravity. Addax's lance shattered, Jonathan's lance glanced off Addax's head, and all of that pressure shoved Jonathan off his horse, backward.

He hit the ground in a heap.

The crowd went wild.

"Stay here," Essien commanded softly.

Catalina grasped her daughter and pulled her well out of the way of the men rushing out of the staging area as Essien ran out onto the field where Addax was coming around by the lists, lifting a hand to the crowd, and Jonathan was flat on his back, barely moving. As Catalina watched, Essien reached Jonathan and bent down over the man to see to his condition. It took a few moments before Essien and a few other men were able to pull Jonathan into a sitting position. The crowd, seeing that he was at least able to sit up, cheered for him.

Catalina thought it was rather sweet that Essien should be so concerned for his brother's opponent. To her, that showed his good character, kindness in a man she'd not experienced before. But now she was standing in the staging area with her daughter, and there were men and horses everywhere, so she thought it would be best if she retreated to the lists, especially with Adabella by her side. Unfortunately, Adabella wasn't so apt to relinquish the puppy, and was concerned that the dog was hungry, so Catalina could see that her next stop would be at the same vendor, who had beef and beans so the dog could eat.

Taking her daughter by the shoulder, she directed the child toward the gate next to the lists. She was about to pass through it and on to the street beyond when she heard her name. Puzzled, she stopped, only to see Lance coming toward her from the staging area.

He was coming in behind her.

"Lady de Barenton," Lance said, "may I have a moment of your time?"

Catalina was immediately on her guard. "Lance, I have nothing more to say to you," she said. "I am not the person who requested the betrothal to Sir Essien and I cannot break it. Nor would I. I am sorry if you feel slighted by this, but there is nothing I can do."

Lance put up a hand to silence her. "I know," he said. "My lady, I was not going to ask you to demand the betrothal be broken. I simply wanted to tell you that I've had an entire night to think about the situation and if I have made you uncomfortable with my suit, then I apologize. You never showed any interest in me, that is true, but I am stubborn. I thought I could convince you to see things my way. I've never had anything belong to me in my entire life and I just wanted something… someone… to belong to me. I saw that opportunity with you."

Catalina eyed him for a moment. Essien thought she'd been

cruel to Lance, and she'd defended herself because he'd been relentless and annoying, so it was difficult not to snap at him again. She was afraid that if she let her guard down, he might resume his unwanted attention. She'd become so accustomed to having her guard up with him that it was difficult to lower it.

"Mayhap you saw an opportunity, but I hope you realize that I did not," she said. "It was not personal, le Kerque. I simply did not want to remarry anyone."

"But now you are pledged to al-Kort."

"I am," she said. "My father will not break the betrothal. He wishes for me to marry, so I shall have to."

Lance simply nodded, as if he'd received confirmation for the last time. The last rejection, the last statement of fact. She didn't want him and he had to accept that. After a moment, he drew in a long, pensive breath.

"But your father did not want you to marry me," he said.

Catalina shrugged. "I would not know his mind," she said. "My father did not share his thoughts with me. I suppose you do not bring what he wants into a marriage."

"I realize that."

"You are not going to file a grievance with the local magistrate, are you?"

Lance shook his head. "Nay," he said, sounding defeated. "Why? You do not want me, so there is no reason to fight for something futile."

"That is a sensible way to look at it."

"Mama!" Adabella tugged at her. "We must feed the puppy!"

Catalina nodded to her daughter. "We will," she said, but her focus returned to Lance. "My apologies. We must go. I wish you well, wherever you end up."

Lance nodded, watching them scurry off with a squirming puppy in Adabella's arms. While Catalina felt some relief to get away from him, Lance could only feel regret. Deep, deep regret.

Yet one more thing he couldn't have in a life that was full of such things.

But now, it was over for good.

⌇

THERE WERE DANCING dogs again.

Catalina had just purchased another bowl of beef and beans when Adabella spied the man with the dancing dogs.

They had to stay for the show.

Catalina ended up holding the puppy as it wolfed down the food while Adabella watched the dancing dogs with fascination. Catalina lingered for a few minutes, feeding the puppy and thinking on her conversation with Lance, but a few minutes turned into a longer stretch because Adabella didn't want to leave. A half-hour passed, at least. She could hear the roar of the crowd in the lists, rising and falling, and she knew the bouts were going on. She wanted to see Essien compete in the finals, so she finally had to break her daughter away from the dogs and drag her, and the puppy, back to the lists.

Adabella wasn't happy and the dog wasn't happy. The moment they came within range of the staging area and the big stable situated on the edge of it, the puppy threw itself out of Catalina's arms and raced across the staging area, back to the barn where its mother was. Adabella started weeping because Catalina wouldn't chase it, so Catalina ended up dragging her crying daughter back to the lists, where the two competitors for the championship were lining up.

It was a stroke of luck that she'd made it back in time, and as she sat down, she could see that Ines hadn't moved from where she'd left her, still sitting with Brielle's children and playing with something that looked like clay or earthenware cows. Christin's children were back, three little boys under the age of seven, and they had their father with them, an enormous man with black hair and black eyes who was a good deal older than his wife. He sat on the bench with his two-year-old son over his shoulder while the five-year-old and seven-year-old were begging him to go down to the field and stand at the railing like their grandfather was. He kept putting his big hand over their faces to shut their mouths, and it did not please them. As they turned to their mother and began to beg, the man with the black eyes noticed Catalina.

"Ah," he said. "Lady de Barenton, I presume?"

Catalina nodded. "I am, my lord."

"I am Alexander de Sherrington," he said. "And you are Essien's betrothed."

"I am, my lord."

He smiled. "I was glad to hear the news," he said. "Essien and I have known each other for a very long time. He's a good man. May I wish you every happiness."

Before Catalina could reply, Harald piped up.

"Essien will do well for himself by marrying her," he said, interjecting himself into the conversation. "He will become the Earl of Mercia upon my death. No man can turn down such a title, even if he does have to marry a widow with children. A title like that will make men overlook much."

It was a callous thing to say. Brielle, Christin, and Alexander were all looking at Harald in various stages of disgust as Catalina lowered her head in shame. Her father was putting a monetary value on her worth as a woman, as a person, and that was obvious. She'd always known that, but he'd never spoken of it to others with her present. It was embarrassing.

"I am not entirely sure the title even matters," Alexander said steadily. "A man does not marry for a title alone. Or wealth. He looks for a woman of good character. At least, I did. But I married Christin instead."

He meant it as a jest. Christin gasped in outrage, turning to him and pinching him on the arm where he couldn't fight back because he had the toddler sleeping on him. But he laughed, low in his throat, grabbing her hand and kissing it before she yanked it away indignantly.

"What my husband is trying to say is that the worth of the woman is as great as her character," she said. "It is in her moral standing, her poise, her graciousness. I've only just met Lady de Barenton, but I would say that Essien is quite fortunate she has consented to marry him."

Catalina looked at Christin, her expression full of gratitude. Christin smiled and winked at her before the roar of the crowd overwhelmed them and their focus shifted to the field. The finalists began to take their positions, horses jittery, knights as cool as ice. There was a good deal riding on this match and the very excitement of it was in the air.

"Look," Christin said, pointing to the field. "It will be Essien against his brother. This should be a fine match because they are both tournament champions."

Catalina could see Essien on the east side of the field now with his falcon-headed standard, while his brother was on the west side, closer to the staging area, bearing his dark green standard with the black dragon on it.

"The finals already?" she said. "I suppose I missed the other bouts while Adabella and I were finding food and dancing dogs."

Christin nodded, her eyes on the field. "Addax unseated Jonathan," she said. "Then it was Cassian and Deinhold, and Cassian won that easily, but the bout between Addax and Cassian was something to behold. Cassian is a champion too, you know. It was a battle of titans."

"Not today, it wasn't," Cassian said as he came into the lists and his daughters began to scream for him. He grinned, picking up the littlest one as he sat behind his wife, next to Catalina. "Today was simply not a good day for me. My shoulder still hurts from yesterday and Addax just made it worse. I kept trying to drop my shoulder to keep it away from him, but he hit it every time. The marshals noticed and that is why I lost the points. And the match."

He was unhappy with the loss while trying to protect a sore body part, and Brielle turned around, looking at her husband.

"You dislocated it yesterday," she said. "No wonder it hurts. The physic had to pop it back into place."

She reached up, rubbing his left shoulder, but he shook his head. "That hurts," he told her, removing her hand. "I need rest if I am going to be any good in the mass competition. Sherry and I are going to take the prize, eh, Sherry?"

Alexander had his eyes on the field, sighing heavily to Cassian's statement. "I'm too old for the mass competition," he grumbled. "That is a younger man's game."

Cassian grinned, putting his hand on Alexander's shoulder. "Come on, lad," he said. "You're not too old. You're just right."

"I agree," Christin said. "He's just right. But I also hate the mass competition because it's brutal and lawless. If he does not wish to compete, he'll hear no complaint from me."

Cassian wouldn't accept Alexander's withdrawal. "Sherry, the younger de Lohr sons are going to compete and they will need your guidance," he said. "You'll have me, Curtis, Roi, Douglas, probably Rhys and Maddoc, and a few more. We'll need a leader."

"Do not do it, Sherry," Brielle said. "Cass will push you into the thick of things to save himself if the going gets rough."

Cassian snarled at her. "My loving wife said that," he said sarcastically, but quickly returned his attention to Alexander. "Please, Sherry. Say you'll participate."

"Hush," Christin said. "The match is ready to start."

All attention turned to the arena floor just as the marshal dropped the flag. Both horses began to charge, kicking up dirt, and the crowd leapt to their feet, screaming. Somewhere, someone even had a drum and was banging it furiously. Catalina didn't even have time to be anxious or excited, it all happened so fast. The horses were running at one another, the lances came into contact with the knights, and both of them shattered. In a big explosion, wood flew into the air, straight for the lists.

Catalina heard Alexander shout first. She noticed the parents covering up the children, so she moved to do the same. Ines was still at Brielle's feet, but Adabella was next to her, so she put her arms around the child to shield her from flying wood, but no one was shielding her. A substantial piece of wood flew into her face, slashing her jawline.

Other people had been hit, too. Catalina knew she'd been struck, but she was checking to see that her daughter was uninjured when she heard Brielle say something about the blood on her face. Suddenly, Brielle and Christin were at her side, using the sleeve of Brielle's broadcloth dress to stem the blood flow coming from the left side of Catalina's jaw. Alexander and Cassian were crowding around, all four of them inspecting the gash.

"That must be tended to," Alexander said. "She caught a good piece of it."

Brielle took her sleeve away, trying to see how big the gash was, before putting the fabric over it again. "I'll take her back to Lioncross," she said. "Cass, can you please collect her children and bring them?"

Cassian nodded, moving to collect the children, of which there were many. Alexander went to help him as Brielle and Christin began to move Catalina out of the lists. No one even bothered to ask Harald to tend his grandchildren because he wasn't in his seat any longer. He'd moved at some point and didn't turn up on a quick perusal of the lists, so between the four adults, they collected all of the children and moved Catalina from the lists. They were hardly to the bottom of the stairs when Essien appeared.

His helm was off and his face was tight with concern.

"God's Bones," he muttered, looking at the blood on Catalina's neck. He'd seen what had happened from the arena floor and come running. "I did that. My God, I know I did that."

"Not to worry, Es," Alexander said. "She's in good hands. 'Tis only a scratch."

Essien didn't answer him. He went straight to Catalina, pulling away the fabric that Brielle had pushed against her jaw only to see a fairly decent gash from where the wood had sliced her. The man looked positively sick.

"I'm so terribly sorry," he said as Brielle put the fabric back. "Are you in much pain?"

Catalina smiled weakly. "None at all, I promise," she said. "I did not even realize I'd been cut until Lady de Velt told me."

Essien wasn't comforted by that at all. "I must go with you," he said. "I will tend her, Brie. This is my fault and I will tend her."

He started to push Brielle away so he could take physical custody of Catalina, but Alexander stopped him.

"Es, they want you back on the field," he said. "The lady will be well, I promise. This will not kill her."

The marshals were standing at the railing below the lists, summoning Essien, but he had little interest in answering them.

"I'll forfeit my match," he said seriously. "I must tend my lady."

"Nay," Catalina said, coming to a halt and preventing him from leading her away. "My lord, please finish your match. You have earned this. You *must* finish."

He looked at her, his eyes full of doubt. "But you are injured," he said. "I must help you."

She smiled. "You have," she assured him softly. "You were kind enough to see to me when you knew I'd been struck by the wood. That means a great deal to me. But now you must finish your match, something you have worked very hard for."

"But—"

"Essien, please."

Essien. She'd called him by his given name, and that did something to him. It made it personal. She wasn't being formal any longer, and somehow that strengthened him. It bolstered him in a way he'd never known before. He was indecisive a moment longer before finally nodding.

"Very well," he said. "If you insist."

"I do. Please."

He took a deep breath, calming himself, but finding that he

wanted to get this match over quickly. He wanted to return to Catalina's side.

"As you wish," he said, reaching out to take one of her hands and kissing it sweetly. "This will not take long."

With that, he headed off, followed by Cassian as Alexander and Christin herded the children. With Brielle still holding the fabric to Catalina's jaw, they headed off in the direction of Lioncross's keep as Essien mounted his steed and collected a fresh lance. Thoughts of Catalina's bloodied face haunted him, so much so that when the marshals dropped the flag and he spurred his horse forward, he used a difficult trick against his brother because he wanted to end the match quickly.

He wanted to get back to Catalina.

Riding at full speed toward his brother, he aimed his lance at Addax until the last second, when he moved it slightly, away from his brother's body. But a split second later, as Addax began to pass by the tip of the lance, he swung it back at his brother, catching Addax in the back of the shoulder with a sweeping motion. The idea was to sweep his brother right off the horse, and he did so most ably. Unable to keep his balance at the unexpected move, Addax was knocked forward, holding on for a few seconds before losing his grip and falling heavily to the earth.

The crowd went wild with glee.

With the championship won, including the horse that his brother was riding—which was, in fact, Essien's horse—he had everything he wanted. He'd finished. He made a sweep in front of the lists to acknowledge his adoring admirers before dismounting, quickly, and pulling his brother to his feet. Making sure Addax was unharmed—which he was, because the man was laughing at the fact that he'd just lost the much-coveted horse—Essien left the crowd cheering as he ran off for Lioncross Abbey.

He had a woman to see.

CHAPTER FIFTEEN

"**T**HERE WILL BE a wedding before I leave for home," Harald said. "There is no reason to wait. Let us see to this wedding and be done with it."

Back in Christopher's solar about an hour after the joust finished, Harald was unwilling to wait a moment longer before seeing his daughter wed. The mass competition was being organized in the great meadow next to the tournament arena, and when Christopher should have been out there, supervising, he was, instead, dealing with Harald's demands. The man had what he wanted and he intended to see it finished.

Immediately.

"As you wish," Christopher said patiently. "There is no reason to be petulant about it. Essien has agreed to the marriage, so it is simply a matter of a priest's blessing. My wife will insist on a mass as well, so that can take place easily in Lioncross's chapel before you depart."

Harald was walking around the solar as he spoke, a sort of stalking gait. He seemed distracted as well as demanding, and when he finally came to a half-full pitcher of day-old wine, he poured a measure into a cup and drank it.

"Excellent," he said, wiping his mouth with the back of his hand. "And Essien can take Catalina and the girls with him when he leaves. There is no reason for them to come back to Eckington with me."

Christopher watched the man pour himself another cup of wine. "As I said before, whatever you wish," he said. "But doesn't your daughter have possessions at Eckington that she should like to collect?"

Harald downed the cup and smacked his lips. "I will send them to her," he said. "She does not have to return."

Christopher frowned. "Why not?" he said. "Why are you so adamant she not return home with you, not even to collect her possessions?"

Harald paused in pouring himself yet another cup of wine, realizing from Christopher's tone how he must be sounding. Like a man eager to get rid of his daughter. He was, but he didn't want his ally to think ill of him for it. Therefore, he settled down in the nearest chair, trying to look relaxed.

"It is not as it sounds," he said. "I simply mean she will want to be with her husband and start her new life. Why return to the old one that will remind her of unhappy times? That is all I meant by it. But I do want the marriage to take place immediately."

"And I told you that we can arrange it."

"Good," Harald said. "I want to speak to Essien, however. Will you summon him now?"

Christopher shrugged. "He's probably with your daughter," he said. "She was injured when a splintered lance hit her in the face. Or did you not know that?"

Harald nodded. "I knew," he said. "Your daughters are tending to her the last I saw. She is here, in the keep, is she not?

There is nothing I can do for her."

It was a little cold, but Christopher was coming to see that when it came to his daughter, Harald *was* cold. He'd never seen that side of him before and, to be truthful, he didn't much like it. He sighed heavily, perhaps with some exasperation, and turned for the solar door.

"I'll send for them both," he said. "We can tell them together that their marriage is to take place before you leave."

"I am leaving in the morning."

Christopher had his hand on the door latch, pausing to look curiously at Harald. Everything about the man just seemed strange and out of character for him. He had never known Harald to be demanding, or apathetic about people, but he'd been both since his arrival. Toward his own daughter, no less.

Strange, indeed.

Christopher opened the door and sent one servant for Essien and Catalina and one servant for his wife. If there was to be any wedding, Dustin would want to plan everything, even at such short notice. She appeared first to the summons, since she was already nearby, and Christopher explained the situation. Since Dustin loved weddings, she was excited to plan this one and dashed off about the time Essien and Catalina appeared. Brielle and Christin were with them, fussing with the clothing Catalina was wearing because it wasn't her own. As they approached the solar door and caught sight of their father, Brielle spoke first.

"Sorry, Papa," she said. "Lady de Barenton had blood on her dress from her wound and we had to find something for her to wear, but I'm too tall and Mama and Cissy are too short, so we're trying to make one of Cissy's dresses fit her while the servants clean the blood from her garment."

Christopher could see that his daughters were trying to pin the dress up a little where it was gapping along the bustline.

"Thank you for taking such good care of Lord Eckington's daughter," he said. "I have a need to speak with her and Essien now. I'm afraid you'll have to fix the dress later."

He indicated for Catalina and Essien to enter the solar, throwing out an arm when his daughters tried to follow. He cocked an eyebrow at them, pointing toward the stairs, silently telling them to go away because he did not want them as part of this conclave. With a shrug, the women turned away, heading back to their business, and Christopher closed the solar door.

Catalina was sitting down in a leather chair, tugging at the linen dress where it was binding her a little. Christopher took a moment to look her over—she was a truly lovely woman with wavy, dark hair and big eyes that were a dusky shade of blue. She also had a big gash on the left side of her jawline, cleaned up and exposed to the air, and Christopher smiled politely at her when their eyes met.

"My lady," he said. "I hear you had a bit of misfortune at the tournament earlier today."

"My lance broke and the wood went flying into the lists," Essien said, answering for her. "Actually, Addax's lance broke as well, so there was a good deal of wood bursting into the lists where everyone was. My lady just happened to catch a shard in the face."

Christopher peered at the wound without touching it. "It does not look too terrible," he said. "Who put the stitches in it?"

"Lady Hereford," Essien said. The man looked positively miserable about what had happened. "She put two very small stitches in the gash. She said it should heal very well and there will hardly be a scar."

Strange how the man was far more upset about it than the woman's own father. Catalina knew this, and she turned to look at Essien.

"It was not your fault," she insisted softly. "I wish you would not be so distressed about it."

His answer was to reach out and take her hand, in front of her father and in front of Christopher, as if he had been doing such a thing all his life. He forced a smile at her.

"I cannot help it," he said. "I know it was an accident, but I feel terrible about it."

Catalina smiled at him and squeezed his hand. He couldn't seem to stop looking at her, stop hovering over her, and Christopher watched it all with some astonishment. He knew that Essien could be emotional about things, but it was clear that the man had no sense of restraint in comforting a woman he felt that he'd injured. But not just any woman—the woman he was going to marry.

Christopher thought this was as good a moment as any to tell them the news.

"Essien, the lady's father and I have been talking and we do not see a reason to delay your marriage," he said. "If you are agreeable, we would like for the two of you to be married this evening, after the games for the day."

That had Essien snapping his head up, looking at Christopher in surprise. "Tonight?" he said.

Christopher nodded. "Any objections?"

Wide-eyed, Essien shook his head. "Nay," he said. "Not from me. My lady? Do you have any objections?"

They were still holding hands as Catalina shook her head. "Nay," she said. "I do not. Where shall we be married?"

"Lioncross has a chapel," Christopher said. "I have put my

wife on organizing the mass, so more than likely, all you need to do is show up and exchange your vows. Dustin will arrange everything you need for the ceremony. Harald? Do you have anything to add to this?"

Harald was over by the empty wine pitcher. He'd been watching the clear affection between his daughter and Essien and, like Christopher, was surprised by it. He came away from the table, moving to stand in front of the pair.

"There are no objections to this?" he said, pointing to Catalina though he was speaking to Essien. "You are agreeable?"

"I am," Essien said. "Thank you for this opportunity, my lord. I am honored."

"Are you actually *happy* about this?"

It was a question full of surprise. Essien didn't really have to think about it. He looked at Catalina a moment before answering.

"I am," he said, his eyes glimmering at her. "Your daughter is a good woman, a kind woman. Thank you for considering me worthy of her hand."

Harald looked at Christopher, clearly incredulous, and Christopher fought off a grin. What had started out as a forced marriage between two people who had no desire to marry had turned into something else. It was rather difficult to believe.

"Astonishing," Harald muttered. "You do understand that you shall be continuing my legacy, as the Earl of Mercia."

"I do, my lord," Essien said. "I shall endeavor to honor the title, always."

Harald's gaze drifted over him, the tall and powerful knight who had been born in another kingdom, someplace far away. He looked like royalty, with his straight, strong features. Harald had seen him in the tournament and knew the man was extraordinarily skilled. What he didn't know was the man's mindset over the gratitude he was showing.

Was there something more behind those brown eyes?

"You do understand that this is an ancient title you shall inherit, don't you?" he said. "I realize you come from ancient blood, but so do I. My family goes back many centuries, to the founding tribes of England. When you assume the Mercian title, I should like you to take my family name—de Efford. That is not uncommon when a man of lower rank assumes a title of higher standing. It honors the legacy the title represents."

Essien could see that the man was trying to manipulate him. He could tell because Harald hadn't looked him in the eye through that entire speech. A man who did not make eye contact had something to hide.

"Did the title come through your father, my lord?" he asked.

Harald did look at him, then. "What does that have to do with it?"

"Is de Efford the family name for the title?"

Harald's features tightened and his jaw began to twitch. Before he could reply, Christopher answered for him.

"Nay," he said. He didn't like what Harald was doing. "De Efford, Lord Eckington, is his father's family name. The Mercian title came through his mother. He did not take her name when he assumed the title, I will point out, so I do not know why he is asking you to take his father's family name. That has nothing to do with the Mercian title."

Called out by the Earl of Hereford, Harald turned red with rage and embarrassment. "Because I have no sons to carry on my name," he said to Christopher. "You have six. I have none. My wife could only produce a daughter and she, in turn, has only had daughters, so it is not outlandish to request that the man marrying my daughter, purely for the Mercian title, take my family name. I have a right to ask that my family be continued."

"I am not marrying her for the Mercian title, my lord," Essien said as the tension in the room escalated. "Truthfully, I do not care about the title. I would take her without it."

Harald rolled his eyes. "God's Bones, lad," he said. "That is a stupid thing to say. I simply want my family to live on through my name. Is that so difficult to understand?"

Essien remained cool. He didn't say anything, choosing to let the silence weigh heavily. That was enough of an answer as far as he was concerned, because he didn't like the fact that Harald de Efford was not only trying to force him into some ridiculous agreement about his name, but he was also belittling his daughter. The entire conversation had been about belittling Catalina.

As if she meant nothing at all.

Essien was going to change that.

"My lady," he said, tearing his gaze away from Harald and looking at Catalina. "What is your wish? If you wish to keep your family name as our own, I will not agree. But if you'd rather become an honored member of the House of al-Kort, the royal family of Kitara, I would be most honored by your worthy addition. The choice is yours."

Catalina had been sitting there with her head down, ashamed by her father's behavior, but Essien's soft words had her lifting her head to look at him.

"You… you are asking my opinion?" she said, stunned.

He nodded. "There is no more important opinion in my world, not now," he said. "Whatever you wish, we shall do."

Her mouth popped open. His answer only seemed to intensify her surprise. She looked at her father, red-faced and angry, knowing what he wanted her to say, silently conveying that she'd better do as he wished. But this was the moment when Catalina de Efford de Barenton was no longer under the control of her father. He didn't want her, and now, she surely didn't need him. And she didn't need that damn name.

This was the moment.

"I do not want the de Efford name," she said, returning her attention to Essien. "It has only brought me shame and loneliness and sadness. Why should I want to perpetuate it? Our marriage will see me take your name, Essien. I will become Lady al-Kort and may I always be a tribute to you and your family."

Essien smiled, feeling proud. Probably prouder than he ever had in his life, in a different way. This wasn't about pride in his accomplishments or pride in his lineage. This was pride in a beautiful young woman telling him that she wanted to be part of his life, part of his heritage.

He was deeply touched.

"As you wish," he said. Squeezing her hand, which he had never released the entire time they'd been in the solar, he turned to Christopher. "When may we be married, my lord? The sooner, the better."

Christopher, too, was experiencing some pride. Essien, the youngest Kitara brother, the one more apt to scream, fight, kick, rage, or weep, was showing some remarkable maturity, both emotionally and spiritually. Addax had always been the dignified one and Essien had always been the unpredictable one. But in this moment, Essien had shown his true mettle.

Christopher could not have been more pleased.

"Let me send for Dustin and tell her we wish to have the

mass soon," he said. "But don't you plan to compete in the mass competition today?"

Essien shook his head. "I already won the tournament," he said. Then he looked at Catalina. "I think I have something better to do than beat on some fellow knights."

Catalina laughed softly, gazing into his eyes. Christopher watched the pair, thinking that, at this point, they probably didn't even realize there were other people in the chamber. He had to laugh to himself, because this was not the Essien he'd informed about the marriage only yesterday.

This was someone else.

"Very well," Christopher said after a moment. "I can see where your priorities lie."

Essien simply nodded, grinning at Catalina, and Christopher gave up trying to get the man's attention. He went to the solar door again and opened it, intending to send a servant for his daughters, but he could see that they were still in the entry. He'd told them to go away but they hadn't gone far, which was typical of that pair. They were obedient when they wanted to be.

"You two," he called to them, motioning them over. "It seems that we are to have a wedding today. Can you find something appropriate for Lady de Barenton to wear if her garment is not yet cleaned of the bloodstains?"

The mention of a wedding had Brielle and Christin gleeful. "Of course!" Christin said. "How much time do we have?"

"Probably about an hour," Christopher said. "Whatever you are going to do with her, do it quickly. Lady de Barenton?"

He was catching Catalina's attention as she sat in the chair, holding Essien's hand. Dutifully, she stood up and, still holding his hand, walked over to the door where Brielle and Christin were. Christopher ushered her through the door, into the waiting arms of his daughters, but he had to hold Essien back because the man was following her. He literally had to pull their hands apart, snorting as he did so, and pushing Essien back into the solar as his daughter whisked Lady Barenton away. Shutting the door, he bolted it and went over to the large table that held his writing kit and papers.

"Now," he said, "I am going to draw up the marriage contract with the terms agreed upon by Lord Eckington. Essien, while I do this, you should come to know your wife's father a little better. You can start by telling him just what you think of his attempts to manipulate you earlier. You are not permitted to be rude, but you are permitted to speak your mind. Go ahead. I will sit here and write up the contract."

Essien looked at Harald, who was gazing back at him with a somewhat defensive expression. And with good reason—in Christopher's opinion, Essien hadn't said anything that wasn't deserved.

In a calm, succinct manner, Essien told Harald exactly what he thought of his attempts and also of how he'd treated his own daughter. By the time he was finished, there wasn't anything left unspoken. Harald knew where he stood and Essien knew where he stood. Glad to be rid of his daughter and her unlikable husband, Harald signed the marriage contract without hesitation.

And so did Essien.

CHAPTER SIXTEEN

A WEDDING.

Lance wasn't invited to Catalina and Essien's wedding. He hadn't expected to be. There had been a preliminary mass competition that afternoon, something he had participated in, but he didn't have any friends at this particular tournament so he couldn't get a group of them together to form a unit. That was what most of the knights did in the mass competition—they simply got together a group of their friends and went around like a gang of ruffians, beating other groups into submission and gaining the upper hand.

Some of the mass competitions could get rather dangerous because in some tournaments, there really were no rules, so the stronger competitors would capture the weaker knights and then ransom them back to their lords. There were also men that would thrash other knights and demand their money. Some even took weapons in payment. But this mass competition was a little more civilized because the Earl of Hereford wouldn't allow the lawlessness that sometimes plagued these events. Therefore, it was simply a matter of knocking men to the ground because the rule was that if someone was knocked down, they couldn't get up and were, therefore, out of the competition. That made it a little easier for those who didn't want to be beaten to a pulp.

Lance was one of them.

But the fact that he had no real friends here meant that when the groups were formed for the mass competition, he was teamed up with men he didn't even know, other men who didn't have any friends or allies in the competition. They were usually the weaker or the newly knighted, so he didn't have much faith in the members of his group, but he gave them a good lecture and discussed strategy with them. A couple of them didn't want to be part of the group after that, so they departed to go it alone, which was figurative suicide in a competition like this. But Lance let them go because he didn't want anybody that wasn't going to actually try to win the event a part of the group.

As if they had a chance.

The biggest problem was the de Lohr group. The de Lohr sons partnered up with family friends, very seasoned and terrifying knights, and became the dominant group in the preliminary event. The only saving grace for the rest of them was that they weren't part of the event very long before they received a summons from Lord Hereford himself. Lance heard other men talking about an impromptu wedding and discovered that the tournament champion himself was marrying the daughter of a de Lohr ally. It was like a gut punch to Lance to realize they meant Essien was marrying Catalina.

After that, he didn't feel much like competing.

Walking away from the group that disintegrated without his leadership, he found his way into the bailey of Lioncross. The chapel was a half-moon-shaped structure built into the southern wall of the fortress. It could hold thirty people at any given time, so it wasn't small by any means. As Lance found himself over by the great hall, he could see movement inside the chapel from where he stood. He saw clearly when they lit candles and that soft warm glow emitted from the lancet windows on the north side of the structure. He could hear the faint drone of scripture recitation as the mass was performed.

His pursuit of Catalina was over once and for all.

She officially belonged to another.

That realization drove him into the great hall, where he found copious amounts of wine in which to drown his sorrows, and he did so for the most part. He was seated by the entry door, watching people come and go, trying to summon the courage to ask Lord Hereford for a position or, at the very least, to refer him to someone who was in search of a decent knight. Perhaps courage would come in a bottle for him, because he wasn't certain it would come any other way. He wasn't usually a heavy drinker, but today, he was going to make an exception.

He figured that he'd earned it.

After pouring himself a third cup of wine, he was heading back to his seat when he noticed that same tattered figure just outside the great hall doors. Quite honestly, it looked like a beggar or some kind of poverty-stricken individual, but certainly not someone who belonged in a grand residence like this. They looked sorely out of place. Setting his cup down, he went outside to confront whoever it was. He probably shouldn't have cared, but he did. Perhaps saving good people from a thief might endear him to Hereford and help his cause.

By the time he quit the hall, the figure seemed to have disappeared. Lance looked left, and looked right, and finally decided to go right because it was closer to the keep. There was a garden over there as well as the kitchens, and there were places to hide. The great hall of Lioncross had flying buttresses against the southern wall, great pillars that braced the stone wall, and he came around one of them only to spy the tattered figure, who was looking away from him.

Quietly, he came up behind him.

"You," he said in a low voice. "What is your business here?"

The figure jumped, startled, whirling around to face Lance, but in doing so, the scarf around its face came away, revealing horribly burned skin and a missing nose. Like a living skull-face. Shocked, Lance reached out and grabbed a bony arm.

The figure, evidently a man, gasped.

"Please, my lord," he begged in a rough voice. "I mean no harm. I truly mean no harm!"

Lance was having a difficult time getting over his revulsion. "What do you want here?" he demanded. "Who are you?"

The skinny, burned figure was terrified. "My name is Al," he said. "More than that, I do not know. I suffered an accident that robbed me of my memories."

He had a slow, deliberate way of speaking, halting and stuttering at times. He was so skinny, so wretched, that Lance was fairly certain he wasn't a threat. A child could have taken him down. But he had to make sure the man wasn't armed.

"Show me that you have no weapons," he commanded.

The man held out his tattered cloak, showing his tunic underneath, and his belt, which had nothing on it. Lance yanked off the cloak, which smelled like rot, and had the man turn around to make sure there was nothing on his backside that couldn't be seen. There was nothing, so Lance gave him back his cloak.

"Then what are you doing here if you have no memories?"

he said. "Lioncross is not a charity. You'll find no alms here."

The man made sure the scarf was wrapped tightly around his face. "I am not looking for charity," he said. "I am looking for Lord Eckington's daughter."

That puzzled Lance greatly. "Why?"

The man shook his head. "I do not know," he said. "But she might know who I am."

That didn't make things any clearer. "Know who you…?" Lance paused, shaking his head. "I am certain she would not know you. Moreover, she was just married, so you cannot see her. She is with her new husband."

The man appeared saddened and confused. "It… it would only take a moment," he said. "Or mayhap Lord Eckington would know me."

Lance was growing impatient. "You have not given me a good explanation as to why I should allow you to see either one of them," he said. "You came here because you think they may know you? That is ridiculous. You must leave."

He grabbed Al by the arm again and began dragging him toward the gatehouse. But the man dug his heels in, pleading.

"Please," he begged. "Please, my lord, will you ask her for me? I do not need to see her if she does not wish to see me, but can you ask her something for me? Show her something for me?"

Lance paused, eyeing him with annoyance. "Show her what?"

The man dug into his layers of cloaks, wafting them around as he did so. That smell of mildew came at Lance again and he had to turn his head away, trying to get some fresh air. But the man finally found what he was looking for and held it out to Lance.

"This," he said. "I was wearing it when I was injured. You can see the shadow of it seared into my hand. When my memory started returning, the name of Eckington came to me. I was told it was a castle in Herefordshire, so I came here. Read the back of the pendant."

Lance looked at it. It was a gold cross, a few inches long, and the front of the cross had red semiprecious stones on it. A few were missing. Turning it over, he read the carefully carved inscription—

Allez avec Dieu.

Go with God.

"So you have a pendant," Lance said dubiously. "What does this have to do with Lady de Barenton?"

Al pointed to the cross. "Because that is gold," he said. "Only someone of wealth could have given me that. A mother. A wife. Even a father. I hope that Lord Eckington or his daughter might recognize it and tell me who gave it to me."

"And that is why you seek them?"

"Aye, my lord," Al said. Then he hesitated before continuing. "Might you tell me Lord Eckington's daughter's name?"

"Lady de Barenton," Lance said. "Does that sound familiar?"

Al thought very hard. "Nay," he finally said. "May I know her first name?"

"Catalina."

That didn't sound familiar to him, because he'd never known the name of Alfred's wife, but it was clear he wasn't ready to give up. "Please," he said again. "Will you show her this? Will you please ask her if it is familiar to her?"

Lance had to admit that he felt rather sorry for the man. There was something quite pathetic about him. He didn't sound mad, and he didn't seem dangerous, so perhaps he really *was* here on a fact-finding mission. Lance looked at the cross again.

"You were over at the tournament field today," he said. "I saw you."

Al nodded. "I was, my lord," he said. "I was hoping to be directed to Lord Eckington, but everyone was very busy. I could not find anyone to help me. At least, not anyone who was not afraid of me and my appearance."

Lance grunted. "Understandable," he said. "Your accident must have been very bad, indeed."

"A fire aboard a ship."

Lance's eyebrows lifted. "How long ago?"

"Two years, my lord."

Around the same time Lady de Barenton's husband died. That popped into Lance's head. He didn't know why, but now this man, and the cross, were making him suspicious. He remembered that Harald told him that Lady de Barenton's husband had been killed in France. Or Flanders. Somewhere over there.

So did this burned man have some connection to that?

He wondered.

"Over at the tournament field, there is a stable block," he said. "Did you see it?"

Al nodded. "I did, my lord."

Lance looked at him. "Go there," he said. "Climb into the loft and hide there. Wait for me. I do not know when I will be able to ask Lady de Barenton about this cross, so it may take time. Wait for me there and I will come to you when I can."

Al nodded quickly. "I will go now, my lord," he said. "Thank you. I've not known much kindness as of late, so your generosity is most appreciated. I will not forget it."

I've not known much kindness as of late.

Lance could relate to that. He hadn't, either, so perhaps in helping this unfortunate soul, he was making himself feel a little better. He didn't receive much kindness, but he could give it.

Small as the gesture was.

Waving Al on, he watched as the cloaked and tattered figure slipped through the gates of Lioncross Abbey, out into the night with the competitors' encampment glowing in the distance. The tournament field was beyond that, and there, Al would find the stable. And he would wait for an answer to his question. As Lance thought of that, he realized that he'd taken the cross just so he'd have a chance to speak with Catalina again.

God, he was pathetic.

So much for ending his pursuit once and for all.

CHAPTER SEVENTEEN

"**I**S SHE STILL out there?"

Standing by the lancet window in their borrowed chamber at Lioncross, Essien nodded.

"She is," he said. "Her mother is trying to convince her to come inside."

Catalina had been seated at a dressing table that Brielle had brought in from another part of the keep. She had been permitted to collect all of her possessions in her father's tent, and Adabella and Ines were safe and happy in the nursery at Lioncross with the other de Lohr grandchildren for the night, so the events following the short mass at Lioncross's chapel had run fairly smoothly.

Except for one.

Rebecca.

Even now, she was standing in the bailey below their bedchamber window, crying as if her heart was broken. She'd been informed of the marriage, like the rest of the de Lohr household, because a special supper was prepared away from the feast for the tournament competitors as Essien didn't want five hundred people celebrating his wedding when all he really wanted to do was celebrate quietly with his new wife.

Therefore, preparations had been made for a small supper that was only attended by the couple, Harald, Christopher and his entire family, plus Addax, David, Peter, Ashton, Rhys and Maddoc, the de Wolfe brothers, Paris, and Kieran. That was the extent of the circle, and it was a lovely meal of roasted chicken to celebrate what had been a quick blessing by the priest from the church of St. Andrew in the village. That blessing followed a wedding mass, and about four hours after Essien won the joust tournament, he found himself with a wife and a new life.

And he couldn't have been happier.

But Rebecca wasn't.

She didn't create a fuss during the mass or the meal, probably because her mother threatened her were she to do so, but now that everything was over, night was upon them and so was her lack of restraint. With the feast for the competitors going on in the great hall, Rebecca planted herself in the bailey and wept below Essien's bedchamber window. Both Essien and Catalina could hear the sounds, now with Dustin trying everything she could to force Rebecca inside.

It was the least bit dramatic.

"I am sorry she is so upset," Catalina said, standing next to Essien as they both peered from the window. "If I thought it would help, I would speak with her. Mayhap to assure her that I will take good care of you and she needn't worry."

Essien put his arm around her shoulders. "I do not think she is worried about someone taking good care of me," he said. "It only matters that *she* is not taking care of me. Thank God."

Catalina laughed softly. "It is difficult to be so young and so in love."

Essien shook his head. "Make no mistake," he said. "She is

not in love. In fact, if none of this had happened, she probably would have forgotten about me by tomorrow, but the fact that I've gotten married before she's had a chance to try to woo me has somehow made this into more of a personal failure to her rather than a lost love."

Catalina looked up at him. "Do you want to hear something odd?"

"What?"

"I have never been infatuated with anyone."

"Never?"

She shook her head and moved away from the window. "Never," she said. "I went to foster very young. Right after my mother died, in fact. I was barely Adabella's age when my father sent me off to Thetford Castle in East Anglia. I was there until he summoned me home to marry Alfred. Believe me, there was no one at Thetford to become infatuated with. They were either too old or too young or too wild."

Essien leaned against the wall by the window, folding his big arms across his chest. "Thetford is de Winter's holding."

"It is."

"No nice, shiny de Winter knights?"

"None worthy of my time."

He laughed softly. "How cruel," he said. "But tell me about your mother. Where was she born?"

Catalina made it over to the bed, looking at the garments that Brielle and Christin and Dustin had loaned her, all spread out over the mattress. "She was from Catalonia," she said. "I was born on the feast day of St. Catalina of Alexandria, so she named me after the saint. Her family name was Antequera, a cadet branch of the House of Trastamara. My great-uncle ruled Catalonia, in fact."

"So you have royal blood," Essien said.

She nodded. "Aye," she said. "Very minor, however. Trastamara is the ruling house of Aragon, and my family is simply an offshoot. My mother had several older brothers and sisters, but she married my father because of the Earldom of Mercia."

"What do you remember of her?"

Catalina shrugged. "She died when I was very young," she said. "In truth, I do not know what killed her. My father would never speak of it and the servants would only tell me that she fell ill with a fever. But I remember her voice. I remember that she had hair like mine, dark and wavy. I remember the feelings of love from her. I think that's why I hug my girls so much. I want them to feel that love, to remember it. I was so young when I lost that security, like you were."

Essien nodded. "I was even younger than you," he said. "Until Hereford found my brother and me in the Levant, my life was a horrendous existence."

She sat back down in the dressing chair, listening with interest. "Do you remember much of it?"

"I remember enough," he said. "It is not something I really speak of because to speak of it makes me live it again, and I do not wish to do that. I will tell you someday, but not tonight. Tonight is for us, not the horrors of the past. I only want good memories of this night."

She smiled faintly. "I would like that," she said. But her smile soon faded. "This has all come about so quickly that I've not had time to be anxious or nervous."

"Why would you be?"

She shrugged, turning back for the mirror and picking up her tortoiseshell comb. "A wedding night is always a nervous time for a bride," she said. "The fear of the unknown, I suppose. The first time, it was because I did not know what to expect, but this time… the same can be said. You and I hardly know each other, Essien. We've not even kissed one another on the mouth. Not even at our wedding mass. And now we are expected to consummate this union. Strangers consummating a sudden marriage."

He came away from the wall, taking her concerns very seriously. "If you do not feel comfortable doing this tonight, we do not have to," he said. "I would never expect you to do anything you are uncomfortable with, Catalina."

He lay down on the bed, on his side, with his head propped up on his hand and a bent elbow. They were nearly eye level as she combed her hair pensively. Truthfully, all she could feel from him was sincerity. He wasn't speaking the words because he thought that was what she wanted to hear.

He meant them.

She hoped he would always mean them.

"Are you always like this, Essien?" she said softly. "So considerate? Or are you only considerate now because this situation is so new? Will you forget in the months and years to come?"

He watched her as she combed her hair, studying her fine profile, her beautiful eyes. "Your father today," he said. "Has he always treated you like that?"

"Always. Why?"

He nodded his head in understanding. "Now your question makes sense," he said. "Will I always be considerate to you? I hope so. I will always try. I will never show you such disrespect as your father does. I am simply not like that."

She looked at him, then. "Alfred was not terribly considerate, either," she said. "You must understand that my experiences with men are my father and my dead husband. If I seem suspicious of your kindness, I hope you will forgive me and be patient. A kind man is very new to me."

"Would you rather I be a tyrant?"

She laughed softly. "Definitely not," she said. "I would rather you be simply Essien, the man who is now my husband."

"Does it make you happy?"

A smile played on her lips. "I believe it does," she said. "I was not so certain about it yesterday, but today… it is my hope that this is the start of something wonderful."

He reached out, taking her hand. "It is," he murmured. "I can feel it. We are going to know happiness that people seldom do."

"Do you truly think so?"

"I do," he said. "But, as I said, I want you to be comfortable with me. I realize that will take time, so take the time you need. If I can help, I hope you will tell me."

She simply smiled at him, looking him over. He was a handsome man as it was, and growing more handsome by the moment in her eyes. There was something very strong and noble about him, like a knight from lore. She could have never hoped to have a man such as him for her husband, but here she was. Here *he* was.

It was like a dream.

"I am comfortable with you," she said after a moment. "I have been since the start. You've never once tried to force anything, and that is appreciated more than you know."

He gave her hand a little squeeze. "This was a surprising situation for us both," he said. "It would do no good to make a tense situation worse. We were both of the same mindset of not wanting to marry."

"I have news on that front."

"What is that?"

"I have changed my mind."

He snorted. "That is good," he said. "Because I have, too. It is good that we both feel the same way."

"Considering we had no choice, that is a good thing."

He winked at her. "Exactly."

Catalina giggled. "Speaking of being forced by Hereford," she said. "Do you live here at Lioncross? Is that where we are to live?"

He shook his head. "Nay, I do not live here," he said. "My brother's properties are to the north, in Cumbria, and I am the garrison commander for one of his holdings, Raisbeck Castle. Lots of sheep and meat and wool. It turns a tidy profit."

"Then that is where we shall live?"

Essien shrugged, rolling onto his back as he still held her hand. "I was given the title Lord Binchester when Addax married and was made the Earl of Deira," he said. "In fact, that makes you *Lady* Binchester. The title came with a castle and other properties attached to it, but the fortress is called Vinovia Castle, named after the old Roman fort nearby. It is smaller, very agricultural, but there is also some limited mining. It supports itself quite well. Raisbeck is a little more challenging in that it is larger, and the land seems to be more fickle than the land I own, so I have been helping Addax with it. But I should like to make Vinovia our home. Just for us and our children."

Catalina liked the sound of that. "Vinovia," she repeated. "That is a lovely name."

"And you will make a lovely Lady of the manor," he said, watching her grin. "Your daughters will have plenty of room to run and play and keep pets. I shall buy them ponies and they can ride them as much as they wish. It will be their home, too, and I want them to be happy."

Catalina's smile faded and she shook her head in wonder. "How remarkable," she said.

"What?"

"You," she said simply. "*You* are remarkable. That you should be so considerate toward little girls that are not your own, but your wife's children from another man, is remarkable to me. How very kind you are to think of them."

He shrugged. "And why not?" he said. "Do not forget that I, too, was treated well by a man who was not my father. He did not marry my mother, of course, but Hereford has set an example of how a man should treat people—friends, family, and allies alike. He never made me feel as if I was not part of his family. I would hope that your daughters feel the same way about me, someday."

"They will be grateful," she murmured. "As will I."

He could see the utter appreciation in her face. "I will be grateful also," he said. "I shall be very proud to tell people that you are my wife, a lady of substance and breeding. Even after knowing you only a day, I feel very fortunate."

It was a sweet thing to say. More and more, Catalina's guard was coming down whether or not she wanted it to. She had been so starved for affection her entire life that now, when a door to the future was cracked open, she wanted to throw it wide open and dash through. There was hope there, something shiny and bright and alluring. She'd heard from others that Essien was a good man, so it was quite possible this was simply Essien being himself. Not an act. Not something to lull her into a false sense of security.

She very much wanted to believe it.

But it also made her want to kiss him.

In her mind, there was nothing more attractive than a kind, handsome man—and in her opinion, she'd just married one. He'd told her that they didn't have to consummate the marriage tonight if she was uncomfortable with it, but that wasn't the case at all. Truth be told, she wanted to consummate it. She wanted him to touch her. He'd done something to her with his sweet words and she wanted to reciprocate the only way she knew how.

By physically demonstrating that appreciation.

Essien was still looking at her when, abruptly, she stood up from her chair and put her hands on his face, planting her lips over his. She kissed him, perhaps a little heavy-handedly and awkwardly because she'd never done that kind of thing before, but Essien quickly got over his surprise. She kissed him once, and then twice, the second time being a little longer and a little more passionate. When she pulled back, looking into his wide eyes, she smiled.

"There," she murmured. "We have kissed on the mouth."

He licked his lips where hers had touched his, as if he could still feel her. "We have."

"May I kiss you again?"

His answer was to put his arms around her, his mouth fusing to hers. The second kiss was far lustier because the moment Essien touched her, all of his restraint seemed to vanish. He was running purely on instinct at this point, much as she was, and they feasted upon one another.

The magic ignited.

Before he realized what he was doing, Essien was stripping off his tunic, his clothing. He had to pull away from her to remove his tunic, but Catalina boldly grabbed the sleeves and yanked it over his head, tossing it onto the floor. He put his arms around her once more, kissing her, touching her, listening to her sigh with pleasure.

But she was only getting started.

Catalina was existing in a haze, one where Essien was the only thing in her world. The smell of him, the feel of him, sparked a fire that was quickly consuming her. Alfred might have been an apathetic husband at times, but he had made sure to teach his wife what she needed to know in order to please a man. Catalina had always hated doing what Alfred wanted her to do, putting her mouth in places that smelled awful and had an odd texture, but he had insisted. Those weren't good memories for her, but there was so much desire at this moment to make new memories with a husband she was very quickly coming to appreciate. Better memories and more pleasurable moments.

For both of them.

Catalina tore her mouth away from Essien's seeking lips and unfastened his breeches, sliding them down to his knees. Whereas Alfred had been feebly hung, Essien's manhood was magnificent. It was already massive and he wasn't even fully erect yet. Gently, she grasped his erection and stroked it, and Essien's eyes rolled back in his head at the sheer pleasure of it. She fondled him for a moment before rolling him onto his back, pulling his boots and breeches completely off, and then climbing between his legs and taking his erection into her mouth.

Essien thought his loins were going to explode. She manipulated him with a surprisingly expert mouth until he was absolute mush in her hands, but it began to occur to him that she'd learned this somewhere. With someone. Reaching down, he grasped her by the hair and pulled her head up.

"Wait," he said hoarsely. "Where did you learn to do this?"

She looked at him, her cheeks flushed with passion. "Alfred," she said. "He taught me. If you do not like this, then I will never do it again. But I thought… mayhap you would like for me to demonstrate what I knew. Are you pleased?"

Essien wanted to say no. What she was doing was a whore's trick. Noble-born women didn't lick their man's cock. Not usually, anyway. But he couldn't quite stop her because, by damn, if it didn't feel like a little piece of heaven. His indecisiveness meant enough of a pause that Catalina assumed he wanted her to continue, so she did. Her tongue did deliciously wicked things to him as her fingers probed the split of his buttocks, fingering his anus and his testicles, and that very nearly sent him over the edge.

He'd never experienced anything like it.

But he didn't want her to pleasure him to the point of release. He wanted to pleasure her, too, to acquaint himself with her beautiful body, so he forced himself to sit up, gently pulling her into a sitting position. Then he pulled the loose-fitting garment she'd borrowed from Christin over her head. When that was on the floor, he took hold of the shift underneath and pulled that off, too, leaving her nude in the dim light of the chamber. Essien took a moment to simply look her over, her big breasts, slender waist, and very round hips. Those were hips that had birthed children, generous and round in all of the right places. This was no skinny, bony lass.

This was a woman.

He'd never seen anything so arousing.

Catalina ended up on her back when he grasped her by the arms and flipped her over, assuming the dominant position. His mouth fixed on her neck, kissing a blazing trail down to her right breast, where he took a nipple in his mouth. She gasped when he suckled her, gently at first, and then with more force. Bolts of excitement ran throughout her body and she couldn't help the gasps of joy. But her unsteady breathing told Essien how much she liked what he was doing to her. Her fingers were in his hair as she held him to her breasts, forcing him to suckle her in the most tender of places.

He answered her command.

Catalina was lost in her pleasure, feeling Essien's heated hands on her flesh, his mouth drawing in tender places. When he began to kiss her belly, it tickled, but she put a hand in her mouth to keep from crying out in sheer delight. Alfred had done this before, but only when they were first married. After that, he didn't put any effort into it, but she still had to pretend that she liked it. But this time, she wasn't feigning pleasure.

The pleasure was real.

Essien moved lower, his mouth now on the mound of dark curls between her legs. Catalina parted her thighs for him, an instinctive move, and he settled his big body in between them, his tongue manipulating her sensitive woman's center. Catalina was quickly reaching her climax and her body was beginning to twitch. Essien could feel it. Not wanting to miss the moment, he lifted himself up and drove deep into her quivering folds.

Catalina's knees came up, her body arching to meet his entry. She was climaxing as soon as he began to thrust, and Essien covered her mouth with his own, drowning out her cries of pleasure. She was tight and hot as he thrust into her, again and again. Catalina's body convulsed with multiple climaxes, her legs shaking uncontrollably, and Essien lost all control. The instinct to mate with the woman was overwhelming. His thrusts were measured and deep, pelvis against pelvis, pleasure against pleasure. Sweat began to glisten. Essien lifted himself up on his arms just so he could watch her beautiful body in the weak light, inspecting this woman that was now his wife.

His wife.

God, he was going to take great delight in filling her full of his seed, imagining the sons she would give birth to. Strong, powerful, intelligent. Never in his life had he imagined having children with anyone, but he was now. This round, ripe goddess was made for his body in hers, for childbearing, for motherhood. Most of all, she was made for him and the heart he kept so carefully protected.

He could already see that he was going to give his heart to her easily.

He only hoped that he could earn hers.

His thrusts grew deeper, harder, as he felt his release approach. Catalina met his thrusts and he could feel her walls throbbing around him. Moaning softly, she reached down to touch the place where their bodies joined, and her caressing fingers threw him over the edge. When his release finally came, his body tensed up so hard that, for a few moments, he saw stars. He plunged into her, grinding his pelvis against hers, and stimulating her passion yet again. Catalina was so highly aroused that in little time, she was climaxing around him again. He could feel her tight walls drawing at him, demanding seed that had already been spilt, but he kept thrusting gently until her spasms died down, enjoying the moment with everything he possessed.

Still joined to her, his body collapsed on hers. He gathered her up tightly, trying not to put all of his weight on her, and just held her. He wasn't usually at a loss for words, but at the moment, he was.

He simply couldn't verbalize the wonder of the experience.

"Are you well?" he whispered. "Did I hurt you?"

She shook her head, her hair against his face. "Not at all," she said. "But… that has never happened to me."

He wasn't sure what she meant. "What hasn't happened to you?"

She pushed her hair out of the way, turning to look at him as he lifted his head. "*That,*" she said as their eyes met. "The burst of stars. The pleasure that men always feel and women seldom do. That is the first time it has ever happened to me."

He grinned, leaning down to kiss her. "Good," he murmured. "I am happy to know that I am the first. Did you like it?"

She giggled, embarrassed. "I did."

"Enough so that if I want to do it again, you will have no objection?"

"I will have no objection."

He kissed her again, cuddling with her, his face in her hair as he inhaled her scent. "May I tell you a secret?" he whispered.

Catalina was greatly enjoying the closeness of him, greedily soaking up every moment of it. "Of course," she said.

"I am glad you wanted to consummate the marriage."

She started to laugh. He started to laugh. Soon, they were laughing like fools, hysterically. It was a release of joy, a release of tension, of all of those feelings they'd had when they'd been forced into this union. In a sense, they were laughing at those who had brokered the marriage, at Christopher and at Harald, because those men could have never imagined that their actions might actually lead to joy. Therefore, it was laughter of celebration. It was such wonderful laughter. They might have continued on all night had they not been interrupted by a knock on the door.

Their laughter quickly died down.

"I wonder who that could be?" Catalina said.

Essien shook his head but didn't reply. He climbed out of the bed, nude, and went to the door.

"Who comes?" he asked.

There was no answer right away. He put his ear against the door, but he couldn't hear anything. Was it a joke? Frustrated that he'd been lured out of a warm bed, he slammed his hand against the panel.

"*Who* is there?" he demanded.

There was a shriek outside, clearly someone who was startled by the bang. "Me! Essien, I must speak with you!"

It was Rebecca.

Essien lost his temper then. With a growl, he yanked the door open with unnatural speed and stood in the doorway, larger than life, as naked as the day he was born.

Rebecca was there, cowering.

"You foolish little chick," he barked. "Did you really come here to speak with me on my wedding night about this imagined romance? I will tell you now that I am tired of your behavior. I do not love you. At the moment, I do not even like you, so go away and leave me alone. I do not want you. I have never wanted you. You are spoiled and ridiculous, and you have a good deal of growing up to do before a decent man will have you, so get out of my sight or I will tell your mother what you've done. If she doesn't spank you, I will. Do you understand me?"

He stomped out after her and she screamed, fleeing down

the stairs. When he was satisfied that she wasn't going to return, he came back into the chamber and bolted the door.

Catalina was sitting up in bed, the coverlet clutched to her naked breast as she looked at him with some disapproval.

"What happened to treating people fairly and kindly?" she asked.

He was irritated. "She has pushed me beyond all tolerance with her foolish behavior," he said. "It had to be said. I should have said it sooner. It is not often that someone drives me to madness, but she has."

"Kind of like Lance driving me to madness?"

He had just lifted up the covers to climb in, but he froze and looked at her. After a moment, a sheepish smile crossed his lips and he finished getting into bed.

"Point taken," he said. "Mayhap I shouldn't have, but she's so damn irritating."

He pulled Catalina into his arms and she cuddled against him. "I do understand such irritation," she said. "It seems that we both had unwanted attention hounding us."

He leaned back against the pillow, holding her snugly. "In your case, I completely understand le Kerque's infatuation," he said. "I cannot fault the man for his good taste. But in Rebecca's case, did she truly think there was even a chance between us?"

"She is young," Catalina said. "You must give her some grace."

"I will give her the palm of my hand to her backside if she doesn't stay away."

"Hereford might have something to say about that."

"Hereford would agree with me."

Catalina snorted softly, feeling drowsy now with his heat and their physical activities. With the steady sound of Essien's heartbeat in her right ear, she drifted off to sleep after inarguably the best night of her life.

And so did he.

CHAPTER EIGHTEEN

H E HEARD THE sniffling.

It was early morning and Jonathan had made his way out to the deserted tournament field. Many of the knights had stored their gear in the stable and he needed his things before the mass competition continued this morning. He happened to be walking by the silent lists when he heard the sniffling. Curiosity had him seeking out the source.

He saw a bright red head sitting in Lady Hereford's seat.

It was Rebecca.

She had a kerchief in her hand, wiping her nose delicately as she sniffled and quietly wept. Jonathan thought of simply slipping away, unnoticed, but a sad young woman weeping alone tugged at him. He didn't have any sisters, but he liked to think of himself as a man sensitive to a woman's fragile emotions. Of course, he hadn't thought that way the evening of the feast when he'd spanked Rebecca soundly for her behavior, but he hated to see a fiery young woman's spirit broken. He rather liked fiery young women when they weren't throwing cherries or pebbles at him.

With a sigh, perhaps of regret, he stepped up into the lists.

"My lady?" he said quietly. "Is there something I can help you with?"

Startled, Rebecca looked at him for a brief moment before quickly turning away. "Go away, Jonathan de Wolfe," she said angrily. "You are not welcome here."

He paused a few feet away, but he didn't leave as ordered. "I come in peace," he said gently. "Is there something I may do for you? A scoundrel I must slay?"

She sobbed. "Aye!" she said. "You can slay Essien!"

Jonathan fought off a smile. "Did he offend you?"

She looked at him. "He… he was horrible to me!" she said angrily. "He told me he did not even like me and that no man would want me!"

Jonathan genuinely had to hold back guffaws of laughter. *Well done, Essien,* he thought. "And when did he tell you this?"

"Just now," she said, jabbing a finger in the direction of the keep. "He stayed the night in our keep, on the good graces of my father, I might add, but still had the audacity to insult me."

"Then why do you not tell your father?"

She seemed to back down a little. "Because… because he is on Essien's side," she said, turning away again and putting her kerchief to her nose. "He is always on everyone's side but mine."

Jonathan knew that wasn't true. He knew what a nuisance Rebecca had been making of herself since the tournament began and even before that. He knew she'd pitched a tantrum after Essien's marriage, carrying on in the bailey for all to see because she believed herself in love with the man. The de Lohr brothers could not have been more ashamed about it. She was silly and ridiculous, that was true, but Jonathan was also under the opinion that people like Rebecca made life exciting.

Without people like that, life would be boring, indeed.

Silently, he made his way toward her, coming to sit a few feet away from her, behind her, as she sniffled. He watched the back of her lowered head for a moment.

"Correct me if I am wrong," he said after a moment. "But Essien was married yesterday. You are aware of that, are you not?"

She didn't say anything until he asked her again, and then she simply nodded her head. "Aye," she muttered.

Jonathan nodded in understanding. "Ah," he said. "So you do know. Therefore, if you've spoken to him this morning, when I know he's not yet emerged from the keep, that must mean you saw him inside the keep. Am I correct?"

Rebecca sighed sharply. "What is your point?"

Jonathan leaned in her direction, his eyes glimmering with mirth. "That means if you've seen him this morning, when I know he's not come out of his chamber yet, then you must have gone to him," he said. "Did you, perchance, knock on his door and interrupt him and he yelled at you for it?"

She looked at him in outrage, gasping. "I knew you would not understand!"

He was trying very hard to keep from laughing. "I *do* understand," he said. "I understand very well. I understand that you, being quite spoiled and headstrong, thought you could convince him to leave his new wife for you. But what you do not realize is that he is already married. No one can break that marriage bond. Even if he did leave his wife for you, he could not marry you. Is that really what you want?"

She scowled at him. "You are ridiculous, Jonathan de Wolfe," she spat. "You do not know my mind."

"I am afraid I do."

"I told you to go away. Why are you still here, talking to me?"

Jonathan let his smile break through, then. "Because I have something to tell you."

"Then be quick about it and leave."

She turned her back on him, furious, and he came up behind her, leaning over so he was close to her ear.

"I know that you are young and beautiful," he said softly. "You have your entire life ahead of you. Do not waste your time on men who do not see that beauty or are occupied with someone else. How would you feel if you were Essien's wife and some foolish girl was trying to take him away from you? Would you like that?"

She was losing some of her huffiness. "Well…"

"Of course you would not like it. You would think that the girl was showing incredible disrespect to you, and you would not like it at all." At that point, all Rebecca would do was shrug, so he continued. "My dearest girl, someday you will find a man who cannot live without you. He will hang on your every word. He will live for the sound of your laughter. Every kiss you bestow upon him will be the best kiss he's ever had. You will not have to work so hard for him as you have for Essien. It will simply happen and you will be so smitten that you will be walking on clouds. Nothing can bring you down. You will love him and he will love you, and all will be right in the world. So do not mourn the loss of Essien. He is not good enough for you. The right man will come, Rebecca. I promise he will."

When he was finished, she turned to look at him. Her features were calm, her big eyes fixed on him. "Do you truly think so?"

He nodded sincerely. "Without question," he said. "You are

a magnificent beauty with much to give a man. Any man would consider himself fortunate. But do not be so impatient. A love worth waiting for is a love worth having."

She smiled at him, though it was reluctantly. Then she chuckled. "You are wise, Wolfie," she said. "How is it a man who spanked me last night is the same man who makes me feel better this morning?"

He grinned. "Because I am magic," he said, holding out a hand to her. "Come along, lady. There is food in the great hall and I want some of it. Come with me and we shall speak of the kind of man you want to marry. I will see if I know of anyone who suits you."

She put her hand in his. "Truly?" she said, hope in her voice. "Do you know of a rich prince who will take me to Rome?"

He led her down from the lists. "You want to go to Rome?"

"I do, very much," she said. "The streets are paved with marble and every house has a golden roof."

He eyed her as he tucked her hand into the crook of his elbow. "Is that so?" he said. "Interesting. I've not heard that. What else have you heard?"

Rebecca told him. He was able to get her off the subject of Essien and on to another subject that she seemed to have a passion for. Soon enough, she would forget about Essien altogether and move on to something else. That was the hope, anyway. As Christopher and Dustin saw Jonathan taking Rebecca into the hall, and she wasn't weeping or carrying on, they both breathed a sigh of relief.

Perhaps the one thing to take a lady's mind off a lost man was, in fact, another man.

Even if that man was the big brute called Wolfie.

Christopher thanked God for Wolfie.

CHAPTER NINETEEN

"MAMA! I WANT to see the dogs!"

Ines was in fine form that morning after a night in the de Lohr nursery. She'd been fed, bathed, and had played with her new friends until the nurse blew out the candles and forced everyone to go to sleep. Even then, Ines and Celestine had stayed up, giggling and playing with Celestine's clay cows. The cows had an adventure with another herd of mean cows who wanted to steal their food, but the nurse shut that down, too, when she realized the girls hadn't gone to sleep.

Still, Ines was well rested and ready for dogs this morning.

It was all she could talk about.

Both Ines and Adabella were walking with their mother, who was on the arm of her new husband, Essien. The girls hadn't attended the wedding mass because Catalina didn't think they would really understand what was going on, so they'd essentially been in the de Lohr nursery since yesterday. They'd missed the wedding and the feast. This morning, Catalina and Essien had explained the marriage to the girls, together, telling them that they would go live with Essien now at his home in the north. Essien even brought up ponies, which thrilled the girls.

At least, it thrilled Ines, but Adabella didn't seem interested one way or the other. She clung to her mother's other hand, solemn like she usually was.

"We will go find the dogs later," Catalina said to her youngest daughter. "But first, we must return to Grandfather's tent and collect the things we left behind."

"Why did we leave them, Mama?" Adabella asked.

Catalina squeezed her daughter's hand. "I simply forgot," she said. "I realized this morning that we'd left behind a satchel containing your shoes and some things for your bath. I suppose I gathered our things so quickly yesterday that I left a few things behind. Essien is taking us back there before he enters the mass competition today."

Adabella looked around her mother at the tall, dark-haired man who was now her mother's husband. The very same man who had given her the puppy. He caught her staring at him and gave her a smile and a wink.

"My puppy," she said. "Where did he go?"

Essien wasn't quite sure how to answer her. He looked at Catalina, who made a face, and he didn't understand why until Ines rushed him and grabbed hold of his legs. He very nearly tripped as he tried not to run her over.

"I want a puppy!" Ines declared. "Addie has a puppy? I want a puppy, too!"

He very well understood why Catalina had grimaced at the mention of a dog. He smiled at Ines, but he was talking through his teeth to Catalina.

"What do I do?" he said. "Help me."

Catalina's response was to grasp her daughter by the hand and pull her away from Essien. "Not now," she said firmly as they continued walking. "We have a busy day ahead of us. You will help me find all of our things left over in Grandfather's tent, and then we will watch Essien at the mass competition. Dogs and puppies will come later."

Ines was yanking on her mother's hand. "But—!"

"Nay, Ines," Catalina said sternly. "Cease your begging. Behave yourself or there will be no dogs at all."

That shut Ines up, but she was very unhappy. Truthfully, Essien felt a little sorry for her. All the child wanted was puppies. He supposed that wasn't an entirely unreasonable request at that age.

"Lady Ines," he said, "if you are a very good girl and do what your mother tells you, I will take you to see the dogs myself. With your mother's permission, of course."

Ines nodded, but she still wasn't entirely happy. Dogs were slipping through her fingers and her world was a darker place for it.

Poor little lass, Essien thought.

He wasn't sure he'd ever learn not to be soft when it came to children.

They exited the gatehouse of Lioncross Abbey and headed for the competitors' encampment, which was alive with men preparing for the first round of the mass competition. Yesterday afternoon had only been a preliminary round, something meant to be a warm-up for the main event, which was today. There was a good deal of activity, in fact, and Essien held tight to the ladies as they passed into the encampment, heading for the de Efford tents.

There was a single fire in the middle of the encampment and the guards were warming their meals on it. It smelled like burned bread and singed meat, but the de Efford soldiers were happily eating the offerings. It was a cold morning yet again, so any warmth was welcome, even if it was scorched food. They knew Catalina on sight, and they were all aware she'd married, so when she entered the encampment with Essien, a big man with big muscles, the guards were respectful.

Catalina took Essien and the girls into the large tent.

"Now," she said, hands on her hips as she looked around, "the first thing I must do is search my father's trunks to ensure that he has nothing else of mine. My father likes to collect things, shall we say, even things that do not belong to him, so I will do that this morning."

Essien looked around at the cluttered tent. There were huge trunks with iron braces and locks against one side.

"Your father takes all of this with him when he travels?" he said, incredulous. "How can a man need so much?"

Catalina threw open one of the trunks. "My father believes in traveling lavishly," she said. "Not only do we have the fortified carriage, but we have two wagons to bring along his things—beds, chairs, trunks. He does not leave much behind."

"I can see that," Essien said. He watched the little girls as they went over to a table with two chairs and began fighting over who was going to sit in one of the seats. "Would it be helpful to you if I took your daughters over to the stable where the puppies are? It might give you a little peace in packing."

She looked at him. "You would do that?" she said gratefully. "That would be so very kind of you. Truthfully, they were with me yesterday when I collected my belongings, and I think I was so eager to get them out of here that I simply overlooked a few things."

He smiled. "Then I am happy to take them."

"But shouldn't you be preparing for the mass competition?"

His smile grew. "That will take me very little time, indeed," he said. "Let me take my wife's daughters over to see some puppies first. It will give me a few moments to spend with them."

Catalina nodded, her gaze moving to her girls as Adabella pushed Ines away from the chair and Ines began to cry. "We've not discussed this yet, but we probably should," she said. "What do you want the girls to call you?"

He shrugged, watching Ines plop on the ground and wail. "Whatever they are comfortable with," he said. "Were they close to their father?"

Catalina shook her head. "Not at all," she said. "They were not male, so Alfred did not have a great deal of time for them. Ines does not even remember her father. She was so young when he left."

"I do not mean to replace him, you know."

"I know," Catalina said. "You do what you are comfortable with. If you wish for them to call you Papa, I am agreeable. But if you wish for them to call you Essien, I am agreeable with that, also."

He smiled faintly as Ines stopped wailing, stood up, and pinched her sister on the leg. "I am their mother's husband," he said. "They can call me whatever they wish because, as their mother's husband, I will love them and spoil them and discipline them if necessary. With your permission, of course."

Catalina snorted. "You have it," she said. "And you can start now."

She pointed to the girls, now in a pinching fight, and Adabella got a good chunk of the flesh on her sister's arm and twisted it. Ines screamed. Squaring his shoulders, Essien bravely entered the brawl.

"Ladies?" he said, going down to one knee as he got in between them. "It would be much better to behave kindly. Only well-behaved ladies are allowed to see the puppies."

As he'd hoped, that shaped them right up. They were young enough that he could use that kind of logic and get away with it. Adabella came out of the chair, standing about eye level with him as he knelt.

"Will my puppy be there?" she asked.

Essien nodded. "I'm sure he will be," he said. "Would you like to see him?"

Adabella nodded vigorously. Essien looked at Ines. "And you?" he said. "May I depend on you to behave yourself?"

Ines didn't answer him so much as stick her finger up her nose in reply. "Why?"

Essien started to laugh, reaching over to pull her finger out of her nose. "Because the puppies are frightened if you are too loud," he said, trying not to let her see him grin. "If you are naughty, they will run from you. You do not want them run away from you, do you?"

Ines shook her head. "Where are they?"

Essien stood up, holding out a hand to each girl. "I will take you," he said. "And you can tell me why you like puppies so much. Do you like ponies, too?"

The girls had a good deal to say on the subject of ponies. They were already telling him about it. Essien winked at Catalina as he led the girls out of the tent, heading for the tournament field and the stable, which weren't too far away. In fact, both could be seen the moment Essien left the tent, and he took the talkative girls in that direction.

Catalina went to the tent flap to watch. Yesterday's tournament champion, a prince to his people, was making the effort to spend time with two fatherless little girls who liked to pinch each other and pet puppies. And he was doing it with such grace. Something in her heart swelled enormously for him, an admiration and adoration she didn't think she was capable of. But Essien had earned it with his gentle treatment of her children. No man, not even their own father, had ever been so kind to them.

But Essien was.

What a wonderful man, she thought.

There wasn't anything about him that wasn't wonderful.

Tearing her gaze away from the trio, she headed back into the tent. She had no idea where her father was, but she wanted to be finished by the time he returned.

With the girls occupied, she quickly went to work.

CB

HE'D BEEN WATCHING.

Truthfully, he'd been watching the bailey since dawn, knowing that, at some point, Essien and Catalina would have to come out of the keep. Essien was here for a tournament, after all, and he had obligations. A marriage wouldn't interfere with that, or so Lance assumed. Moreover, Lance had spent the night thinking about the things Essien was doing to his new bride. He went back and forth between being angry about losing the woman and resigning himself to the fact that he had. Even if he told himself, more than once, that he had to move on, he couldn't seem to do it.

Not really.

And he had an excuse to talk to her.

He'd held on to that cross all night, tucked away in the coin purse at his belt, waiting for the right time to show it to Catalina. Perhaps it would come to something, but perhaps not.

What she ultimately thought of the cross didn't matter to him. He was just using it to speak to her.

So, he waited.

At some point, right as the sun began to peek over the eastern horizon, Harald made his way into the great hall where there were tables with watered wine and boiled fruit juice, bread, and warmed-over meat from the night before. There were men wandering in and out, taking food with them or sitting down in front of the warm fire and having a meal with friends before the day began.

Only the allies and friends of de Lohr were allowed in the great hall on a morning like this, as the rest of the competitors were expected to feed themselves and be self-sufficient. The feast in the evening was for everyone, to celebrate the events of the day, but there were many tournaments where the sponsor didn't supply meals at all. Lord Hereford did it out of generosity, but this tournament was only five days long, whereas many of them could be a couple of weeks.

Therefore, Lance remained in the great hall and made sure to eat good meals, because once this tournament was over, he honestly didn't know when he would eat like this again. It wasn't as if he didn't have any money, because he did, but for him, the future was clouded. He hadn't yet been able to ask Lord Hereford if the man could refer him to anyone who was looking for a well-trained knight, so he was still feeling some sense of trepidation where the future was concerned.

The truth was that anything could happen.

But until then, he had a mission to complete. As Harald poured himself a drink but made the servants wait on him, Lance continued to watch the bailey for Catalina and Essien. He was finally rewarded for his patience when, about an hour after sunrise, the very woman he was looking for emerged from the keep in the company of her new husband and her two daughters. They looked like a nice little family, and Lance couldn't help but feel some jealousy.

Still, it didn't deter him from what he needed to do. Catalina and Essien seemed to be heading out of the bailey, probably toward the mass competition field, so Lance decided to follow. He tried to stay well back from them, following at a distance, but the truth was that the pair wasn't looking at anything other than each other. Lance could have been right behind them and they more than likely wouldn't have noticed. Once they went through the gatehouse, Lance could see that they were heading straight into the competitors' encampment, and given the fact that Harald's encampment was right at the edge, he was able to see when they entered the big de Efford tent.

And then he sank back against the great hall of Lioncross, in the shadows, and waited.

Lance wasn't going to approach Catalina with Essien around. He thought ahead to the mass competition, and knowing Essien would be competing in it meant that Catalina would be alone, at least while he was on the field. He was starting to think that it might be the best time to approach her, being alone as a spectator, when Essien abruptly emerged from the tent with Catalina's daughters in tow. He had them by the hand and was leading them in the direction of the tournament field. Lance watched them until they disappeared from view.

That meant that Catalina was alone inside the tent.

He had to move now.

Quickly, Lance came out of the shadows of the gatehouse, quickly moving toward the encampment. Harald's men were on guard, but they knew him and didn't try to stop him. They were well aware that he'd been relieved of his post, but there wasn't one man there who wasn't fairly apathetic toward Harald. The appearance of Lance didn't mean much to them unless he was going to set the tent on fire or something else so blatant, so Lance simply walked by them, his focus on Harald's big tent. Once he reached the flap, he stuck his head inside and saw Catalina on the opposite side, going through a trunk.

He stepped inside.

"My lady?"

Startled, Catalina whirled around to see Lance standing by the tent opening. After a moment of trepidation at his appearance, a mood reflected in her expression, she simply turned around and resumed what she was doing.

"I was married last night," she said. "If you know what is good for you, you will not be here when my husband returns. I do not think he would like it if you were here, alone, with me."

"I realize that, my lady," Lance said. "But I do have a purpose."

"What purpose?"

"I have been asked to show you something and to ask you if you know where it comes from."

Catalina had a few items in her hands, standing up from the trunk and looking at him in puzzlement. "You *what*?"

"I have an object I would like to see if you can identify."

"What kind of an object?"

"I will show it to you if you will give me a moment of your time."

Catalina grunted impatiently. She still had a few things in her hands, now putting the items on the nearest table. Brushing off her hands, she faced him.

"Very well," she said. "What are you supposed to show me?

And who asked you to do it?"

"A man who calls himself Al," Lance said. "I saw him lurking on the grounds of Lioncross last night, wrapped up in a cloak and something around his head, covering up everything but his eyes. I caught him, thinking he was a thief, but he told me that he was looking for either you or your father. It was an odd story, really. He said that he'd had a terrible accident a couple of years ago and did not remember his identity, but he had something in his possession that he thought you could identify. He said that you might know who gave it to him."

Catalina was clearly impatient. "That sounds very strange," she said, moving to open another trunk. "If he does not remember his identity, why would he think I could?"

"I do not know, my lady, only that he hoped you could."

She sighed and turned back to the trunk in front of her. "Show me what it is and let's be done with it," she said. "I am very busy."

Lance reached into his coin purse and dug the cross out. Catalina was digging through the trunk when he extended the cross to her. She noticed that he was holding an item out to her and, pausing in her rummaging, took it from him. She didn't look at it right away. As he stood back politely, she finally tore her attention away from the trunk and looked at the item in her hand.

Her first glance was unreadable. She simply looked at it. But she looked again, more closely, and as Lance watched, her eyes widened and she seemed to stagger sideways. It was as if a great, unseen wind was blowing at her, trying to knock her off her feet. She had to grab on to a chair to steady herself.

"My… my…" she gasped. "My… *God!*"

She nearly shouted the last word, and Lance's brow furrowed. "Do you know what that is, my lady?" he asked.

Catalina couldn't even answer him at first. When she did, all that came out was a cry of anguish. In fact, it made Lance flinch because it was so loud. Suddenly, de Efford soldiers were in the tent flap, making sure Lady Catalina wasn't being attacked, and Lance simply looked at them and shrugged his shoulders. He didn't know what was going on any more than they did. Catalina shrieked again and practically fell into the chair she'd been gripping, still looking at that small, twisted cross. Lance waved the soldiers away before approaching her, slowly.

It was clear that something was very, very amiss.

"My lady?" he said timidly. "What is it? What is wrong?"

She was staring at the cross, unable to speak. As Lance watched, her eyes filled with tears and she began gasping.

"Wh-who…" she stammered. "*Who* gave this to you?"

Lance pointed in the general direction of the tournament field. "As I said, I saw a man lurking about here," he said. "My lady… he was horribly scarred. I've never seen anything like it. He said it was a fire that had injured him so. He—"

She screamed again, leaping to her feet and putting her hands over her ears. "Nay!" she cried. "Nay, do not tell me! I do not want to hear any more!"

"I do not understand."

She suddenly whirled on him, rushing to him and trying to give him the cross. "Take this back to the man," she said in a panic. "Tell him I do not know what it is. I do not know anything about it. Lance, do this for me and do not tell a soul of this incident, and I shall make sure you have a good position, somewhere. But you must forget about this and never speak of it again. Will you promise me?"

He was confused, but he was also concerned. She was horribly overwrought and he had no idea why. He didn't take the cross from her, merely eyed it.

"My lady, are you in trouble?" he said, reaching out to steady her because she was trembling so badly. "If you are in trouble, let me find your husband. He will want to know."

"Nay!" she cried again, stepping back from him and tripping over the borrowed dress she was still wearing from yesterday. She ended up on her bottom on the cold earthen floor. "You will never speak of this to—"

She was cut off when Harald suddenly appeared in the doorway. He'd been returning from the great hall of Lioncross, nearing the edge of the encampment, when he heard the screaming coming from his tent. That had sent him on the run, noting that his own soldiers seemed concerned but indecisive, so he burst into the tent to see what was amiss. One look at his daughter on the ground, with Lance standing over her, and he was filled with rage.

Shock and rage.

Even if Harald didn't particularly care about his daughter, he was enraged that Lance should be here. *Again.* After Harald had banished him, the man had had the gall to return. Perhaps he was even beating on Catalina because of the sins of her father. The fact that she was here was puzzling, too, but he didn't stop to ask questions. All he knew was that his daughter was on the ground and Lance was standing over her, and he was compelled to punish the man. He grabbed the first thing he could find, which happened to be an iron sconce near the door.

He wielded it like a club.

"*You!*" he boomed. "What are you doing here?"

Before Lance could speak, he had a sconce flying at his head as Harald tried to decapitate him. He ducked it, but in doing so, he put his arm up to protect himself, and that push-back motion sent Harald's momentum sideways. The old man, unused to swinging heavy sconces around, stumbled to his left, unable to stop himself.

Unfortunately for him, there was a big wooden rack that held the weapons for his guards right in his path. The swords were all stored with the blade side down, but the spears and maces were not. There were two particular maces that had bulbous, spiked ends and then enormous, daggerlike spikes coming out from the top of the bulbs, pointing straight up. Harald's momentum had him crashing into the rack of weapons and the daggerlike spike of one of the maces ramming straight into his throat while the spike from the other mace pierced his right eye, through his brain, and emerged through the back of his skull.

Harald collapsed on the cache of weapons, dead.

Catalina's screams could be heard all over the encampment.

CHAPTER TWENTY

"WELL," ADDAX SAID, "isn't this cozy? You look like a family man already, Es."

Essien and the girls had just made it to the tournament field when they ran into Addax, who had come to get some of his gear that had been stowed in the stables. Essien and the girls came to a halt as they met up with Addax, with Essien breaking into a big grin.

"You wanted me to marry and have a family, didn't you?" he said. "Meet Lady Adabella and Lady Ines, Catalina's daughters."

Addax smiled at the little girls. "Greetings, ladies," he said. "I am Addax. Essien is my brother."

Adabella and Ines looked at Addax, at Essien, and back again. When it became clear that they weren't going to say anything, Essien urged them gently.

"You may greet him," he said. "It is good manners to do so."

Ines held up a hand and gave him a weak wave, but it was enough. Addax dipped his head in response.

"I saw you at the tournament," he said. "Did you like watching the horses run and the men poke each other with lances?"

Ines nodded.

"Do you like horses?"

Again, Ines nodded. "Do you have a horse?"

"Do I have a horse?" Addax repeated, feigning great interest in her question. "I do, in fact. I have several. I am a knight, like Essien. We fight for Lord Hereford and the king, and we ride horses as part of that vocation."

Ines pointed to the tournament field. "You ride horses there, too?"

"I do," Addax said, smiling at the bright toddler. "I rode in the tournament, too. My horse's name is Daregan. Would you like to see him?"

Both girls nodded. "Can I ride?" Ines asked.

Addax shook his head. "Not him," he said. "He is big and mean. But I think we can find you a pony to ride. I think Lord Hereford has a few."

That had Ines jumping up and down with glee. Even Adabella appeared interested. The puppies were evidently forgotten with the lure of ponies, and Addax was whipping them up into a bit of a frenzy about it. In fact, Ines started yelling about ponies and Essien put his hands up in surrender.

"You can take them to see the ponies now," he said. "You started this, so you can finish it. I can help Catalina finish packing. She may need help."

Addax found himself swarmed by little girls. "Why not come with us?" he said, but seeing the rather lascivious expression on Essien's face, he understood completely. "Ah, I see. It's like that. I take it that last night went… well?"

Essien nodded slowly. "Well, indeed," he said. "*Quite* well."

"And you'd like to get back to her?"

"If I may?"

Addax snorted. "Go ahead and help your wife," he said. "My new nieces and I shall become better acquainted. But I cannot be away for too long. I need to get out to the competition field, and so do you."

Essien ignored the suggestion of a tight timeline and waved his brother off. "Take your time."

Addax started laughing, knowing Essien hadn't even heard him about the tournament field, as he led the girls away, telling them that he would buy them each a pony and that Essien would have to take care of it. That had Essien laughing as he turned around, heading back to the encampment with the anticipation that he might have some private time with his wife. Truthfully, he was quite excited about it. It was true that they'd made love most of the night, but it had been a whole four hours since he last touched her in that way, and he wasn't sure he could survive much longer.

He picked up the pace.

Essien was thinking on how much privacy they would actually have, predicated on the fact that Harald hadn't been there when they arrived and, hopefully, hadn't returned. Or wouldn't return anytime soon. He was within twenty yards of the edge of the encampment when he began to hear screaming.

Concerned, Essien continued his brisk walk, and the de Efford encampment began to come into view. He saw the de Efford soldiers looking frantic, and that sent him into a panic. He took off at a full run, bolting into the encampment and into the tent only to see Catalina standing in a corner, screaming at a horrific sight—Harald was on the ground with pikes and sharp things all around his head, blood everywhere, and Lance bending over him.

That was all it took for Essien to launch himself at Lance. The man never stood a chance.

CHAPTER TWENTY-ONE

"LET ME SEE if I understand this," Christopher said as he grimly surveyed the tattered remains of the de Efford tent. "You heard the screaming and came into the tent, where you found Harald dead and Lance bending over him."

He was addressing Essien, who was holding Catalina tightly, trying to calm the woman down. The truth was that the tent had been destroyed because of the fight between him and Lance, though he'd mostly destroyed it throwing Lance around until he finally rendered the man nearly unconscious. Somewhere in the process of that fight, Rhys and Maddoc had joined in because they were in the competitors' encampment and had heard the noise. Also joining in had been William, Paris, and Kieran, who had taken Lance out of the tent and beaten him within an inch of his life when Essien told him what he'd seen. After that, they took him over to the vault of Lioncross, where the man was currently locked up.

But he'd left a hell of a mess in his wake.

"Aye, my lord," Essien said, his entire body tight with distress. "Catalina tells me that Harald must have thought Lance was trying to harm her and attacked him. What you see of

Harald happened when Lance defended himself, only I did not know that until well after de Wolfe and Hage took Lance to the vault."

"So Harald attacked Lance?" Christopher asked. "With what?"

Both Catalina and Essien pointed to the iron sconce halfway across the tent. "That," Catalina said, sniffling. "Lance and I were speaking, and when I stepped back from him, I tripped. I was on the ground when my father entered. He must have thought Lance was attacking me, so he believed that he was defending me."

Christopher nodded, digesting what he'd been told, digesting the horrible scene around him. David was standing next to his brother, watching Alexander and Rhys as they tried to figure out how to extract Harald's head from the weaponry without making more of a mess. Maddoc had gone with William and the others to put Lance in the vault while Peter and Ashton, who'd shown up after the fact, spoke to the guards outside to find out what those men had seen.

Meanwhile, the mass competition was about a half-hour off and they could hear the crowds already at the competition field. Christopher knew that all of these knights wanted to compete, so he had to make a decision.

"Right," he finally said. "I will speak with de Kerque and see what he says about this. Essien, you should take your wife and leave this mess. I'll have my men clean it up and prepare Harald for his return to Eckington."

Essien nodded. "Aye, my lord."

He pulled Catalina along with him as he moved to exit the tent, but Christopher's gaze trailed after him. He stopped Essien before the man could leave completely.

"Es," he said softly. "You do realize what has happened, don't you?"

Essien looked at him with some confusion. "My lord?"

"You are now the Earl of Mercia," Christopher said. "These men, Harald's men, are now yours. All of this is yours. When you are ready, you have some decisions to make."

Essien had to think on that revelation. It hadn't occurred to him that he'd now inherited the titles. In fact, that had been the furthest thing from his mind. He looked at Catalina, who was looking back at him with equal surprise at the realization. But he simply nodded, mostly to Christopher, and quit the battered tent, leaving Christopher standing with David.

Once they were gone, David shook his head at the state of the tent once more before leaning over Rhys and Alexander as they worked like a pair of surgeons on Harald's head.

"Lady Mercia said that Harald fell into the weapons?" he said. "I suppose that is not impossible, but he must have had quite a bit of momentum to do it."

Christopher was watching the men also. "This situation is very strange."

"Why?"

Christopher also shook his head. "I am not entirely sure," he said. "Harald was adamant that his daughter wed, so she did. I heard from Addax that he'd evidently released le Kerque from his oath because the man had designs on his daughter, and when she married Essien, le Kerque felt cheated."

"And?"

"*And* why was Lance back here with Lady Mercia?" Christopher said. "I did not ask her why he was here, though I should have. Christ… is it possible she was having an affair with le Kerque? Did Essien step into a twisted situation, something that was my mistake?"

"I doubt it," David said. "But I definitely think you need answers from Lady Mercia when she calms down."

"Something tells me that her husband will, too."

ⁿ

CHRISTOPHER WAS RIGHT.

Essien *did* need answers.

He took Catalina toward the tournament field because the girls were over there, somewhere, with Addax. They knew nothing about what had just happened in the de Efford tent. Truthfully, Essien wasn't really sure what had happened himself, but he'd refrained from interrogating Catalina about it because she'd been so hysterical.

She wasn't hysterical any longer.

He came to a halt and released her from his embrace.

"Now," he said quietly, "we are out of earshot of everyone and you have regained your composure, so I have a question."

Catalina nodded. "Of course, Essien," she said. "I will answer anything."

"Why was Lance in the tent with you, alone, as soon as I left?"

She could hear the hazard in his tone and it occurred to her what he might be thinking—that there was something clandestine going on between her and Lance, something she'd been hiding from him the entire time. Of course, that wasn't the case.

It was worse than anything he could imagine.

Her eyes began to well up again.

"My God," she breathed. "I think we are in trouble, Essien."

He frowned. "What trouble?"

She was still sniffling as she produced the bent cross, extending it to him. "Lance brought me that."

He took it curiously, looking it over. "What is it?"

Catalina wiped her eyes. "It is why Lance came to see me," she said. "He said that there was a man lurking around Lioncross and Lance thought he was a thief. He confronted the man, who proceeded to tell him that he had come here because he was looking for me."

Essien still wasn't clear. "What does that have to do with this cross?"

"Because the man needed help in identifying it," she said. Then she broke down in tears. "Essien, you do not understand. I gave that cross to Alfred when he departed for France."

Now, the situation was starting to make some sense. Horrible, disorienting sense. "*What?*" Essien spat. "This belonged to Alfred de Barenton?"

Tears streamed down her face. "It did," she said. "There is an inscription on the back."

Shocked, Essien flipped the cross over. He could barely make out the etching. "*Allez avec Dieu,*" he read, his voice trembling. "Go with God."

Catalina was sobbing. "Go with God," she confirmed. "I had a goldsmith in Worcester put those words there. Lance said that the man did not remember who he was because of a terrible accident, but somehow, he was led here, to me. I do not know how he came here, but he did. He wants to know if I know who gave him that cross, and I am afraid… I am afraid it is Alfred returned, Essien. I'm afraid my husband has come back."

She was weeping so hard at that point that he could hardly understand her, but he understood enough. It was absolutely astonishing. He could see how upset she was and he pulled her into his arms, holding her tightly.

He didn't know what else to do.

"I have not asked what happened to Alfred," he said hoarsely. "I knew you would tell me in your own time, but now, I must ask. What happened to him?"

Catalina clung to him. "Alfred had a brother in France, a warlord, who had property," she wept. "His brother needed help with a warring neighbor, so Alfred took one hundred men and sailed to Calais, only he never made it. I received word that the ship went up in flames within sight of Calais and all aboard were lost. He was burned alive."

Essien was starting to see where this was going. "So you never had a body to bury?"

"Nay," she whispered. "The ship sank with all aboard, or so I was told."

"Who told you?"

"His brother."

"Then it is possible Alfred survived and is only now returning."

"That is my fear."

Essien felt sick. Sicker than he'd ever felt in his life, more desperate and disappointed than he'd ever felt in his life. In fact, his entire life was playing out before his eyes, and if what Catalina said was true, and Alfred was alive, then the rest of his life would be without her.

There was no way he'd be able to survive the pain.

There had to be a way out of this.

"Listen to me," he said, struggling against the gloom that threatened to consume him. "We do not know any of this for certain. You said that Lance brought you the cross?"

She nodded, wiping at her nose. "He did," she said. "That is why he was in the tent, Essien. He must have seen you leave, because he came in right after you were gone. I told him to leave, but he did not. I hope you know that I would never do anything to shame you or hurt you. And you certainly know how I feel about Lance, so there is no love lost there. I promise you, there was nothing clandestine about his appearance."

He nodded, kissing her forehead and pulling her into a gentle embrace. "I know," he said, though he'd felt guilty for even entertaining such a thing. "I should not have sounded as if I did not trust you, for I do. But we have a problem to solve."

"We do."

His brow furrowed thoughtfully. "It seems we must start with Lance," he said. "He had contact with this man, so we must find the man and straighten this out. It could be anything, Catalina. Mayhap the man merely found the cross and made up a story. Mayhap he knew Alfred and is trying to assume his position. You must not believe the worst. Not when I know you and I are so strong together. We *will* be strong together. We must have faith."

The simple words of encouragement bolstered her. His strength gave her strength, but it didn't chase away the fear. "It will be a simple thing, truly," she said hoarsely. "I will know if it is Alfred the moment I see him. Either it is him or it is not. There will be no question."

"Then you must see him."

"I must."

That was the crux of the situation—she had to see the man who had brought the cross, and Essien was starting to feel sick again. He was trying to stay positive, but it was difficult.

"If it *is* Alfred, then understand something," he murmured. "He was gone for more than two years. You were informed of his death. I realize that the law allows for seven years until a missing person is declared legally dead, but you had it on good authority, from his brother, that he *was* dead. You and I were married because you believed that you were a widow. I will fight this all the way to Rome, Catalina. You are *my* wife. Whether or not Alfred has returned is immaterial. He does not get to come back and throw your life into chaos. We have not touched the edge of heaven only to have it torn away from us."

Catalina hugged him fiercely before finally looking him in the eye. "I am not entirely sure how the church will see this," she said. "They may be sympathetic, but then again, if my dead husband is discovered alive, they may simply look at the marriage and not the circumstances."

Essien knew that. God, he knew it. The fact that it had only been two years would work against them. He sighed faintly and let her go, gazing steadily into her eyes.

"Then I will ask you this," he said, hardly able to bring the words forth. "If this man is, indeed, Alfred, what will you do? He is the Earl of Mercia now, not me. He has everything I thought was mine, including you. Will you go with him and assume your role at his side?"

Catalina looked up at him, into that handsome face. She could see the torment in his eyes and, truthfully, she had enough of her own. In her mind, and heart, there was only one answer to give.

"Nay," she murmured. "I will not go with him. I have a little money. We can take the girls and flee to Scotland. Or to Ireland. Or anywhere you wish to go. Essien, it is true I did not want to marry you. We have established that. But now I cannot imagine my life without you. If it is possible for love to happen in just a few short days, then it has for me. I will hold you in my heart, and only you, from now until the last breath the world ever draws."

He drew in a long, fortifying breath and reached out to grasp her hand, bringing it to his lips. He closed his eyes tightly as he kissed her flesh, sweetly.

"My love for you will endure," he whispered. "When we become stars, we will be bound by time and space, to one another, for eternity. There is no life without you, Catalina. Whether or not this man is Alfred, it does not matter. You belong to me as I belong to you."

She clasped his hand with her free hand and the two of them stood there a moment, foreheads touching, holding hands tightly. It was a powerful moment, one that elevated their new relationship to something bigger, better, and enduring. Sometimes love wasn't readily obvious in a relationship. It could take months or years to develop. But sometimes, love recognized love at the onset. Old souls, perhaps, coming around again to find one another. Remembering the love of past lives, of past times. That was what had happened with Essien and Catalina.

Love recognized love.

"Mama!"

They were jolted from their thoughts by a familiar shout. They looked over, toward the long stable near the tournament field, to see both Adabolla and Ines on a pony being led by Addax. It was a pretty blond pony and the girls were having a marvelous time. They waved at their mother. But Catalina took one look at her daughters and whimpered.

Essien heard her.

"Nay, my love," he murmured. "Show no weakness in front of them. Children need for their parents to be strong in the face of a crisis. I watched my mother and father in the face of my father's failing kingdom, and never did I feel afraid or lost because they were strong. We are strong."

Catalina sucked in a deep breath, struggling for composure. "You are correct, of course," she said. "We are strong."

"*We* are."

With that, Catalina lifted her hand to her daughters. "That is a beautiful pony," she called to them. "Are you enjoying him?"

The girls waved back, declaring their undying love for the animal. Catalina and Essien went over to meet them.

"His name is Algernon and he used to belong to Rebecca," Addax said. "Now, he is growing fat for lack of use. The stable master said that you can probably have him just for the asking, so I leave that up to you to ask Hereford."

Essien nodded, unable to reply at the moment, as Catalina went to the pony and scratched his nose.

"He's beautiful," she said. "How fortunate that Sir Addax found him for you. Did you thank him?"

Both girls turned to Addax. "Thank you!" they said in unison.

Addax smiled. "My pleasure, ladies," he said. Then he spoke mostly to Catalina. "I was telling them about the first pony I ever had. My grandfather, Bodhi, gave him to me. It was a beautiful pony the color of sand and I named him Makara, after a sea serpent."

"Makara!" Ines said happily, patting the horse's neck. "His name is Makara."

"A fine name," Addax said. Then he handed Essien the lead rope that was still in his hand. "I have entertained them, but I must gather my things and head to the competition field. And so should you."

Essien finally found his tongue. "Something has happened, Ad," he said in a low voice. "I have need of you."

Addax didn't like that tone. He was puzzled for a brief moment, but he didn't question his brother. "I am yours," he said. "What do you need?"

Essien held up a discreet hand, asking for patience, as he turned to Catalina. "My sweet, please take the girls into Lioncross's bailey," he said. "Find a servant and send him for Lady Hereford. When she comes, tell her what has happened."

Catalina looked at him seriously. "Everything?"

"Everything."

She nodded reluctantly. "Very well," she said. "But you are not coming with me?"

Essien shook his head, handing her the lead rope. "Nay," he said. "I have a good deal to do, but I want you to ask Lady Hereford if you may remain in the chamber she loaned us for the time being, since you have no tent or shelter to return to. Ride the girls around the bailey until they are tired of it and then retreat to the chamber. Stay where I can find you. Will you do this for me?"

"I will do anything for you," Catalina said, great sincerity in her expression. "I will go now."

"Good," Essien said. "Go straight through the gatehouse and summon Lady Hereford. I will come to you later."

Catalina simply nodded. Blowing Essien a kiss, she turned the pony around and headed in the direction of Lioncross's bailey. Essien and Addax followed along behind her at a distance until they saw her pass through the gatehouse and into the bailey. Once she was safely inside, Addax turned to his brother.

"Now," he said quietly, "what is going on?"

Essien wasn't even sure where to start. "It has all happened so fast," he said. "When I left you with the girls and returned to Catalina, before I even reached the tent, I heard her screaming. When I ran inside, I found her father dead on the floor and her father's former knight, Lance le Kerque, bending over the man. Naturally, I thought the worst, so I thrashed le Kerque."

Addax's mouth was hanging open. "My God," he said. "Le Kerque killed de Efford?"

Essien shook his head. "Not intentionally, I've discovered," he said. "It seems that de Efford returned to the tent and found le Kerque with my wife, alone, and he must have thought that the man was trying to assault her, so he attacked him—only le Kerque dodged out of the way and de Efford impaled himself on some weapons in a stand. The action killed him."

Addax was shocked. "Oh, Es," he said, hand over his heart in a gesture of sincerity. "I am so sorry. This is a terrible way to start off a marriage."

Essien snorted ironically. "More than you know," he said. "According to Catalina, Lance was there because he wanted to show her something."

"What?"

"A relic she gave her first husband, Alfred, before he went to France."

Addax's brow furrowed in bewilderment. "A relic?" he repeated. "But… but how did le Kerque have it?"

"Because there is a man here, at the tournament, who brought it," Essien said. "Le Kerque saw the man yesterday and thought he was a thief because he was lurking around, but he was evidently looking for Catalina. He gave le Kerque the cross and asked him to have her identify it. Ad… she thinks the man is her first husband. She thinks he has returned."

That statement brought a universe of horrific implications with it, and not one of them was lost on Addax. He watched the face of his brother, a man who was usually passionate about life and almost always happy, but in this case, he was pale and full of sorrow. The man's eyes were virtually dead at the potential of losing the woman he'd just married. A woman he was clearly mad about.

It wasn't as if his brother had a different woman every night. Not in the least. Essien wasn't like that. It was true that he liked the company of women, and there had been a couple throughout his life that had been somewhat special to him, but nothing like Addax had witnessed over the past day. Essien had gone from being staunchly resistant to marriage to extraordinarily grateful that he had been pushed into it.

At the marriage mass the day before, Addax could never recall seeing his brother so happy. He'd had a glow about him that was very unusual and certainly not indicative of someone who was unhappy with the situation. For her part, Catalina had been gracious and kind and lovely, and Addax remembered thinking that he was sorry his own wife was missing the ceremony. Emmeline would have loved it. It did Addax's heart good to see his younger brother so happy. Now, that happiness was being threatened.

Addax did what any good brother would do.

He wanted to make it right.

"Where is this man?" Addax asked quietly. "The one who brought the cross. Where is he?"

Essien shook his head. "I do not know," he said. "Le Kerque does, and he is in the vault."

"Then let us go and ask him," Addax said, grabbing his brother by the arm and pulling him along. "We will ask him where the man is and then we will find him."

They were heading toward the gatehouse, where the vault was, and Essien walked alongside his brother. "Catalina said she would know him on sight," he said. "I told her we would go together."

Addax came to an abrupt halt and faced him. "Nay, you will not," he said, his voice low and harsh. "You will *not* go together. You will not take her anywhere near him. I will go to him, and when I do, you will not have to worry about this any longer. The problem will be gone and buried. Literally. Do you understand me?"

Essien did. "Ad, I cannot ask you to do such a thing."

Addax's dark eyes were glittering. "You did not," he said. "But I will not risk my brother's happiness, or his entire life, over the return of some man who was supposed to be dead. Where has he been all of this time? And why did he choose this particular time to return if, in fact, it *is* him? *Why?*"

"I do not know," Essien said. "Addax, you are speaking of the man who fathered those two little girls you just spent time with. You would kill their father?"

"I would save my brother's world. That is the only way to look at it."

"But—"

"Essien, listen to me," Addax muttered. "Do you remember when I was betrothed to Emmeline, how we believed her husband to be dead? Do you?"

Of course Essien did. Addax had been in love with the beautiful Emmeline, who was married to a man who mistreated her horribly. When the man disappeared on a trip into town and no body was found, they assumed him dead. It was a natural assumption. But the man wasn't dead, in fact. He'd been badly injured, and had no memory of who he was, until Addax happened to see the man in a village one day. All of the man's hopes and dreams to marry the woman he loved came crashing down when he saw her husband working as a servant in a tavern.

It had been horrific.

But fate had other plans. A series of events saw the man killed that very day, in front of Addax, no less, and the problem was solved. No one ever knew that Addax had seen Maximilian de Grey, Emmeline's husband, and when he was killed, Addax made sure the man was properly buried. But he never told anyone, save Essien and another close friend who had witnessed the entire event. Odd how Essien's life was now playing out along those same lines.

A husband who wasn't dead.

History was repeating itself.

"Of course I remember," he finally said. "How could I forget? Your life was nearly ruined."

Addax nodded. "I know," he said. "I also know that if you had been next to me the moment I spied Maximilian, you would have taken fate into your own hands. If the runaway horse hadn't killed him, you would have. Do not deny it because I know you would be lying."

Essien sighed heavily and averted his gaze. "This is different."

"How?"

"Because it is," Essien said, more firmly. "This man we seek has not harmed anyone. He was not horrific to his wife, or beat her, or slandered or abused her. He was going to war. He was reported dead. But he may not be dead. He is simply returning to the life he knew."

Addax was shaking his head even before his brother finished. "He's been gone for two years," he said. "Why did he not come back sooner? Mayhap he's been running all over Europe, spending money and reluctant to come back to a wife he does not treasure. Mayhap he is only here because he had nowhere else to go. Do you really wish that upon Catalina? That is a horrible existence."

"You do not even know if any of that is true."

"If you will not let me do this for you, then let me do it for her."

That brought Essien great pause. He knew that Catalina had been unhappy with Alfred. He further knew that she was wildly happy with *him*. They were wildly happy together.

Let me do this for her.

Was it possible that Addax was the only one willing to fight for Catalina's happiness?

"Oh… Addax," Essien said, wiping his hand over his face in a weary gesture. "Are you certain this is something you want to do?"

"Of course it is."

"But *why*?"

They'd come to the gatehouse by that point. In fact, they could look inside and see Catalina leading the girls around on the blond pony over on the south part of the bailey. Addax let go of his brother and looked at him with anguish in his expression.

"Because I've spent my life trying to protect you," he finally said. "When we were young children and our father was facing the loss of his country—our country—I could do nothing to help him. I could do nothing to protect you. When we were being used by the merchant as slaves, starved and beaten, I could not protect you. All I have ever wanted to do is protect you, Essien. You are my brother. You are the only family I have. Let me *do* something now. Let me save your happiness because, as your big brother, that is my right. It is my right and my honor to make your life easier because there were so many times when I couldn't. *Please*, Es. Let me do this for both of us."

Essien had tears streaming down his face by the time his brother was finished. There had been such pain in his words, the helplessness of his position as the older brother, the protector, and being unable to do anything when their situation was out of control. Now, he saw something he could help with, something he could prevent. He could protect his brother's happiness, even if it required being brutal to achieve it. Addax wasn't seeing that—he was only seeing the hope of the situation.

Hope that Essien's happiness could survive.

"You are my big brother," Essien said, wiping at his face. "You are the greatest man I know. I will always, always respect and admire you. You do not have to kill for me."

"Aye, I do. And I will."

It was a heartbreaking, terrible situation. Essien reached out, grasping his brother by the arm as he struggled for something to say. But his thoughts were interrupted by the approach of Christopher and David as the two of them headed toward the gatehouse.

They were coming from the encampment and the de Efford tent, where they'd been discussing the situation. They knew what Addax and Essien knew, that Lance was in the vault. The man who seemed to hold the key to everything. When Addax and Essien looked over at them, David lifted a hand in greeting.

"Ah," he said. "Four earls in one place. I do not think I've seen so many earls since the last gathering of warlords for

Henry."

It was true. The Earls of Hereford, Canterbury, Deira, and Mercia were all standing in one place. But it also underscored the gravity of the situation where it pertained to Essien. He might not be Mercia at all, and as painful as it was, he hastened to tell them.

They had to know.

It was like a nightmare for Essien having to relive it, telling Christopher and David everything that Catalina had told him about the cross and the man that Lance had been in contact with. But in the same breath, it was clear that so much made sense now. Christopher and David had been wondering why Lance was in the de Efford tent, and now they knew.

There was something more to the story.

A mysterious man was the very heart of this entire situation.

"And we think this man who gave Lance the cross is still here, at Lioncross?" David finally said.

Essien nodded, trying not to look entirely miserable. "Aye, my lord," he said. "We have come to ask Lance if he knows where the man is. Mayhap he is in the village, at a lodging. I want to know where he is and I want to talk to him."

That was understandable. Christopher felt bad for Essien, having married a woman whose first husband might be still alive. In fact, he felt quite guilty about it.

"Come with us, then," he said. "We were going to interrogate le Kerque and get some answers. A man is dead and I must have all of the facts. But you can ask him about the man who gave him the cross. That is your right, Essien."

Essien nodded. "Thank you, my lord."

"Peter and Ashton questioned the Eckington guards,"

Christopher said. "They could not offer much more to the story, as they were outside nearly the entire time. But they did confirm that Harald was enraged by Lance's presence in the tent. One man saw him grab the candle sconce next to the door."

"Then there is truth that he attacked le Kerque?" Essien said.

"There seems to be," Christopher replied. "But we must speak with Le Kerque. I want to hear his side of things."

With that, the four of them headed into the southern section of the gatehouse. They entered the guard room, a big room with a dirt floor and a blazing hearth, and then passed through a sturdy wooden door that led to a narrow staircase leading down to the vault below.

The iron sconces in the stairwell were fitted with blazing tapers, casting light and black smoke into the air. The fat of the candles burned dirty. They had to be careful going down the steps because they were stone, and damp, and one slip would send them straight to the bottom. Christopher went down first, followed by David, Addax, and finally Essien. The main area of the vault below was vast, hard-packed earth that had been lined with stone, and it was built under the wall rather than the gatehouse because the constant traffic on the ground above could make the vault itself unstable. There were five different cells—four smaller ones and then a larger one that was tucked into a corner.

Christopher had had the vault dug out several years ago after he converted the abbey portion of the castle to the knights' quarters, so as far as vaults went, this one was newer and relatively nice. It was low-ceilinged, however, so Christopher and Essien had to be careful not to hit their heads.

William, Paris, Kieran, and Maddoc were waiting for them as they reached the bottom.

"My lord," William greeted Christopher. "The prisoner is conscious."

Christopher peered past the young knight, seeing a figure in the cell behind him, but he was unable to see much more than a dark figure until he took the fish-oil lamp that Maddoc was holding and held it up so he could see Lance better.

The man had been beaten within an inch of his life.

Given what Christopher had been told about Lance's purpose in the de Efford tent, it was clear that the man hadn't deliberately done anything to Harald, nor had he touched Catalina. Events out of his control had made him appear guilty of murder. Of course, the younger knights didn't know that and had treated him accordingly. Christopher couldn't fault them for that, really. They were young and eager and very highly trained, keen on a world of right and wrong. That was the knighthood, and they were knights.

Justice was their vocation.

Especially against a wicked knight.

"Thank you, de Wolfe," he said. "I will deal with the prisoner in my own way, but I thank you for taking charge of him."

"My lord, you may need us," Paris said seriously. "Le Kerque is a fighter. Kieran could barely subdue him. It took William and I to help get him down to the vault."

Christopher looked at Kieran, quite possibly the most muscular young knight he'd ever seen, and the man didn't have a fraction of de Norville's arrogance. He seriously doubted that Kieran would have trouble with any man alive. Therefore, he tried to keep a straight face in the wake of Paris' boast.

"I understand," he said steadily. "But, as you can see, I've brought reinforcements. If the four of us cannot handle him, we'll send for you."

Paris looked at David, at Addax and Essien, and nodded reluctantly. "If you are certain, my lord," he said.

"I am," Christopher said. "In fact, you need to get over to the competition field. I know my sons are already over there, preparing, and they will be starting the event soon, so you do not want to miss it. You are on their team, are you not? You must hurry."

"And you are certain that you can handle le Kerque alone?" Paris said, giving it one last try.

"I am," Christopher said decisively. "Maddoc, you go with them. They'll need your strength."

Maddoc was already heading for the stairs. "Do you know where my father is, my lord?" he asked.

Christopher gestured up the stairs. "The last I saw him, he was in the de Efford tent, trying to separate Harald from the weaponry through his head," he said. "Go, now. All of you."

Kieran and Paris were now following Maddoc up the stairs, but William remained. His gaze was on Christopher.

"I was rather hoping you would be in the competition, my lord," he said. "My father used to tell stories of you back in the day. He said you were unbeatable."

"I still am," Christopher said, his eyes glimmering. "Be glad that you do not have to face me."

"I would like to, my lord. Very much."

"Be careful what you wish for."

"Mayhap someday?"

"Mayhap."

William grinned, as did Christopher. After patting the young knight affectionately on the cheek, Christopher turned back to the cell as William ran to catch up with his friends. Handing the lamp off to David, he took the key off the wall and unlocked the cell.

"Le Kerque, we have some questions," Christopher said as he stepped in.

Lance was sitting on the straw, his back against the cold, stone wall. His face was battered, one eye nearly swollen shut.

"I am certain you do, my lord," he said with a battered mouth. "I will tell you what I told those idiots who just left. I did not kill Harald de Efford."

"I know," Christopher said. "Lady Mercia has absolved you, but I want to hear it from you. What happened?"

Lance shrugged, perhaps with some relief to hear that Catalina had defended him. "I am not entirely sure," he said, shifting painfully where he sat because he had a cracked rib or two. "I went to speak with Lady al-Kort, but I suppose we are calling her Lady Mercia now?"

Christopher nodded. "That is what she is," he said. "Essien is the Earl of Mercia with Harald's death. Now, proceed."

Lance did. "I went to speak with her," he said. "During our conversation, she became upset and stumbled back onto the ground. I was moving to help her up when Lord Eckington entered and… and the man went mad. I do not know why, but he shouted at me and swung an iron sconce at my head. I put up my arm to block it, but the force of my raised arm knocked Eckington sideways and he fell into the weapon stand. I swear upon my oath that is all that happened. There was nothing more."

"You did not push him?"

"Nay," Lance said firmly. "All I did was put my arm up, though I may have pushed at the sconce to keep it away from my head. I do not remember if I did, but whatever I did was enough to send Eckington falling into the weapon stand. His daughter screamed, Lord Mercia came into the tent, and after that… there was a row."

Christopher grunted. "I would say so," he said. "Mercia had every right to, Lance. I am certain you can see his perspective, coming into a tent where his wife is screaming and her father is dead on the floor. It is natural that he would think the worst."

Lance fixed on Essien, then. "I do not blame him," he said, mostly speaking to Christopher, but shifting his focus after that. "I never touched your wife, my lord. I swear it."

Essien was trying not to become angry or agitated. "Mayhap you did not," he said. "But you waited until I was out of the tent before approaching her."

"That is true," Lance admitted. "But I had something for her and I thought it would be better to deliver it to her in private."

"You mean the cross?" Essien said. "She told me about it. What I want to know from you is where the man who gave it to you is."

Lance sighed heavily. "I told him to wait for me in the loft of the stable next to the tournament field," he said. "You've not seen this man, my lord. He looks as if he has been roasted alive and lived to tell the tale. *Horrifying* is how I would describe him, so I told him to stay out of sight."

"Did he give you his name?"

Lance nodded. "He said it was Al," he said. "Beyond that, he could not tell me more. He was in a terrible accident that evidently robbed him of most of his memory. If you see him, you will understand."

Essien looked at Addax. "Al," he whispered. "Her husband's name was Alfred."

Addax didn't know what to say. He could see despair sweeping over Essien and he wanted to comfort him, but there would be no comfort until they found this man and got to the bottom of things.

"So this man wanted you to believe that he is Lady Mercia's first husband, back from the dead?" Addax said, because Essien was quickly falling into ruin. "Did he tell you that?"

Lance shook his head. "Nay," he said. "He did not tell me that and I did not get that impression, but it did seem to me that he was simply looking for answers. He was looking for who, and what, he was, and he was hoping Lady Mercia might be able to tell him based on that cross."

"And out of the goodness of your heart, you are helping him?"

There was sarcasm in that question, but Lance only saw the irony of it. "Mayhap," he said. "I understand a little about people being lost and looking for answers. I've been lost and looking for answers my entire life, ever since Juston de Royans took me into foster and gave me the name of le Kerque. It was his mother's name, you know. He tried to give me a world to belong to, knowing I could never be part of the world that bred me. So I carried his mother's name, but it was not mine. I have a different one."

The conversation had taken a huge swing, away from the man who had given him the cross and venturing into a realm of lost or found or belonging. No one was really sure what he was talking about. As Addax reached out to Essien, grasping the man's arm to give him some sense of comfort, Christopher and David were still mulling over Lance's swift turn of focus.

In fact, they were a little startled by it because of the mention of one name…

Juston de Royans.

He was a man who had fostered and mentored both Christopher and David, and a host of other great knights of their generation. Juston de Royans was a knight's knight, a man who'd molded the knightly sensibilities of a generation. To discover that Lance had also been part of the men under his wing was surprising to say the least.

"You fostered with de Royans?" Christopher said, unable to keep the awe out of his voice.

Lance didn't reply right away. He simply averted his gaze from the de Lohr brothers, watching Addax comfort Essien and wishing that he'd had a brother he could turn to like that. In fact, the sight of two sets of brothers standing before him did something to him. The very thing he'd kept buried deep inside him, the very thing that had made him who, and what, he was, was starting to come forth, erupting like a volcano.

The hurt.

The anguish.

The lack of belonging.

"Aye," he finally said. "I fostered with de Royans. I know that the two of you used to serve him. He was your teacher, your counselor. He mentored many of the great knights of your generation. I know of your relationship with him. The entire time I was at Bowes Castle, I heard of nothing else."

Christopher and David looked at each other, puzzled. "I do not understand," David said, his focus shifting back to Lance. "What do you mean that you heard of nothing else but my brother and me?"

Lance sighed sharply. "I was brought to Bowes Castle by my mother when I was very young," he said. "I am told that I was barely more than an infant, for I do not remember. My mother was a serving wench in a local tavern and my father was an elite knight. Unfortunately, my mother was married to another man at the time I was conceived, and this man would not accept me as his son, so I was given to Sir Juston's wife, Lady Emera. She is the one who raised me until de Royans took over my education. She's the only mother I remember, but she was not my real mother."

Christopher crouched down a few feet away. "Was your father one of de Royans' knights?" he asked. "Is that how you ended up at Bowes?"

Lance nodded. "Aye," he said, finally looking at Christopher. "You can ask de Royans if you do not believe me. He has seen eighty summers by now, but he is still alive the last I heard."

Christopher shrugged. "I will not ask him anything," he said. "But I am quite puzzled by this entire conversation. We did not come to discuss your past, but Eckington's death and your role in it. Let us return to that subject, please."

Lance didn't want to hear that. Beaten and bruised, he struggled to his feet, though for him, it was an act of rage. His entire body was quivering with anger, with disappointment, and he didn't care that Christopher wanted to discuss something else. *He* had something to say to Christopher and David and he was damn well going to say it. He'd waited a lifetime to say it.

He might never have another chance with the two of them, together.

"I will return to the subject after I say what I need to say," he said, glaring at Christopher and David. "Aye, I fostered with Juston de Royans because of my father, a de Royans knight. Because I was his bastard, I could not secure a decent enough position once I came of age. Even with de Royans' connections, positions were difficult to come by because I did not bear my father's name. Therefore, I have spent my life as a bachelor knight, mostly. I was a mercenary for a while, but the money was better on the tournament circuit. I have been riding the circuit regularly for the past ten years, in England and in France, but a chance meeting with Harald de Efford in London saw me swear fealty to him. I did it because he was a de Lohr ally, a neighbor. I did it because Eckington is situated near Lioncross Abbey."

Christopher frowned. "What good would that do?" he said. "I do not know you."

"But I know you," Lance said, his eyes beginning to well up. "You are my uncle, my lord. You see, my mother's name was Edie, and she was a serving wench at The Lion and the Lamb, a tavern north of Bowes Castle. My father's name is David de Lohr. I am the result of their brief liaison."

One could have heard a pin drop in that cold, stale cell. Christopher stood up, making a conscious effort to close his gaping mouth, as he looked at his brother. David, however, wasn't showing as much restraint—the man looked as if he'd been struck on the side of the head with a club. His eyes were wide, his jaw slack, and he ended up grasping the side of the cell to keep his balance. Even Addax and Essien, back by the cell door, were looking at Lance in shock. That, most definitely, wasn't something they had expected to hear.

No one had.

Least of all David.

After several seconds of genuine shock, David came away from the cell wall and moved in front of his brother, so that he was looking at Lance head-on. Even though the man's face was bruised from the beating he'd received, the features were nonetheless clear.

David stared at him, drinking it all in.

"You… you are Edie's son?" he said, his voice full of astonishment.

Lance nodded. "And yours."

That had David shaking his head in disbelief. He didn't say anything right away. He simply stood there with his head wagging back and forth. When he finally spoke, it was in an anguished hiss.

"I do not mean to insult you, but how do you know?" he said. "Your mother… I was not the only man she was friendly with, I'm ashamed to say."

Lance shrugged. "I do not remember her, so your words have no meaning to me," he said. "My birth name is Nathan Smith, as Edie's husband was a smithy, but he knew I was not his son. He is a dark-haired, dark-eyed man, and as you can see, I am not. Edie gave me over to de Royans for safekeeping because her husband threatened to kill me. It was de Royans who changed my name to Lance le Kerque. But Nathan was a son of King David from the Bible, and that is why I bore that name at birth. Because you, David, were my father."

David was swimming in a sea of denial, paddling frantically, but the truth was that he was starting to drown in the face of irrefutable evidence. "Edie was blonde," he said. "You are blond and I am blond, but that is not unusual coloring. It could be that you take after your mother and she simply lied that I was your father."

"David," Christopher said in a low voice. "*Stop*. He looks like you. He looks a good deal like Daniel. Surely you can see that."

David could, but he wasn't going down without a fight. Denial was turning to anger. "Very well," he said. "Let's say you are a de Lohr. What do you hope to gain by telling me? Do you wish to be another son of mine, entitled to an inheritance or money?"

Lance could hear the suspicion in his voice. "Nay," he said with a sigh. "I can see that this is not welcome news, but it is of no matter. I was hoping to find a family, a place where I belong, but I can see that is too much to ask. Mayhap you can simply give me my freedom from this cell and I will leave you in peace."

Watching the scene, Christopher wasn't hard pressed to admit that he was heartbroken by it all. David was wallowing in shock, and Lance wasn't going to press him. A man, by his own admission, who had never had anyone or anything that belonged to him. No family, no name. He'd told David with the hope of finding that family, but David wasn't ready to give it. At least, not at the moment.

Perhaps they had to let it all sink in first.

Lance was a de Lohr.

"Lance, you have your freedom," Christopher said. "You are free to leave the vault, but please do not leave Lioncross. Not yet. This is a complex situation that cannot be solved in a day. You must give us time to come to terms with it."

Lance simply nodded. He was so disappointed that he was sick with it. Yet another rejection. He didn't know what he had expected, but he had hoped for a different outcome. On unsteady feet, he walked past Christopher, past David, and came to the cell entry where Addax and Essien were standing. With eyes that were dull with pain, he looked at the two brothers.

"I will take you to the man you seek," he said. "You may ask him your questions, for I do not know more than what I have already told you."

With that, he headed over to the stairs, taking them slowly with his beaten body. After what Addax and Essien had just heard, they didn't push the man. Essien couldn't even manage to still feel irritated with him. Clearly, Lance had been harboring his own secrets, a heavier burden than most.

They followed Lance up the stairs and into the sunshine beyond.

CHAPTER TWENTY-TWO

THEY WERE ON the hunt for puppies again.

After walking in circles in the bailey of Lioncross, Adabella soon became bored and, after her, Ines became bored. Adabella began speaking of her puppy and her sister caught on. Soon enough, they were begging to see the puppies again and nothing Catalina said could distract them.

They were wild for puppies.

Unfortunately, the pony couldn't compete with the lure of little dogs, especially when Adabella was genuinely under the impression that the puppy Essien had given her was, in fact, *her* puppy. It had run off, back into the stable next to the tournament field, and she wanted it back.

No amount of convincing otherwise could distract her.

After the third time around the bailey, Catalina had yet to see a servant she could send for Lady Hereford. She wasn't sure where they all were, but they weren't in the ward. She tried to get the attention of a soldier or two, but they were more focused on what was happening beyond the wall with the mass competition in the distance. She hated to disobey Essien, but she simply hadn't had the opportunity to send for the woman.

Perhaps a quick jaunt over to the tournament field, to the stable where the puppies were, could soothe her restless daughters and she could return to the bailey without Essien ever knowing she'd left it. Moreover, he'd only asked that she remain where he could find her. He hadn't specified where. With Ines verging on a tantrum, she took the pony by the lead and headed for the gatehouse.

Unbeknownst to her, she had just missed Essien, Addax, Christopher, and David as they'd gone into the vault. She was moving quickly, pulling the pony with Ines on its back and Adabella skipping alongside her. She was starting to curse the fact that Essien had brought the puppy into their lives, but in the same breath, it made her smile because it had made Adabella so happy.

Essien seemed to have that gift with the women in the family already.

Past the gatehouse they went, heading toward the competitors' encampment and the tournament field beyond. She could see, clearly, her father's encampment. His soldiers were still there and the tent was still in disarray. She thought that she caught sight of Christin's husband still in the tent, but she wasn't sure.

She didn't even know if her father's body had been taken care of.

In truth, she felt no real grief at his death. He probably wouldn't have felt any grief in the event of her death, either, so she didn't feel guilty over it. She was sorry for the way he'd died, however. That had been shocking and awful. But now that he was gone, perhaps she felt some relief. Relief that she no longer had to deal with her father's mistreatment and apathy.

It was a strange feeling, indeed.

She led the pony past the competitors' encampment, passing through an area that still had some vendors, and on through the gate that led to the staging area. Off to the east, she could hear the crowd at the competition field, the low hum of excited spectators. The long stable block was in front of her, but just as she came near, she heard an indignant female voice behind her.

"That's *my* pony!"

She turned to see Rebecca heading toward her with Jonathan at her side. Remembering what a fuss Rebecca had put up the night before about her marriage to Essien, Catalina braced herself for the incoming storm.

"Good morn to you both," she said pleasantly. "Lady Rebecca, my girls are so happy for the loan of your pony. Sir Addax found him in Lioncross's stable and let the girls ride him. I hope he did not do wrong, did he?"

She had just outlined the entire situation for Rebecca, who was frowning deeply until she met with Catalina's polite words. After that, there wasn't much of a fit she could pitch about it, especially considering she hadn't ridden that pony in years.

"Well," she said, trying not to sound like a complete tyrant, "next time, he should ask."

"Of course," Catalina said. "I am very sorry he did not. Would… would you like to walk with us? We were just going inside the stable because there are puppies in there and my daughters want to see them very badly. Please come with us."

Rebecca was completely thrown off guard by Catalina's kindness. She looked at Jonathan, who lifted his eyebrows encouragingly at her. He'd just spent an hour inside the great hall lecturing her about being kind to others and how the loss of an infatuation meant nothing in the grand scheme of things. When she didn't reply right away to Catalina's offer, he did.

"That is a very kind invitation, my lady," he said. "I think Lady Rebecca would like to see the puppies, but I am expected at the competition field. May I leave her in your care?"

"Of course," Catalina said, reaching out to take Rebecca's elbow companionably. "Come with us, my lady. I want to hear about your love of ponies. Or do you have a horse these days? I'm certain you must have a beautiful one."

As Jonathan smirked and headed off toward the competition field, Rebecca found herself being pulled away by her mortal enemy. Well, not so much her mortal enemy as someone who had caused her a good deal of anguish. Not that she'd *deliberately* caused it, but she had caused it, nonetheless.

… hadn't she?

There was no solid answer to that question as Catalina herded Rebecca into the stable, along with the pony and the two little girls, and Rebecca simply went with it. When Jonathan was away completely, Catalina leaned into Rebecca as if they were old, dear friends.

"Sir Jonathan is quite handsome," she said, giggling. "What a fine match he would be for you. So dashing and strong."

Rebecca looked at her in surprise. "Wolfie?" she said. Then she frowned. "He is like one of my brothers."

"But he is *not* one of your brothers," Catalina said. "He is a de Wolfe. They breed very handsome men."

Rebecca couldn't dispute that. She shrugged. "Mayhap," she said, ambivalent. "I've not thought on it."

"You must," Catalina said, giving the arm she was holding a squeeze. "Look how beautiful you are. You could command the greatest husband in all of England. If Jonathan is not to your liking, then you must think high, my lady. Very high. Mayhap there is an eligible prince somewhere for you. I hear there are very handsome princes in Saxony."

Rebecca was softened by the flattery in spite of herself. She was also increasingly baffled at her own behavior. Here she was, being pulled along by her hated enemy, the woman who'd married the man she couldn't live without, and she was *letting* her. Why was she letting her? She wasn't resisting in the least. Catalina was sweet and charming, sweeping Rebecca off her feet with kindness. At that moment, something Jonathan said came back to her.

How would you feel if you were Essien's wife and some fool- ish girl was trying to take him away from you?

Here she was, with Essien's wife. And she was the foolish girl, yet Lady al-Kort was being so kind. Since she'd never met the woman before yesterday's wedding, she'd made up all sorts of terrible things in her mind about her, but the reality of Catalina was quite sobering.

Rebecca was starting to feel stupid.

"Saxony," she said after a moment. "That is far away, isn't it?"

Catalina nodded. "Far away, indeed," she said. "But the land is beautiful, I hear, with big mountains and big rivers. Don't you want to travel someday?"

Rebecca nodded. "Someday, for certain," she said. "I want to go to the Levant where my father fought with Richard. Papa said it was a beautiful and mysterious land."

They were in the stable now, and the girls, who had run on ahead, had already found the puppies. They were screaming with delight.

"Here," Catalina said, tying off the pony in one of the stalls next to a bucket half full of grain. "We'll leave your pony here whilst we visit with the puppies. What is the pony's name, anyway?"

Rebecca looked at the little beast. "George," she said. "There was a lad named George from Gloucester Castle who used to visit. He was a horrible child and tried to cut my hair with a dagger once. I named the pony after him so I could ride him and kick him and make him do what I wanted."

She was serious, and Catalina fought off a grin. "Ah," she said. "A most appropriate name, then. The pony is very obedient, thanks to you."

Rebecca had forgotten all about George de Clare, and seeing the pony again reminded her of that awful little boy. But it was also a good memory, too.

"George was so terrible that my brother, Westley, helped me get revenge on him," she said as Catalina led her over to the mass of wriggling dogs. "When we had visiting nobles, my mother would make a small feast for the children to mirror the big feast for the adults. Wesley put a handful of pepper in the gravy. We pretended like we wanted the gravy and George, being selfish, stole the whole bowl and drank about half of it before he realized it was full of pepper. He was never cruel after that, knowing we would punish him."

Catalina grinned. "How wonderful it must have been growing up with siblings."

"You do not have any?"

"Nay," Catalina said, shaking her head. "It was just me. That is a lonely way to be."

They were distracted by little girls and lots of puppies. One of them wandered over to Rebecca, who picked it up and cuddled it.

"I do not know if my mother will let me bring him in the keep," she said, kissing the dog's head. "Although she has had dogs before. Why not me?"

"True," Catalina said. "Why *not* you? I would wager that when you show her the puppy, she will be unable to resist."

Ines chose that moment to show her mother a white puppy and tell her that she wanted it very badly. She *had* to have it. "Mummy, please!" Rebecca watched Catalina with her young daughter, seeing how gentle she was with her. That made her increasingly curious about the woman.

Perhaps she wasn't as bad as Rebecca had made her out to be.

"Your wedding yesterday," she said hesitantly. "Were you happy with it? What I mean to ask is if it was something that made you happy. Most girls dream about their wedding, but yours happened very quickly."

Now they'd ventured onto the subject of the wedding and Catalina wondered where this was leading. She hoped that she wasn't about to be lambasted for her marriage to Essien, so she braced herself.

"My first marriage took place in Hereford's cathedral," she said. "It was big and bright. My father invited everyone he'd ever met, I think. It was a massive celebration for a marriage that was not worthy of such a thing. But yesterday's mass was much more peaceful and intimate with so many of Essien's friends. And your family was there. It made it so very special."

Rebecca was listening. She might have been spoiled and headstrong, but she was intuitive. "What became of your first husband?"

"He died," Catalina said. "He was traveling to France to help his brother in a war and the ship caught on fire."

"Oh," Rebecca said, sorry she'd asked. "Do you not mourn him?"

Catalina shook her head. "Nay," she said. "Not ever."

"You said your marriage was not worthy of the big mass?"

Catalina's gaze moved to her daughters, now up and chasing the puppies around the stable. "It was not," she said. "But it gave me the two greatest gifts I could ever receive. Therefore, I do not regret it. But it was nothing special. Not every marriage is."

"And your marriage to Essien is?"

Catalina was careful in her reply. "I do believe it is special," she said. "Sometimes, you meet someone whose heart speaks to yours. I've heard it happen to others, but never to me. But I think… I think Essien's heart speaks to mine and mine speaks to his. But it has to come naturally. You cannot force something like that. You have to find that one person in this world that feels the same way about you that you feel for them, and that is a rare thing. When it happens easily, it is the most special thing in the world, I think."

Rebecca pondered that. She, too, was watching the little girls play as the puppy in her arms fell asleep. She had finally come to the conclusion that Catalina wasn't the monster she'd built her up to be. She was just a woman who had married Essien, and so much of what Jonathan had said to her made sense. There had been no crime committed against her by Catalina. The woman had been forced into the marriage just as Essien had been, but she seemed to be content with it.

Happy, even.

"I do wish you good fortune, my lady," Rebecca said. "I know that I was upset about it, but the truth… the truth is that Essien never belonged to me. But now he belongs to you and I wish you well. I truly do."

Catalina smiled at her. "Thank you," she said sincerely. "I

promise that I will take good care of him. You needn't worry because I will make sure he is happy, always. And I promise you that, someday, you will meet someone whose heart speaks to yours. You'll know it right away and it will make every heartache you've ever experienced fade away. You won't even remember them anymore."

Rebecca smiled reluctantly. She was feeling quite ashamed for her behavior now. She'd started to say something when movement behind Catalina caught her attention. She could see someone wrapped in cloaks coming down the ladder from the loft, stumbling through the hay on the ground at the base of the ladder, before heading in her direction.

Catalina caught Rebecca's expression and turned to see a tall, skinny figure swathed in cloaks and scarves coming near. The girls were far enough away, playing with puppies, that they didn't even see the figure, but Catalina and Rebecca did. Catalina stood up first, followed by Rebecca, as the figure came close.

They were preparing to defend themselves.

"I am sorry to interrupt," the figure said, mouth muffled by the fabric around his face. "Might I have some water? If you can tell me where the well is, I can draw it myself."

He sounded sickly and pathetic. Both of them could see how badly he was trembling and how weak he was. The cloaks he wore, and there were layers of them, were dirty and tattered and they could smell him from where they stood. The only thing they could see of him were his eyes, and the skin around them was scarred and red. As both women stared at him, something occurred to Catalina.

He is wrapped up in a cloak and something around his head, covering up everything but his eyes.

That was what Lance had said about the mysterious man who had given him the cross. Therefore, Catalina knew instantly who it was and her heart surged into her throat.

My God… He'd found her.

Somehow, he'd found her.

"Who are you?" Rebecca demanded, cutting into Catalina's train of thought. "What are you doing here?"

It was an aggressive question, and Catalina hoped it wouldn't set the man off. She had no way of knowing if he had violent tendencies, so she did the only thing she could do—she tried to ease the situation. Her daughters were here and she needed to protect them from someone who might be out to harm them all. She had no way of knowing.

Carefully, she proceeded.

"This is a man in need, Lady Rebecca," she said calmly. She took a step toward the man, indicating for him to sit on an old stool amongst the straw on the ground. "Sit down. We'll bring you some water. Have you eaten? Do you wish for some food also?"

The man didn't seem too apt to sit down in the stool that Catalina was indicating. "I do not wish to be trouble," he said. "But I will take any sustenance you might have. Even oats for the pigs will suffice."

He didn't sound violent. In fact, he sounded quite weak and pathetic, so Catalina turned to Rebecca.

"We must help this poor man," she said quietly. "Will you look around and see what the stable boys have left behind? Sometimes they have wine and bread around should they become hungry. Look around and see what you can find, please."

Rebecca nodded, though she was still on her guard. Nonetheless, she turned around and began to hunt for anything the stable hands might have had stashed away. Catalina was right— often, those who worked in the stables kept food around for themselves. Working the stables could mean long, difficult hours. Adabella and Ines, seeing that Rebecca was looking for something, joined in the hunt, and the puppies followed.

"We will find you something," Catalina said to the man. "Are you traveling somewhere?"

He did sit down, then, and through his cloak, Catalina could see that his legs were no bigger than bird's legs.

"Nay, my lady," he said. "I have reached my destination, I think."

"Do you have a name?"

"Al, my lady."

"Where are you from, Al?"

He paused. "I do not know," he said. "I have come to Lion-cross in the hope that someone here can tell me that."

Catalina watched him. She could see the outline of his face through the scarf and she could see that he had no nose. At least, there was nothing there where a nose would be. The very eyes that she'd told Essien she would recognize if, in fact, the man was Alfred were quite weary. She could see that in everything about him—bone weariness.

Despair.

Given she knew why he was here, there was no reason to drag out the situation by playing games. She simply didn't have the time. Reaching into her purse at her side, she pulled forth the old, twisted cross.

She held it up between them.

"Did you give this to a knight and ask him to seek Lord Eckington?" she asked. "Was that you?"

When the man realized what she was holding, his eyes widened in shock and perhaps also fear. He backed away from it as if the object radiated fire, directed at him. There was an aversion there, something to be feared. But after a moment, he seemed to calm a little, his gaze never leaving that small, twisted object.

"Why do you have it?" he finally asked.

"Please answer me," she said. "I will not be angry. Did you give this to a knight?"

He hesitated before nodding, once. Catalina looked at the small golden cross with the carnelian stones. After a moment, she smiled, but it was nearly a grimace.

There were a lot of memories in that little cross.

"I remember when I gave it to Alfred," she said. "I wished him well and he departed."

The man's gaze lingered on her for a moment, flickering and fearful. "Who are you?"

"Lord Eckington's daughter."

"Catalina?"

"Aye."

It was the lady herself. He hadn't known her on sight, but here she was, standing in front of him. What a beautiful woman she was and, somehow, more memories of Alfred speaking about his wife came back to him. He'd spoken of her beauty. But Rebecca came around the corner and interrupted the moment as she brought a napkin that had bread and some kind of jerky in it, as well as a pitcher with some very stale wine.

"Here," she said, handing the items to Catalina. "This is all I could find."

Catalina took the food, handing it over to the man, who stood up quickly and extended a hand that had three fingers burned to the nubs. He took the food, turning his back on her as he moved his scarf aside and began wolfing down the bread.

"I am sorry," he said, mouth full as he tried to keep them from seeing his face. "I have not eaten in some time. I am very sorry."

"Do not apologize," Catalina said. "Here—take the wine or you'll choke."

He did, drinking it down and spilling it all over himself. Catalina and Rebecca exchanged concerned glances at the actions of the poor, wretched creature.

"You are injured," Rebecca said, trying to get a look at what was under the scarf. "Are you in pain? Do you need help?"

The man shook his head, coughing as he choked on the wine. "Nay, my lady," he said. "I am healed from my injuries, though the scars remain. I am not in pain."

Rebecca was still trying to get a look at him. "But how did you hurt yourself?"

He managed to swallow the bite in his mouth. "Fire," he said. "There was a fire and I was burned. I spent time in France, being tended to by priests, before I made my way back to England."

He shoved more bread in his mouth as Rebecca moved closer. "How terrible," she said. "Won't you come and sit down? Surely you must be exhausted."

He saw that she was coming closer and quickly pulled the scarf over his face. "Please, my lady," he said, holding out a hand to stop her. "You do not want to see more of me. It would haunt your dreams."

Rebecca paused. "Very well," she said. "But will you at least sit?"

He nodded. But then he turned to look at Catalina and held

up his hand, the one with the missing fingers, and she could see a faint outline of the cross seared on his palm.

"It was so hot that it burned my hand," he told her, his voice hoarse. "But I knew… it was important. I saved it from the fire."

Catalina nodded, seeing that he was quickly becoming distressed. "Please," she said, indicating the stool again. "Sit down again. We will find you more food. I will find you more food and Lady Rebecca can sit with you, if you like. She is very kind. You needn't be afraid."

Wearily, he sat on the stool again as Rebecca lowered herself to her knees a few feet away, facing him. She began talking to him about his travels and where he had been, something he seemed unclear on—but he had been to London, and Rebecca took the conversation from there. She talked about the cathedral and the woman on Wick Street who made dresses for her mother. She spoke of anything she could think of, and at that moment, Catalina ceased to see the spoiled girl who had caused so much trouble. She saw a young woman trying to help.

It was a remarkable thing to witness.

Behind Rebecca, about twenty feet away, were Adabella and Ines, lying on the ground as puppies walked all over them. Her girls were happy and occupied and the very man everyone had been searching for, the mysterious visitor who had caused such an uproar, was being tended to by a gracious daughter of de Lohr. Catalina kept her gaze on the scene, walking backward until she came within line of sight of the entry door. Beyond that was the staging ground and the gate that led out to the lists, the village, and the castle. She was hoping to find a servant to send for Essien, but as she turned her head to look, she could see her husband coming into the staging area along with Addax and Lance.

The very men she wanted to see.

At least, Essien was the one she wanted to see. She was puzzled why Lance was with him, but she couldn't stop to think about that now. Keeping an eye on Al and Rebecca, she made her way over to the stable entry. When Essien saw her, he began to run, and she ran out to meet him. His arms went around her as they came together and he hugged her tightly.

"What are you doing here?" he said, sounding concerned. "You were supposed to remain in the bailey. What did you—?"

She put her fingers over his lips to silence him. "I found him," she said simply, taking Essien by the hand and pulling him toward the stable. "The man who gave Lance the cross. I found him. Well, he found me, in truth. He was in the stable."

Essien's eyes widened. "He's in there?" he asked. "Damnation! Let me—"

"Nay," Catalina said, putting her hands on his chest as he tried to move past her. "There is no need for violence or force, Essien. He is very calm. He is talking to Rebecca. He is hungry and confused, so do not be harsh with him. There is no need."

"Rebecca?" he repeated, confused. "What is she doing in the stable?"

"A story for another time," Catalina said quickly. "Please, Essien. You must be calm, I beg you."

Essien was geared up for a fight, but his wife's plea and Addax's encouraging expression forced him to cool. After a moment, he nodded, a silent agreement to behave, as Catalina took his hand again and led him into the stable.

It was just as she'd said.

With Adabella and Ines in the distance rolling around in hay and playing with puppies, Essien's eyes found Rebecca's bright red hair as she sat on the ground next to a man swathed in cloaks and tattered remnants. The stable was dim, with light coming from the entry and a few windows, so Rebecca and the man were mostly sitting in shadows. They could hear the soft hum of conversation as Rebecca spoke of fried balls of dough she'd had in London and how the cook at Lioncross couldn't quite replicate them. But the knights must have made a sound as they approached, because Rebecca quickly looked up at them, followed by the man in rags.

Thinking he was about to be grabbed and put in the vault, or even attacked, the man suddenly lurched to his feet and tried to run, but he tripped over Rebecca and sprawled on the floor of the stable. Rebecca, ignoring the fact that she'd just been kicked in the shoulder, jumped up and put herself between the man and Essien and Addax.

"Nay!" she said. "Essien al-Kort, you'll not hurt this man. He's done nothing!"

"He has not come to hurt him, I promise," Catalina assured her. "Rebecca, this man had something that belonged to my dead husband. That is why he is here. He is not a random visitor. Did he tell you that?"

Rebecca looked puzzled. "Nay," she said, frowning as she looked at the man now picking himself off the ground. "Why did you have something that belonged to her first husband?"

The man was trembling terribly, making standing up something difficult. His eyes darted between Essien and Addax and Lance nervously. He recognized Lance, and that only seemed to frighten him further. He tried to answer, but no sounds were coming out until he emitted something that sounded like a groan.

Then he burst into tears.

"Forgive me," he said, sobbing. "I had nowhere else to go. I had to come."

By this time, Adabella and Ines had seen the fall, heard the weeping, and they were frightened. They ran to their mother, who could only pick up one of them. She wasn't strong enough to pick up both of them for any length of time. Rebecca rushed to her side and took Ines, who was more than happy to go to the nice lady with the pretty hair. In fact, she wasn't scared anymore, as she was simply fascinated by Rebecca's mane. As she played with her hair, Essien spoke steadily to the man.

"My name is Essien," he said. "This is my brother, Addax, and you have already met Lance. Are you the man who gave him Alfred's cross to bring to Lord Eckington's daughter?"

The man nodded, still weeping. "I... I wanted to know if she could identify it," he said. "I took it."

"That is not what you told me," Lance said, entering the conversation. "You told me that you were wearing it when you were injured and you lost your memory in the accident. When your memory started returning, the name Eckington came to you, so you made your way here to see if you could discover where you came from. *That* is what you told me."

The man looked at Lance, who looked as if he'd been on the wrong end of a fight. "I did," he said, wiping his eyes. "I did tell you that."

Lance pointed at Catalina. "Do you know who this woman is?"

The man looked at her, his sobs fading. "She was very kind to me," he said. "So was the other lady. Very kind."

"That was not the question," Essien said. "Who is this woman?"

He was gesturing to Catalina. The man stared at her for a moment. "Lord Eckington's daughter," he said. "*Catalina.* She told me."

Essien frowned. "She *told* you?" he said. "You did not recognize her? For if you were wearing the cross when you were injured, as you told Lance, then that would make you Alfred de Barenton. *Are* you Alfred de Barenton?"

The man froze. The interrogation was coming quickly, from angry men. He blinked rapidly as if unable to process the questions he was being asked. They wanted answers he could not give them. His gaze moved to Catalina, standing next to Essien, and she seemed to understand his pain and hesitation. So much was said with his eyes that his lips could not convey.

Catalina did understand, in fact.

She knew the truth.

"Nay," she said to her husband. "He is not Alfred. I told you that I would know instantly by simply looking at his eyes. Alfred had blue eyes. Our visitor has brown. Not even a fire can change a man's eyes from blue to brown."

There it was. The answer they'd both been seeking since the horror of the discovery of the cross. So simple, yet so true, and Essien nearly collapsed with relief. In fact, he turned to Catalina and threw his arms around her, holding her tightly and trying desperately not to weep himself. As they embraced one another, seemingly lost to their mutual relief, Addax approached the man in the tattered cloak.

"Where did you get the cross?" he asked quietly.

The man held up his hand. "I took it as the fire burned," he said, showing Addax the cross-shaped scar on his palm. "Alfred was already dead when I took it from him. I was burned, too, but I did not die. Priests tended me until I could return to England."

Addax understood. "And your memory?" he asked. "Are

you lying about that, too? You knew enough to find Lord Eckington at Lioncross. How did you accomplish that?"

The man could see suspicion turned upon him. "I remembered Eckington," he said. "I heard it from Alfred. I truly did come here in the hope that someone would know Alfred, and…"

"And being disfigured, they would think you were him."

The man sighed heavily. "Aye," he said. "There was that hope. But the lady knew his eyes. I did not stop to think that mine would be so different. But not remembering who I am, I did not think it would be so terrible to become Alfred."

That explained a great deal. Addax looked at Essien, who was just releasing Catalina from his crushing embrace. All that mattered to the two of them was that the mysterious man was not Alfred. Addax had told Essien that he would save his happiness regardless of the personal cost, but that wasn't necessary now. The fates had been kind to Essien in this case— the cause of their fear was just a pathetic, lonely man with nowhere to go and no concept of what he had stirred up with the cross he'd stolen. But all that mattered was that the situation was over.

Essien and Catalina would have a lifetime of happiness now.

"I cannot give you the answers you seek," Addax said to the man. "But I can provide you with a warm meal, a bed, and mayhap an opportunity to lead a productive life. I have properties in the north and we are always looking for good men to tend the sheep or to other things around my domain. Do you have any talents that you recall? Anything you were skilled at?"

The man looked at him in awe. "Why… why would you do such a thing?"

Addax smiled faintly. "Because that is what a good man

does," he said. "He helps the unfortunate, and you seem to be more unfortunate than most. Now, tell me—do you have any skills?"

The man shook his head. "I cannot recall," he said hesitantly. "Though I do seem to remember a familiarity with weapons."

"Weapons?" Addax said, indicating for the man to follow him. "That is a place to start. Every armory needs someone to keep it in good order."

The man seemed quite surprised by the suggestion. "But… my lord," he said. "No man can look upon me and not cringe. I am not one to stay in the light."

"Armories are usually dark and dingy," Essien said. "Mayhap it will be to your liking. If you are honest and diligent, that is all anyone will ask of you. But if you'd rather wander and try to discover where you've come from, that is your choice. No one will hold you."

The man looked at Addax, at Lance, and finally to Essien and Catalina as they continued to revel in an important moment. He took a deep breath and returned his attention to Addax.

"I have very little to offer," he said. "But it would be nice to have a roof over my head in exchange for work. I can see that whatever I was looking for, it is not part of Eckington."

"Nay, it is not," Addax said. "But I will find you a place to belong if you want it."

"I want it, my lord."

With that, Addax and the man headed out of the stable, talking about weapons. Before they could leave entirely, Catalina stopped them.

"Wait," she said, leaving Essien and catching up to them.

She had something in her hand, extending it to the man. "I want you to have this."

It was the cross. Timidly, he took it from her, but his eyes were full of disbelief. "Why should you give this to me, my lady?" he said. "I stole it. I do not deserve it."

"You do," Catalina insisted softly, folding his gnarled fingers over the pendant. "I want you to have it. Sell it for the money. That should help you get a start on your life, money to feed and shelter you. Please take it. You risked much to bring it here, so you should keep it. I have no use for it any longer."

"If you are certain, my lady."

"I am certain."

The man was deeply grateful. Nodding his thanks, he departed the stable with Addax as Catalina returned to Essien. As they wandered off together in a tight huddle, that left Lance and Rebecca standing awkwardly. Rebecca held Ines in one hand and Adabella in the other, since her mother had set her to her feet in order to embrace Essien. Seeing that Essien and Catalina were in a world of their own, Rebecca pulled the little girls back over to where the puppies were playing so their mother and her new husband could have some time alone. That was her wedding gift to them. That left Lance by himself, trying not to look at Catalina and Essien.

But even he could see their joy.

Perhaps, one day, he'd find his own.

With a smirk at how the entire circumstance had played out where Lady de Barenton, now Lady Mercia, was concerned, Lance headed out of the stable, into the day beyond. He still had no woman, no name, and no position, but somehow, it didn't matter. Coming to Lioncross had been a life-changing moment for him in many ways. He'd been able to accomplish, at least with David, what he'd set out to accomplish. Perhaps it would go somewhere, perhaps not. But he felt oddly stronger for it.

For Lance le Kerque, everything was going to be okay.

And for Essien al-Kort and Catalina de Efford de Barenton, Lord and Lady Mercia, everything was most definitely going to be okay. A forced marriage had changed their lives, but in a most unexpected way. The very thing they'd fought against had become the very thing that would save them. As Catalina had told Rebecca, her heart recognized his.

And his, most assuredly, recognized hers and would continue to, forever.

Until the world took its last breath.

EPILOGUE

Tournament at Warstone Castle
Seat of the Earl of Wolverhampton, Robert de Wolfe
Ten months later

"HE'S NOT DROPPING his left shoulder," David muttered to his brother. "He's keeping it in position, asking for you to hit it. Again and again."

In full armor, astride a horse that was only put to work at tournaments, Christopher was tightening up the strap on the steel protection on his right forearm. He'd just made two passes against William de Wolfe in front of a crowd of tournament fanatics that were standing twenty deep in some places. The lists weren't big enough to hold everyone who wanted to witness the legendary Christopher de Lohr, winner of multiple jousts, and William de Wolfe, the most cunning knight to walk the earth since King Arthur and his Round Table of warriors. It was a battle of the titans at Warstone Castle, seat of the Earl of Wolverhampton, Robert de Wolfe, and most of the Welsh marches had turned up for it.

Truly, a bout to behold.

"He's doing it out of arrogance," Christopher muttered.

"I've already shattered two lances on him. He wants me to shatter a third, and the match will go into another round if our points are even."

"I think they are."

"I do, too," Christopher said, finishing with the strap. "David… I do not think I can go another bout with de Wolfe. I'm exhausted as it is."

"Jesus," David hissed. "Whatever you do, do not tell Dustin. She'll drag you off this horse and you'll have to forfeit the match. She's not stopped yelling at you since you told her that you were going to compete."

Christopher eyed his wife, sitting in the lists next to Robert and his lovely wife, Gisele. "I know," he said. "Christ, what was I thinking when I said I'd do this? De Wolfe goaded me into it."

"He surely did," David said, grinning. "He played on your monumental pride and you took the bait. And here you are, you old idiot."

He said it a little too angrily and Christopher rolled his eyes. "Then let me see if I can knock that whelp off his horse," he said. "I swear to you that if I do, I will dance on him while he's still on the ground as I steal his horse. I will celebrate this victory until the end of my life."

"Which may come sooner than you think if you do not pay attention to this match," David said. "Look—there goes Sherry, over to the enemy side. What in the hell is he doing?"

Christopher lowered his visor. "I do not want to know," he said. "By the way—have we heard anything from Rhys? He was supposed to be here this morning. He sent word yesterday that he would be arriving."

David helped him adjust the helm. "He will be here any moment," he said. "But do not worry about him. You must focus on keeping your head on your shoulders because there is a wolf on the attack."

Christopher finished with the helm. "Come along, then," he said. "Lead me to the start so we can get this over with."

As David took hold of the charger's reins and began to lead the horse back to the starting position along the guides, Alexander was indeed heading into the enemy camp. On the west side of the guides, William was lined up and ready for his next run. Paris and Kieran were with him, as were a few other knights who had come all the way down from Northwood Castle, where they all served. They, too, wanted to see William subdue perhaps the greatest living knight. When Alexander approached, Paris went to chase him off but Kieran stopped him, shaking his head.

"What?" Paris demanded. "Why did you stop me?"

Kieran's dark eyes were intense. "Because that is Alexander de Sherrington," he said in a low voice. "Mayhap you do not remember that he is one of England's greatest assassins. He would kill you with his thumb and forefinger, and you would never see it coming, so if he wants to speak with William, we will let him. Sherry can have whatever Sherry wishes."

Paris knew he was speaking the truth, but he still made a face and postured like he didn't care. He was arrogant, but he wasn't stupid. He and Kieran and the others watched as Alexander stood at William's left flank.

"My lord?" William said when he saw Alexander standing there. "Is something amiss?"

Alexander shook his head. "Nay," he said. "I've come to tell you that Chris will be aiming for your lance and your arm next, so be on your guard. But if you aim for anything other than his left shoulder, or hurt that man in any fashion, there is nowhere in this world you can run that I will not find you. If I find you, I will do unspeakable things to you and you will not survive. Am I making myself clear?"

William's gaze was steady. "Did he send you here to tell me that?"

"Nay," Alexander said. "He does not know what I am saying, and if you live through this, and he asks, you will tell him that I simply wished you well against a legend. And that is all I am going to do—wish you well. But remember who you are competing against. You have done a splendid job, William, but you have the rest of your life to continue to make your mark. Chris has already made his. Let him keep it."

With that, he walked away, leaving William mulling over his words. After a moment, he smiled and lowered his visor.

The stage was set.

As the roar of the crowd rose to deafening proportions, every knight who was competing at the tournament, and every squire, every page, was lined up on the south side of the tournament arena, watching the match from a distance. That included Addax and Essien, who had come all the way down from Cumbria for this. They'd even traveled with William's group from Northwood part of the way, and by the end of it, they were ready to throttle de Norville and bury the body. But even so, they were quite interested in this match, just like everyone else.

History was being made this day.

"There will never be another match like this one," Addax said, watching Christopher adjust the strap on his lance. "De Wolfe has taken the north by storm, you know. They say there is no man finer in battle. And Hereford... Well, his legend needs no introduction. We already know his greatness."

Essien nodded, watching the marshals take their places. "This pass will determine if Hereford passes the torch of greatness on to William or if he keeps it a little while longer."

"True," Addax said. "Speaking of greatness, how was your wife feeling this morning?"

Essien looked at him. "Well," he said. "Why do you ask?"

Addax shrugged. "Because Emmeline said the woman ate nonstop yesterday," he said. "Anything she could get her hands on. And it did not upset her stomach?"

Essien grinned. "It did not," he said. "She was eating again this morning when she awoke, and is probably eating now. My son demands a good deal of food because he is going to be big and strong like his father."

Addax chuckled. "Let us pray," he said. "Emmy's pregnancies were not so easy. It was difficult to convince her to eat at times."

Essien was still smiling, spying his wife across the arena because she was wearing a gorgeous blue garment. She stood out. At six months pregnant, she was showing nicely and Essien could not have been prouder.

Or more in love.

"Not my beloved Cat," he said. "God has been good that she has been so well."

Addax had to grin at his lovesick brother. As the bout was about to get underway, he glanced down the line of knights standing at the railing. Jonathan was standing next to Essien and he was cheering for Christopher because his own brother had knocked him out of the semifinal rounds. Beside him stood Ashton, who had made it down from Pelinom Castle, where he usually served, and Peter, who was calling reassurances to his father on the field. Cassian, of course, was present, but Brielle was pregnant again and hadn't made the trip. It was the familiar crew of men, all of them joined together once again to watch this historic event.

One that happened in a heartbeat when the marshal finally dropped the flag.

As an entire arena of rabid fans watched with anticipation, William de Wolfe and Christopher de Lohr charged one another with lances leveled. The horses they were riding were big, heavily muscled, and made for the sport. For each inch of ground the horses covered, time seemed to drag out. It was going more slowly. It was going in reverse until they came within range of each other. There was a cataclysmic crash and wood went flying into the air as lances shattered, but William also lost his grip on his lance and the thing went flipping into the guide, destroying it. Losing a lance, or being unseated, meant the bout was over and the points went to the competitor who had retained his lance and his seat.

There was a winner.

The legend had retained his title.

People went mad with excitement. They began to throw flowers and coins and anything else they could get their hands on down to the field. It was positively raining all sorts of things. The knights watching the event on the south railing began to flood onto the field, heading for the champion as he drew his horse to a halt.

Christopher de Lohr was that champion.

Still.

"Well done, my lord!" Addax called to him as he drew near. "A worthy match!"

Christopher handed his lance down to Peter and Alexander, who reached up to help him. But once the lance was handed down, Christopher flipped up his visor and sought out William, on the other side of the arena.

"Stay here," he told those around him. "I will return shortly."

With that, he cantered across the dirt, reining his horse over to William, who was in the process of handing his helm down to Paris. He hadn't dismounted yet. Kieran had hold of the horse, checking the animal for any damage. Christopher pulled his horse alongside William.

"You two," he said, indicating Paris and Kieran. "Leave us."

The two knights did, but Paris was reluctant to move until Kieran dragged him away. When they were out of earshot, Christopher looked at William.

"A fine match, William," he said, his blue eyes twinkling. "Your father would have been proud."

William dipped his head in thanks. "I hope so, my lord," he said. "Thank you for the honor today of riding against you today. It was a privilege."

Christopher nodded, his gaze moving down William's arm, to the hand that had gripped the lance.

"And for me," he said. "But I did not hit you hard enough to dislodge the lance."

"You hit harder than you realized."

"Nay, I did not."

"Then I must have had a weak moment."

Christopher couldn't decide if he was furious or amused at what he suspected. "No de Wolfe has a weak moment," he said. "It is not in your nature."

William shook his head. "Nay, it is not," he said. "But it is not in your nature, either. You were going to kill yourself rather than forfeit a bout, no matter how exhausted or advanced in years you were. A man your age should not go up against younger men with better stamina."

Christopher frowned at the truth, insulting though it was. "William, if you threw this match, I will have the marshals set the guides up once more and we shall go again," he said. "Once I knock you from your horse, and I *will* knock you off, I am going to beat the guts out of you and use your rotten hide as a rug in front of my hearth. Then you can talk to me about old men and stamina."

William was trying desperately not to laugh. "My apologies," he said. "I did not mean it as it sounded, only that you have earned your reputation. You should not jeopardize it against someone as unworthy as me."

Christopher shook his head reproachfully at the smooth-talking young knight. "You are a devil," he growled. "Answer my question—did you deliberately lose your lance?"

William's eyes were glittering with warmth at a man he loved and adored. "Of course not," he finally said. "I would never do such a thing. I lost my grip on it and it simply slipped out of my hand. I lost to a legend today, quite fairly. And I am proud of it."

With that, he directed his horse away, leaving Christopher both fuming and touched. There was no question in his mind that the knight known as the Wolfe had thrown the match. But he wasn't going to argue with him.

God bless the man.

Wherever Edward de Wolfe was, Christopher had a feeling the man was very proud.

And so was Christopher.

會

"I AM GOING to be ready for de Wolfe in the mass competition," Essien said. "With his loss to Hereford, the man will be out for blood."

Addax waggled his eyebrows in agreement. A couple of hours after the tournament had ended, they were preparing for a preliminary bout in the mass competition. Preparing along with them were other members of their team in Ashton, Peter, Cassian, and Alexander.

It was a hell of a team.

"Wolfie is siding with his brother," Cassian reminded them. "The man is unbeatable in a mass competition. We should have enticed him over to our team."

"With what?" Essien wanted to know. "He'll laugh if we offer him money."

"Give him somebody's sister," Ashton said, looking at Cassian. "You have two sisters-in-law who are available."

Cassian scowled. "Rebecca would rip off his arms and beat him to death with them," he said. "And Olivia is too young."

"I heard that William and Wolfie's father married their mother very young."

"Not *that* young."

Ashton conceded the point. "I suppose," he said. "All I know is that I am going to try to stay away from him. I would like to leave the competition with my head intact."

"Ash, you're nearly as unbeatable as he is," Essien said. "And speaking of unbeatable, the rumors are flying that William threw his bout against Hereford. That's what some people are saying. Have any of you heard that?"

Alexander lifted his head from where he'd been securing his scabbard. "None of that talk, Es," he said, his voice low. "That can ruin a man's reputation."

Essien looked at the man. "I didn't say it," he said. "I simply said that I'd heard rumors. My suggestion was going to be that we quash them as we hear them. It doesn't do William or Hereford any good for those to be making the rounds."

Everyone was in agreement. As they returned to the last of their preparations, the tent flap opened and Maddoc entered. He was met with a chorus of greeting.

"We finally made it," he said, his young face flushed because he'd run all the way across the competitors' camp to find Addax's tent. "We met with terrible weather in Wiltshire and that slowed us down tremendously. But I'm finally here and I'm ready to put down a beating on anyone who opposes us."

He was smiling with delight as Alexander gave him an affectionate pat on the side of the head. "Good lad," he said. "But you missed the bout to end all bouts. William de Wolfe against Hereford."

"I know," Maddoc said. "I heard that Hereford soundly beat him."

Alexander eyed him. "And that was all you heard?"

Maddoc nodded. "Aye," he said. "Why? Is there more to it?"

Alexander shook his head, thankful that the knight hadn't heard those rumors they'd just been discussing. "Nay," he said. "Gather your things, lad. We must get to the field."

"I will," Maddoc said. "But I came for another reason— Addax, Lord Hereford wants to see you and Essien in his tent immediately. He said to come with all due haste."

Addax and Essien collected the clubs they intended to use, since no blades were allowed in the mass competition.

"Very well," Addax said. "Did he say why?"

Maddoc shook his head. "Nay," he said. "But he said to hurry."

Addax walked past him, toward the tent opening. "Where is your father?" he asked. "Is he going to be on our team?"

Maddoc shrugged. "Doubtful," he said. "He's with Hereford."

No more questions were asked. With no particular sense of urgency, Addax and Essien made their way across the encampment, toward the enormous blue-and-yellow tent on the north side where Hereford had established himself.

The day around them was sizing up to be a bit turbulent as a storm began to roll in from the west. They could see it on the horizon, having already rolled over Wales and Shropshire, now heading for Wolverhampton. The clouds were dark and even at a distance, they could hear the thunder.

Essien paused to watch it for a moment.

"That is going to turn the mass competition into a lovely, muddy mess," he said unhappily. "Emmy and Catalina must not be allowed to stand out in the muck and watch."

Addax paused, seeing what looked like a bad storm heading their way. "Agreed," he said. "Come along—let's get this over with so we can find our wives. The last I saw Emmy, she wanted to go to the vendors' village because a merchant had brought in a collection of silk scarves. If she does not need one more thing in her trunks, it is silk scarves."

"But you gave her money, anyway."

"Of course I did."

Essien chuckled. "Catalina will buy a scarf and tell me it is for the baby," he said as Addax flipped the tent flap back. "Every time she buys something now, no matter what it is, she tells me it is for the baby. I am starting to become suspicious that it is not."

Addax grinned at a wife trying to slip something past her

adoring, and perhaps oblivious, husband. They came upon the main tent at this point, and as they entered, they came face to face with Christopher and Rhys, who were nearly standing at the doorway to greet them.

"My lord," Essien said. "Maddoc said you wanted to see us?"

Christopher nodded as Addax greeted Rhys. "I do," Christopher said. "I'm sorry to take you away from the start of the mass competition, but this is something rather important that cannot wait. I think you'll understand when I finish telling you."

Both Addax and Essien nodded. "Of course, my lord," Essien said. "How may we be of service?"

Christopher motioned them deeper inside the tent. They followed him, still not sensing anything out of the ordinary. As Essien took Addax's club and set it against a table along with his own, Christopher spoke quietly.

"Something has come to light that I sought to investigate before bringing it to your attention," he said to them. "I will come to the point on this, but there is a bit of an explanation behind it, so I beg patience. The situation is as follows—at the Lioncross tournament last year, Rhys came to me with interesting information. It might have involved you, but also, it might not have. We did not know for certain. We discussed telling you both about it, but decided against it because we wanted to investigate it further before bringing you in on it."

Addax cocked his head curiously. "What is it, my lord?"

Christopher looked at Rhys, who took the hint and continued. "It was, indeed, an interesting situation," he said. "I have a neighbor who is a merchant. He has a fleet of ships that sail all over the known world, but mostly to places like Tripoli and

Alexandria, Naples and Athens. Those kinds of ports. The man knows kings and pashas and emperors the world over, and last year, he returned from a very long journey. I know this because when he is gone, I send men to guard his lands. He returned and had a feast to thank me for helping him. At the feast, I met his new wife, a woman from Alexandria. Of course, my wife spent most of her time speaking with her, and Elizabeau thought that she was elegant and kind, very well read. I, too, spent a few moments speaking with her, and when I asked if she had been born in Alexandria, she told me that it was not the city of her birth. She had been born in Kitara."

That brought a reaction from Addax and Essien. "A citizen of Kitara?" Addax repeated, surprised. "In Alexandria?"

Rhys nodded, looking to Christopher at that point because he knew more about Addax and Essien's background than Rhys did. But Christopher was busy pouring two measures of wine, handing them to the al-Kort brothers.

"Drink that," he commanded softly.

Essien downed his without question, while Addax was a little slower. He lifted the cup to his lips but paused before drinking.

"Why must we drink this?" he asked.

Christopher motioned to it without answering and Addax reluctantly knocked it back. It was strong stuff and fire coursed down their throats, but it was a bracing jolt. Only when the cups were set aside did Christopher continue.

"Addax, I truly do not mean to draw this out, but I want you prepared," he said. "You should be aware that the name of his neighbor's wife is Adanya. Isn't that your sister's name?"

Essien's features were full of shock as Addax simply stared at Christopher with no visible reaction. At least, not yet. It took several long moments for the question to sink in.

"Aye," he finally said. "She was my younger sister."

"And you have no knowledge of what happened to her?"

"Nay," Addax said. "She was with my mother when we were separated. She was no older than my youngest child, who has not yet seen two years."

Christopher went to them both, gripping Essien's arm with a big hand while laying his other hand on Addax's shoulder. It was a reassuring, fatherly gesture. When he spoke to them, it was quiet and gentle.

There was no easy way to tell them what he had to.

"Lads," he finally said, "I think we have something of a miracle because Adanya came to France with her parents. Evidently, her mother's father was the ruler of Alexandria, but when he was deposed, Adanya married Rhys' neighbor and the entire family fled to France. Rhys only knew Adanya's mother's name—he did not know her father's name—so he returned to France after the tournament last year, at my request, and sought them out. He told Adanya and her mother and father about you two, the Kitaran princes, and it seems that they know you. Lads, we found your mother and father, hiding in plain sight in France."

With that, he nodded to Rhys, who quickly left the tent. As Addax stood there, dumbfounded, Essien pulled away. He wandered over to a corner of the tent, overwhelmed and bewildered. His hands were on his mouth, on his forehead, in his hair, and back again. His agitation and confusion were evident.

"That can't be true," Essien said. "It's *not* true. Our father died. He died defending his legacy."

Addax had his hand over his mouth as if to hold back the

cry of disbelief. "My God," he breathed. "And you know this for certain?"

Christopher nodded. "Your father is called the *Kaara Ejadar*," he said gently. "The Dragon King."

"Did he tell you that?"

"Adanya did. And so did you."

That made Addax suck in his breath. He was trying so desperately to keep his composure, but it was slowly slipping away. "Oh, God," he finally said. "Never… I never dared to hope. I never dared to even think that my father could have escaped the carnage. We left him at Lankara. That is where he made his stand. God in heaven, are you telling me that he actually *survived*?"

Christopher could see how shaken he was. How shaken they both were. He still had his hand on Addax's shoulder. "Aye," he said hoarsely. "That is exactly what I am telling you. King Amare survived the onslaught of his brother, Prince Ekon. As he told me, he managed to escape by sea and make his way to Egypt, where he knew his wife would be, if she had survived. And she had."

Addax had to turn away. Actually, he staggered away, heading to where Essien was standing. He put both hands on his brother's shoulders, steadying himself, steadying Essien. His head was swimming with the news.

"Jesus," he finally said. "I've never fainted in my life, but at this moment, I feel as if I'm close to it. I do not understand how any of this is possible. *How* is it possible?"

"Be strong, my son," came a voice from the tent flap. "In the face of whatever this life will bring you, be strong, be honest, and be loyal to those you love. You promised me that you would. Now, I find you a great man in a land full of people who love you. You have both made me so very proud."

Addax and Essien whirled to the sound of the voice only to be confronted by a vision they only believed they would see again when they entered heaven's gates. If there had been any doubt in their mind that their father had actually survived, it was dashed to bits by the sight in the tent opening.

A vision, larger than life.

Amare, still as tall and strong, but with hair that was quite gray, was standing there, looking at his sons as if beholding a vision of angels. There were no words for the love radiating from his eyes, from the pride and the joy that was bursting forth from his very manner. Absolute elation was in everything about him.

He'd found his boys.

He was as surprised as they were.

Addax could see the gladness in his father's expression. He tried to open his mouth to respond, but nothing came out. He blinked and tears streamed down his cheeks.

Abba, he thought.

My abba.

"You said those same words to me as we fled for our lives those years ago," he finally managed to say. "I listened to them. I obeyed them. But I never forgot who spoke them to me, Abba. *You* did."

"I did," Amare said, taking a step closer, looking over both men. "When I saw you last, you were both so small. Now… look at you. So strong and powerful. Essien, you've grown so tall. You are taller than I am."

Hearing his father speak his name did something to Essien. *That voice.* He'd heard it in his dreams, but those dreams had faded. Hearing it again shook him to the bone. He turned his back on the man and burst into tears.

"I've spent my entire life not remembering you," he wept, his hand over his mouth. "It was too painful to do so. I've told Addax that I did not remember much from Lankara, but the truth is that I remembered enough. I remembered the pain, the fear. It hurt too much to remember it all, so I did not. You *were* gone, Abba. But now you're not. You're here."

"I'm here," Amare said, tears in his eyes. "I'm here because I never gave up hope. I never stopped hoping that someday, we would find one another again. I never stopped hoping and praying that wherever you were, you were happy and content. That is all I ever asked of God—to protect you and keep you safe. But I never gave up hope that, someday, I would see you both again. I am here *because* of hope, Essien. Because people who knew you and loved you found me and brought me here. God was working through them, my son. He knew how much I missed you both."

Addax couldn't take it anymore. He went to his father and threw his arms around the man, and together they quietly wept with joy. But Essien stood there, his back to them, weeping for reasons he didn't understand. It was a painful standoff, and Christopher went to Essien, putting his hand on the man's shoulder.

"Es," he whispered. "Go and greet your father."

Essien couldn't quite do it. "You are the only father I remember," he said. "I am a man of two worlds—Kitara, where I was born; England, where I grew up. This is my home… isn't it? Am I not English?"

"You *are* English," Christopher said, his own eyes welling. "You are a great and noble English lord. But you were born a prince of Kitara and you cannot forget that. You cannot ever forget where you came from. Turn around and face your father, the king. Let the man see his youngest son, the *dosara beta*. He has come a very long way to see you."

Dosara beta. Second son. That's what Essien was. He had to be reminded of that because, as he'd said, he was a man of two worlds. An English lord with non-English origins. He wasn't ashamed of that in the least, but as time passed, it had been simply easier to forget something he didn't really remember.

Perhaps, now, it was time to remember.

Perhaps he needed to try.

"He is a ghost to me, my lord," Essien said. "He is—"

"Es, *listen*," Christopher said, interrupting. "I gave you the opportunity to make something of your life, and you did. I could not be prouder of you if you were my own son. But Amare gave you life. He *is* your father. We both are. It is well and good that you should embrace us both as men who have raised you and consider yourself richer for it. Not many men can say they were raised by a legend as well as a king."

Essien lifted his head, looking at Christopher, who forced a smile at him and nodded his head in silent encouragement. Then he put both hands on Essien's shoulders and turned him around to face his father about the time Kiya and Adanya entered through the tent flap. Adanya had changed a great deal, but Kiya hadn't. She looked nearly the same. Addax went to his mother and sister, embracing them with more tears, as Essien faced Amare. They looked at each other for a few moments before Amare spoke softly to him.

"Jab tak ham dubarah nihen malin ge," he said. "Do you remember what that means?"

Essien did. He nodded, feeling the tears coming again. "Until we meet again," he murmured.

Amare smiled tremulously. "Well?" he said. "Here we are, meeting again."

"I thought you meant in another lifetime."

"I meant in any lifetime. You are my son and I will never leave you."

He was patting his chest as he spoke, indicating that even apart, they had always been together in their hearts, and all of Essien's resistance fled. He rushed to his father, hugging him so hard that he lifted him off the ground. He didn't let him go, not even when Kiya and Adanya came to embrace him. Still, Essien held on to his father and, soon enough, the entire family was one big hug, everyone with their arms around each other, everyone weeping with the joy of a most unexpected reunion. It was like the first day in heaven, being reunited with people who had not seen one another in ages. It was a second chance with loved ones.

It was difficult for anyone witnessing the encounter not to feel the love.

Seeing that Essien had finally accepted his father, Christopher left the tent, giving the family some privacy. Rhys was standing outside and Christopher joined him, hearing the roar of the crowd over at the mass competition field.

"I hear that cheer in the distance and I imagine it is for the reunion of the royal house of Kitara," Christopher said. "Christ, Rhys. Of all the winds of fate the world had to offer, they actually blew in our direction for once. We were able to reunite a family that was separated so long ago. I still can hardly believe it."

Rhys nodded. "I know," he said. "It's a truly remarkable story. Have Amare tell you about it sometime, the tribulations he went through when he fled Kitara after the entire city was burned and there was nothing left to defend."

Christopher looked at him. "How did he end up in Cairo?"

"He said that he knew his wife would go there," Rhys said. "She was born there. When he arrived and there were no boys, he tried to find them, but it is a big world. He had no way of knowing where they had gone."

Christopher glanced at the tent behind him. "He's found them now," he said quietly. "Truly, a miracle."

"Indeed, it is."

"Speaking of a big world, how is my nephew faring in yours?"

The subject shifted from Addax and Essien to Lance le Kerque, who still kept the le Kerque surname. At least for the time being. Much had happened on that front, too, in the past several months.

"He is doing well," Rhys said. "He may not bear the de Lohr name, but he has the heart of a de Lohr. Lance is the garrison commander of one of my brother's smaller outposts at Marzan, and I've heard that he has met a local lass that he intends to marry. He's well liked by the villagers at the castle, so I think the move to France was a good one for him. As long as he remained in England, he would be forever under the de Lohr shadow, but in France, he is simply another good knight. We are fortunate to have him."

A smile tugged the corners of Christopher's lips. "I am glad to hear it," he said. "He has finally found a place where he belongs."

"He has."

It did Christopher's heart good to hear that. "I know David remains in regular touch with him and their relationship has reached a cordial level, but you are right," he said. "If Lance remained here, he'd forever be in the de Lohr shadow. This way, he is a man of his own, serving a duke. There is prestige in that."

More cheers from the field distracted them, and they made the decision to head over to the mass competition, leaving the House of al-Kort reveling in their reunion. Before the hour was out, however, Amare and Kiya met their son's wives and their grandchildren, truly a remarkable day for all concerned.

The House of al-Kort was whole once again.

For Essien and Catalina, it was particularly poignant. Three months later, on a cold winter's night at Vinovia Castle in Cumbria, a little boy came into the world, helped in his efforts by his grandmother, Kiya. She was the first one to hold the child, who was named in the tradition of his father's name—an Egyptian first name followed by names from his parents' heritage.

Osiris Bodhi Cristopher was a big name for a very little boy.

And Amare was the second one to hold him.

But his mother and father were proud of the name, proud of his bloodlines, and proud of his origins. They were proud of the deep and abiding love they shared that had created him. While Catalina slept in the wake of her son's birth, Essien sat up with Amare, holding Bodhi long into the night, for on a night not dissimilar to this one, Amare had sent his sons into the unknown to save their lives. But on this evening, the world came full circle for them all. Life for the House of al-Kort, instead of ending, was renewed.

Jab tak ham dubarah nihen malin ge.

Until we meet again.

When Amare had spoken those words, he meant it.

Finally, so had Essien.

CB THE END ಬಿ

Children of Essien and Catalina

(Following his brother's lead, the children were given both names from Essien's culture and the land of their birth, names of men that Essien wanted to honor, so the children could choose which names they wished to use. It should be of note that all of them chose to use their first names, from their father's culture)

Adabella Catherina (daughter of Alfred)
Ines Sofia (daughter of Alfred)
Osiris Bodhi (pronounced BOE-dee) Cristopher
Alexandra Elissa
Darshan Eduardo
Kai Alejandro
Deven Carlitos
Rohan Guillermo
Shaan Domingo
Tarun Esteban

Author's Afterword

I hope you enjoyed the tale of Essien and Catalina. I love that I was able to give the Kitaran princes their own tales, exploring their lives as men not born in England, but living in an English world. Now, given the trade routes of the time, it is absolutely possible that Amare, having escaped destruction, ended up in Egypt, where he knew his wife would have gone. And it is equally possible that Adanya married a traveling merchant and because Kiya's father had been deposed as ruler of Cairo (and the ruler during that time period in history was, in reality, deposed), Kiya and Amare would choose to travel with her to her new husband's home because it was safer for them. I feel bad that Amare and Kiya have been running for so many years, and that's why I had to bring their running to a halt. Now, they're in England, with their sons, and living a life of peace they deserve—together.

Something I want to mention—the very incident that Lance speaks of as his conception is in a book I wrote long ago called *Lord of Winter*. If you haven't read it, it's a must-read. It shows Christopher and David as young knights, among other names you'll recognize, so definitely pick up a copy. And you'll see how Lance was conceived. Additionally, if you've not read *The Wolfe* or *Rise of the Defender*, then you must. That is where William de Wolfe and Christopher de Lohr get their start, so the end of this book really was legendary. Two icons, who have their own giant series, facing off against one another. Did William really throw that final match? Only William knows. And me. And I'm not going to tell.

Also—do we know where the mysterious man who called himself "Al" came from? I think it's fair to say that he was part of Alfred de Barenton's contingent of soldiers, so he was simply a soldier. Maybe a sergeant, someone in the command structure, but other than that, his background is unremarkable. He'll probably never remember everything, but with Addax, our benevolent king, helping him, at least he has an ending.

On another note, the big question I'm going to get is about Rebecca—she's the only de Lohr child that hasn't had a book written about her. The answer is YES, she will have her own book, and it's waiting in my queue to be written. The title, you ask? What else—*Lion Tamer*. And her hero is going to be none other than Jonathan de Wolfe. Yes, Wolfie will have his day, too—with Rebecca. That is going to be one explosive story and I can't wait to get it to you. However, if you'd like a list of the characters in this novel and their respective stories (that they are the hero and/or heroine of), here's a list of must-read books:

Addax: The Black Dragon

Cassian/Brielle: The Dark Conqueror

Alexander/Christin: A Time of End

Peter: The Splendid Hour

David: Steelheart

Christopher: Rise of the Defender

William: The Wolfe

Paris: The Wolfe/The Best Is Yet to Be

Kieran: The Wolfe (and several other stories where he's an

important secondary character)

Ashton: Not yet, but his will be coming in Lord of Havoc, possibly 2027

Jonathan: As discussed above

And with that, all is peace and love for the princes of Kitara and their families. But they sure had a difficult time getting there.

Jab tak ham dubarah nihen malin ge.

Until we meet again,

Kathryn Le Veque Novels

Medieval Romance:

De Wolfe Pack Series:
Warwolfe
The Wolfe
Nighthawk
ShadowWolfe
DarkWolfe
A Joyous de Wolfe Christmas
BlackWolfe
Serpent
A Wolfe Among Dragons
Scorpion
StormWolfe
Dark Destroyer
The Lion of the North
Walls of Babylon
The Best Is Yet To Be
BattleWolfe
Castle of Bones

De Wolfe Pack Generations:
WolfeHeart
WolfeStrike
WolfeSword
WolfeBlade
WolfeLord
WolfeShield
Nevermore
WolfeAx
WolfeBorn
WolfeBite
WolfeHound

House of de Norville:
The Best Is Yet To Be
Castle of Bones
Nevermore

The Executioner Knights:
By the Unholy Hand
The Mountain Dark
Starless
A Time of End
Winter of Solace
Lord of the Sky
The Splendid Hour
The Whispering Night
Netherworld
Lord of the Shadows
Of Mortal Fury
'Twas the Executioner Knight
Before Christmas
Crimson Shield
The Black Dragon
God of Vengeance

The de Russe Legacy:
The Falls of Erith
Lord of War: Black Angel
The Iron Knight
Beast
The Dark One: Dark Knight
The White Lord of Wellesbourne
Dark Moon
Dark Steel
A de Russe Christmas Miracle

Dark Warrior

The de Lohr Dynasty:
While Angels Slept
Rise of the Defender
Steelheart
Shadowmoor
Silversword
Spectre of the Sword
Unending Love
Archangel
A Blessed de Lohr Christmas

Sons of de Lohr:
Lion of Twilight
Lion of War
Lion of Hearts
Lion of Steel
Lion of Thunder

The Brothers de Lohr:
The Earl in Winter

Lords of East Anglia:
While Angels Slept
Godspeed
Age of Gods and Mortals

Great Lords of le Bec:
Great Protector

House of de Royans:
Lord of Winter
To the Lady Born
The Centurion

Lords of Eire:
Echoes of Ancient Dreams
Lord of Black Castle
The Darkland

Ancient Kings of Anglecynn:
The Whispering Night
Netherworld

Battle Lords of de Velt:
The Dark Lord
Devil's Dominion
Bay of Fear
The Dark Lord's First Christmas
The Dark Spawn
The Dark Conqueror
The Dark Angel

Reign of the House of de Winter:
Lespada
Swords and Shields

De Reyne Domination:
Guardian of Darkness
The Black Storm
A Cold Wynter's Knight
With Dreams
Master of the Dawn
One Wylde Knight

House of d'Vant:
Tender is the Knight (House of d'Vant)
The Red Fury (House of d'Vant)

The Dragonblade Series:
Fragments of Grace
Dragonblade
Island of Glass
The Savage Curtain
The Fallen One

Great Marcher Lords of de Lara
Lord of the Shadows
Dragonblade

House of St. Hever
Fragments of Grace
Island of Glass
Queen of Lost Stars

Lords of Pembury:
The Savage Curtain

Lords of Thunder: The de Shera Brotherhood Trilogy
The Thunder Lord
The Thunder Warrior
The Thunder Knight

The Great Knights of de Moray:
Shield of Kronos
The Gorgon

The House of De Nerra:
The Promise
The Falls of Erith
Vestiges of Valor
Realm of Angels

Highland Legion:
Highland Born
Highland Destroyer
Highland Slayer

Highland Warriors of Munro:
The Red Lion
Deep Into Darkness

The House of de Garr:
Lord of Light
Realm of Angels

Saxon Lords of Hage:
The Crusader
Kingdom Come

High Warriors of Rohan:
High Warrior
High King

The House of Ashbourne:
Upon a Midnight Dream

The House of D'Aurilliac:
Valiant Chaos

The House of De Dere:
Of Love and Legend

St. John and de Gare Clans:
The Warrior Poet

The House of de Bretagne:
The Questing

The House of Summerlin:
The Legend

The Kingdom of Hendocia:
Kingdom by the Sea

The BlackChurch Guild: Shadow Knights:
The Leviathan
The Protector
The Swordsman
The Tempest

Guard of Six:
Absolution
Insurrection
Obliteration

Regency Historical Romance:
Sin Like Flynn: A Regency Historical Romance Duet
The Sin Commandments
Georgina and the Red Charger

Gothic Regency Romance:
Emma

Historical Fiction:
The Girl Made Of Stars

Contemporary Romance:

Kathlyn Trent/Marcus Burton Series:
Valley of the Shadow
The Eden Factor
Canyon of the Sphinx

The Eagle Brotherhood (under the pen name Kat Le Veque):
The Sunset Hour

The Killing Hour
The Secret Hour
The Unholy Hour
The Burning Hour
The Ancient Hour
The Devil's Hour

Sons of Poseidon:
The Immortal Sea

Pirates of Britannia Series (with Eliza Knight):
Savage of the Sea by Eliza Knight
Leader of Titans by Kathryn Le Veque
The Sea Devil by Eliza Knight
Sea Wolfe by Kathryn Le Veque

Note: All Kathryn's novels are designed to be read as stand-alones, although many have cross-over characters or cross-over family groups. Novels that are grouped together have related characters or family groups. You will notice that some series have the same books; that is because they are cross-overs. A hero in one book may be the secondary character in another.

There is NO reading order except by chronology, but even in that case, you can still read the books as stand-alones. No novel is connected to another by a cliff hanger, and every book has an HEA.

Series are clearly marked. All series contain the same characters or family groups except the American Heroes Series, which is an anthology with unrelated characters.

For more information, find it in **A Reader's Guide to the Medieval World of Le Veque.**

ABOUT KATHRYN LE VEQUE

Bringing the Medieval to Romance

KATHRYN LE VEQUE is a critically acclaimed, multiple USA TODAY Bestselling author, an Indie Reader bestseller, a charter Amazon All-Star author, and a #1 bestselling, award-winning, multi-published author in Medieval Historical Romance with over 100 published novels.

Kathryn is a multiple award nominee and winner, including the winner of Uncaged Book Reviews Magazine 2017 and 2018 "Raven Award" for Favorite Medieval Romance. Kathryn is also a multiple RONE nominee (InD'Tale Magazine), holding a record for the number of nominations. In 2018, her novel WARWOLFE was the winner in the Romance category of the Book Excellence Award and in 2019, her novel A WOLFE AMONG DRAGONS won the prestigious RONE award for best pre-16th century romance.

Kathryn is considered one of the top Indie authors in the world with over 2M copies in circulation, and her novels have been translated into several languages. Kathryn recently signed with Sourcebooks Casablanca for a Medieval Fight Club series, first published in 2020.

In addition to her own published works, Kathryn is also the President/CEO of Dragonblade Publishing, a boutique publishing house specializing in Historical Romance. Dragonblade's success has seen it rise in the ranks to become Amazon's #1 e-book publisher of Historical Romance (K-Lytics report July 2020).

Kathryn loves to hear from her readers. Please find Kathryn on Facebook at Kathryn Le Veque, Author, or join her on Twitter @kathrynleveque. Sign up for Kathryn's blog at www.kathrynleveque.com for the latest news and sales.